"You asked for my help, Miss Winters."

Her fingernails dug into her left palm. She picked up the journal, shaking it in his direction. "Were you going to give me this if I hadn't walked in on the two of you?"

"And here I thought you trusted me." His voice was nonchalant.

"I don't trust you at all. A *sin* would be less dangerous."

He was suddenly directly in front of her, having moved too quickly for her to react. He ran his thumb over the leather top of the journal, the tip brushing her fingers.

"That's a shame, Marietta." His voice held the low hum of an ocean wave at night. "If you don't trust me, your brother is going to hang." His fingertips moved along the side of her hand and then lifted. The most dangerous man she'd ever met crouched in front of her. "And I guarantee that you will still be serving me. Three services. Three tasks. Three nights of sin?"

Other **Avon Romances**

Anne Mallory

Three Nights Of Sin

AVON

An Imprint of HarperCollinsPublishers

This is a work of fiction. Names, characters, places, and incidents are products of the author's imagination or are used fictitiously and are not to be construed as real. Any resemblance to actual events, locales, organizations, or persons, living or dead, is entirely coincidental.

AVON BOOKS
An Imprint of HarperCollins*Publishers*
10 East 53rd Street
New York, New York 10022-5299

Copyright © 2008 by Anne Hearn
ISBN: 978-0-06-124241-0
www.avonromance.com

First Avon Books paperback printing: May 2008

Avon Trademark Reg. U.S. Pat. Off. and in Other Countries, Marca Registrada, Hecho en U.S.A.
HarperCollins® is a registered trademark of HarperCollins Publishers.

Printed in the U.S.A.

10 9 8 7 6 5 4 3 2 1

To Bella Andre, Jami Alden, Barbara Freethy,
Jacqueline Yau, and our favorite
Starbucks haunt for tolerating hours of
silent typing interspersed with raucous
(and at times "eccentric") conversations. ☺

Acknowledgments

Special thanks, as always, to Mom, Matt, and May. Words can't express the ~~wonderfulosity wonderfulness~~ magnificence of your red pens. And to Dad and Paige for your unending support.

Three Nights
Of Sin

Chapter 1

London, 1825

T he brass ring in the lion's mouth glimmered in the faint light of the gas lamps. Fierce yellow eyes surveyed her from above the loop, questioning her nerve. Marietta Winters curled trembling fingers around the bottom of the metal and forced it against the door knocker.

The brisk night air sliced into her skin. She adjusted her loathed shawl more tightly around her shoulders and pressed her ear closer to the door.

Nothing.

She looked into the lion's eyes, swallowed, then rapped the knocker once more.

Silence echoed in the night, only the shifting breeze an answer to her desperation. She wondered if this was to be the end of her search—an empty hall and no one at home. Another closed door. The final nail in Kenny's coffin.

No. She couldn't think that way.

A faint trembling shook her. Nerves and stress and fear. She hadn't slept in days. Hadn't eaten a real meal in twice that time—a loaf of bread stretched between. Her older brother's insistence on no one knowing their straits had turned the food money into Mark's new cloak for the races, new boots for Kenny, and a shawl for her.

Utter stupidity.

And yet had she just kept her mouth shut . . . not argued with Mark—their row causing Kenny to flee the house . . .

The trembling grew worse. She had to hold it together. A broken rhythm caused her head to whip up. Footsteps, not tremors. Someone had paused for a moment. The footfalls grew nearer, the heavy clack of a man's boots pounding against a marble floor.

She straightened, inclined her head and tried to still the desperate beat of her heart.

The steps stopped on the other side of the oak frame. *Please, oh please, let him be at home.* She had nowhere else to go. All other doors had been closed.

The oak swung with nary a sound, nary a creak.

She squinted at the sudden brilliance. A large man leaned against the door, bright light from the hall backlighting him and casting his features into relief. "Yes?"

His voice was gravelly. And annoyed. No pleasantries, then. Not that she had expected any. No respectable woman would be calling at this hour of the night. Rockwood had urged her to send a note in the morning to set up a meeting, but she couldn't afford to wait that long—she'd never avoid the mob

2

during the daylight hours. And Rockwood, with his talk of this mysterious man, had given her a thread of hope that she couldn't bear for sleep to break.

"I need to speak to Mr. Noble." She wished her voice was stronger, calmer.

The man looked past her, scanning the street, before returning his gaze. She wished she could see his features beyond the shadowy contours of his face. "Bit of an odd time to be calling for tea."

She clutched her reticule. "Yes. But it is urgent that I speak with Mr. Noble." She swallowed. "Please."

"Mr. Noble isn't taking *visitors* this time of night. Return in the morning." His voice was still gruff, but the edge that had been there before softened into something deep and crisp.

Her pride had once been a mile wide. So fierce and strong that she'd thought she could survive on the trait alone. The constant ache in her belly, the desperation, Kenny's fate . . . all had shown her otherwise. She fumbled in her reticule for the card she had stuffed there two hours ago. "Please. I can't return in the morning. Please. Here." She thrust the card forward. Anything, anything, to gain her entrance.

His shadowed eyes surveyed her for a long moment. Long fingers reached forward to grip the card. She let his fingers remove it from hers with reluctance, taking the chance that this man, this servant, might rip it in two. He gave the card a cursory glance and flipped it over his fingers, the card traveling down to his smallest finger and than flipping back. A game for him, but that card represented her brother's life. His eyes held hers, piercing through the shadows.

She tilted her chin up. Her pride may have been trampled, but her determination ran deep. She would see Mr. Noble.

Something changed in the man's posture, though she couldn't pinpoint what in the dark. He stepped back. She offered up a quick prayer and ducked inside.

The hall was lovely, the address expensive, so it shouldn't have surprised her, but the gold, navy, and mahogany shades were tasteful and elegant without being overstated. Mr. Noble was obviously someone who showed his wealth well.

She turned to say something and felt her mouth drop before she snapped it close.

"Thank you for letting me wait inside." She gripped her reticule to keep her hands steady. As if throwing herself on the mercy of a stranger in the dead of night wasn't enough to disconcert her . . .

Tall and rather well made, the disheveled but expensive cut of his clothing displayed strong shoulders with no padding in sight. There was considerably less clothing on this man than she was accustomed to seeing. Jacket, vest, cravat, and anything else that he might have worn had been shed so that he sported only a white shirt, open at the collar, and black trousers. He was slimmer than the boxing brute she had first thought him, though by no means skinny. She swallowed, refining her first thought—he was *extremely* well made.

And his face . . . A wave of warmth caressed her from the roots of her hair to the tips of her toes. Long dark lashes brushed over brilliant green eyes. Eyes that most women would kill for. But no woman would call him pretty. His cheekbones were too stark. His jaw too strong.

A compelling face, arresting, *sensual*. He had a masculine beauty that was nearly otherworldly.

But there was a cynical bend to his left brow. A tilt to his head. A jaded expression that said he knew the exact reaction his looks provoked.

One dark brow rose higher.

She blinked, heat suffusing her as she realized she'd been blatantly staring.

"I need to speak with Mr. Noble. Please. I know it is late, but . . ."

Women likely threw themselves at this man's feet every day, but that didn't cure her embarrassment nor assuage her desperation. Unless he could charm the guards into releasing Kenny, or stop the mobs from tearing anyone associated with him apart, this man's beauty would do her little good.

Unreadable green eyes surveyed her. She met his stare, forcing the heat from her cheeks. She would not back down. Noble was her last resort. Her last bastion. The one sliver of hope she had left.

He gestured with his arm and pivoted, striding down the hall, the prized card that had gained her entrance loosely clasped between two of his fingers. She hesitated for half a second, then followed.

He led her into a dimly lit study. A fire crackled in the hearth. Papers littered a deep mahogany desk, piles of books and documents stacked haphazardly across the surface. He flicked the card onto the desk, and it was instantly swallowed.

He pointed to a chair and then disappeared back into the hall without another word spoken.

She tentatively perched at the edge of the burgundy chair. Perhaps the man was a relation? An odd valet? The cut of his clothes was fine, even in dishabille, but his mannerisms were reminiscent of a butler. How he pointed to her chair, the motion to follow from the hall. The way he walked, as if attempting to blend into his surroundings, and *almost* succeeding. A task of Sisyphean proportions. Not with that face. Not with the way he filled his clothes or held himself.

The beautiful man strode back through the door, grabbed a tome from one of the floor-to-ceiling bookshelves and rounded the desk. The book thumped onto the tottering stack. *Debrett's Peerage.* He dropped into the large chocolate leather chair and leaned back, drumming his fingers on the only uncovered portion of mahogany.

"Now, what is it you need so desperately that you had to appear at such an hour, Miss . . . ?"

She was speechless for a moment. "I need to speak with Mr. Noble."

"Then congratulations, you have achieved your purpose. Shall I see you to the door?" He motioned behind her, his eyes piercing. His body was languid in the chair, belying his expression and the tilt of his dark head. Commanding, yet dissolute.

Her shoulders tightened. "You are Mr. Noble?"

"I am."

Her breath caught at the formal admission and expression in his sharp, abnormally vivid green eyes. The mannerisms he had displayed before seemed ludicrous all of a sudden—an impulsive flight of fancy on her part. The man seated in front of her looked as ruthless and capable as she'd been told.

Something in her rebelled. "But you answered the door. And your dress." She waved a hand at his simple white shirt, loose and slightly rumpled above black trousers.

His brow rose and he picked up a half coiled piece of wire and began winding it around his finger. "It's the dead of night. My butler, and two of my footmen, are out on a task for me. If we are making assumptions . . ."

His eyes passed over her mussed hair, which had long since escaped its pins, to her clutched hands and battered reticule, down to the mud-stained hem of her dress. "You look as if you are two steps from being a washerwoman, yet your bearing speaks otherwise. You hold your head as if you possess breeding. Not that a member of the—" He gave her another once over. "—gentry, is it?—would be afforded more good-will from me than a washerwoman. I've often found the opposite to be true. A washerwoman earns her place in this world, after all."

She had a sudden fierce desire to show him what she could do with the *earned* pistol hidden in her torn dress pocket.

"How did you come across this card?" He plucked it from the mess, twirling it negligently between his fore and middle fingers. "Rockwood's card. One would assume he gave it to you."

"How did you . . . ?" There had been no identifying marks on the card. Nothing to say Rockwood had possessed it. It had simply said MR. NOBLE in a gilded but plain script.

"What is your name?" he asked, instead of answering.

His eyes held a vast well of impatience, but there was a hint of something else there that gave her the slightest bit of hope. Curiosity.

She cleared her throat. She wanted to hold onto that slice of hope. She didn't want to give him her name. The dried spit on her hem and scrubbed tomato splotches on her back and knees were reminders of what happened when she did.

"Marietta Winters."

His eyes narrowed and the tips of his fingers whitened around the card. "I see. And what, Miss Winters, are you doing inside of my study at this hour?"

"I need help."

"Don't we all." He tossed the card onto the cluttered desktop and negligently began coiling the wire again, his eyes sharp. "Why come to me?"

"I was told you helped those in need." She called on everything inside of her to keep the desperation from showing.

"How interesting."

Her throat tightened. "Was Mr. Rockwood mistaken? Have I wasted precious time in coming to you?" Dashed, just like that. The sliver of hope dimmed. Foolish of her to think otherwise—hope had long since abandoned her.

Yet she raised her head higher, determination outstripping reason. A stubborn mouse on a desperate quest. And like a bird of prey, he watched her. He hadn't *stopped* his predatory assessment since he'd opened the door. It was unnerving in more ways than one, and if she weren't so mulish, she might have succumbed to the sharpness there, the hit to her pride.

His head tipped. "Surely Rockwood explained how I work. I rarely accept charity cases from members of the ton."

His tone was mild, almost curiously still, even with the thread of arrogance running beneath. She grasped the edges of her dignity. "He said your services cost ten thousand pounds."

"They do."

"Or . . . " She swallowed. Here was where the danger lay. "Or three favors."

He kept coiling the wire. "And did he explain what type of favors I might ask?"

"No," she whispered.

A dark grin flashed across his face. "Good on Rockwood."

She remembered the vaguely terrified expression on Rockwood's face as he'd talked about Gabriel Noble. *The man makes dukes tremble, Marietta, be careful.* If there had been another way . . .

She looked at the man dominating the space across from her. Arrogant and cold. If there was another way . . . but there wasn't. She was penniless. The law against her. Ostracized. Rockwood had taken pity on her, mainly due to the longstanding ties between their families.

Gabriel Noble . . . he was going to make her toil for every last bit of his help. He would break her remaining pride. She could see it in his icy emerald eyes.

But Rockwood had told her in no uncertain terms that if there was one person who could help her, it was Noble. And she had no other choices. Not if she was going to save Kenny.

"My brother was taken by the night watch two evenings ago." She'd been awake and running for help ever since. Fear and abject obstinacy were the only things keeping her upright. "They are charging him with murder. A—" She swallowed. "A constable said they are going to attempt to hurry through a trial." She looked blindly down, unable to focus. "They mean to hang him."

"The Middlesex murderer."

Her head shot up. "He is not!"

"That is what they mean to hang him for, though, is it not?"

The faded red splat of a tomato stain glowed on the fabric above her kneecap. She squeezed her eyes shut.

"News travels fast in my circles." His voice was silky and smooth, but still ice cold. "And even if it didn't, it's hardly a difficult thing to determine between your appearance, the timing, and your last name."

"Then . . . then you know—"

"That your brother is Kenneth Winters? Seems likely."

"He's not a murderer." Her lips pressed together.

"Of that, I have no idea."

Silence sat like a stone. Noble seemed quite willing to let it gather moss.

But he hadn't said no yet. "Will you help me?"

"Help you prove your brother innocent? Or help

10

you avoid any more brushes with the locals?" He motioned to her dress.

"Help prove my brother's innocence. You have to understand." She leaned forward, feeling that pernicious spark of hope once more. "Kenny could never have done something like that. He wouldn't hurt a soul."

"I've heard that from others, ones who were as guilty as jackals." He continued coiling his wire, as if she were an insignificant gnat and he too full of ennui to even swat her. "Why not hire a Runner? Or an investigator to clear your brother? They are much cheaper, I assure you."

His detachment prodded her anger, made her feel something other than soul deep despair.

"All funds are going to a barrister to help in court." And wasn't that a pity. She had smelled the gin on the barrister from the doorway of his office. But Mark had assured her of the man's credentials, and she'd stayed quiet for once. Mark wanted to help their brother too. She just hoped it had been the wisest use of their remaining monies. "And Mr. Rockwood pointed out that if anyone could help, 'twould be you. And the payment of the favors—"

"I repeat that a Runner or investigator would be much cheaper. In *every* way." He continued coiling . . . coiling the unending wire. "What type of favors do you think I might ask?"

"I don't know," she murmured. It could be anything. She had realized that as soon as Rockwood had reluctantly repeated the terms of Noble's agreements.

11

But she had little choice—her brother was going to hang for crimes he didn't commit. It was evident that the law enforcement did not intend to do any further investigation. They wanted to calm the public. Needed someone punished for the crimes. Quickly. The trial would be a spectacle—enough of a sham to assuage the public that justice was being served. And Kenny—young, stupid, darling Kenny—would be executed.

No one would lift a finger, and the mob would be happy, too happy, with the living effigy they could burn.

She needed Noble, yet Rockwood had been insistent that she be very sure of her willingness to sell her soul before asking him for help. *No one* turned down Noble's favors. No matter what they were.

"I won't murder or hurt anyone."

She thought she caught a glimpse of amusement in his eyes before it disappeared. He leaned forward again. His eyes lovely green chips of ice. His body larger than moments before. "Be assured that if I asked it of you, you *would* comply."

She found it difficult to breathe as his eyes seared into hers.

Whatever showed on her face must have been satisfactory, because he relaxed back into his chair. His eyes scanned her for ten tense beats of her heart. He gave a slight tilt of his head. "However, I doubt such actions would be necessary. But don't think of setting terms. There are only *my* terms. Do you understand?"

A thread of tension uncoiled from her gut even as

his statement about her future formed a new one. It sounded like he was going to help her. *Someone* was going to help her. "And you will gain my brother's release?"

He tilted his head farther, a lock of jet hair falling across his forehead. "If I take your case and he's innocent, yes. If he's not, no, and you will still owe me the favors, whether you wish to or not."

Outrage rose in her, despite the persistent fear. "How do I know you will be fair in determining his innocence? Better for you to simply proclaim his guilt and collect."

He shrugged nonchalantly, as if they were discussing the evening's menu. "That is a possibility. However, much as I'm sure Rockwood told you, I am my reputation. I doubt many would avail themselves of my services if I did that to my . . . clients."

His lids dropped halfway over his eyes, and she shivered. Rockwood had said she could trust Noble with the job. That he always completed his tasks.

"If I take your case, you will not argue with my tactics. You will help me when I require it. You will do exactly as I say throughout. *Everything* I say."

His gaze raked over her. Chills, hot and cold, skittered through her, battling between his words and the look in his eyes. Her heart beat much faster than she preferred.

"Marietta Winters, the question then becomes, do *you* accept?

Chapter 2

He had sent her home without allowing her to answer.

I find myself intrigued, Miss Winters. But I don't take cases like yours without probing further. Besides, you need time to decide yourself. You will essentially be mine once this task is complete. There is no going back on the deal, once accepted. Give your answer to my messenger at noon, and I will give you mine at dark.

Such parting words had done little to reassure her. She'd tossed and turned to the steady ticking of the clock, to the dawn seeping through the darkness, to flashes of taunting bright green eyes laden with shadows.

To perfect lips forming commands and demanding her soul.

An ink blot formed as she set pen to paper.

Dear Mr. Noble,

I find you outrageous and arrogant, regardless of whether your reputation demands such behavior. Still, I accept your conveniently vague terms.

She crumpled the paper into a ball and chucked it next to the other five around the waste basket, hidden in the morning shadows.

Dear Mr. Noble,

You leave me little choice. My brother's life is at stake. I accept your veiled threats couched in indistinct terms.

Crumpled ball number seven.

Dear Mr. Noble,

The longer the delay, the worse for my brother. I accept you are an arroga—

Number eight plopped to the floor of the basket like a slab in a tomb. It was obvious that she had to keep the correspondence short.

Dear Mr. Noble,

I accept.

Awaiting your reply,

She signed her name and sealed the note.

A knock at noon announced the arrival of the messenger. It struck her that Noble had never asked for her address.

Their temporary butler hovered—no *cowered*—near the hall as she opened the door in his stead.

"Murderer!"

"For shame!"

The messenger boy hurried inside as she slammed the door on the shouts from the street. Tinkling glass indicated another meeting of object to window in the drawing room. They had been most successful in hitting that window, situated as prominently as it was. The boy bobbed his head as she handed him the note. He held one out to her in return.

Marietta stared at his outstretched hand. "What is this?"

"A note for you."

She clutched the paper in her slightly shaking fingers. "Thank you. You may use the back entrance, if you wish."

"Much obliged, miss." He bobbed his head and walked down the hall.

With a sharp glance at the still stationary butler, who had no doubt soaked in every nuance of the conversation, she retired to her room.

The note was short. Sloping letters and elegant swirls. She was to stay inside until Noble came at eight. She bristled at the command even as a resounding *thunk* indicated what sounded like a head of cabbage hitting the bricks outside.

She had until the evening to change her mind, but the long daytime hours only reinforced her motivation. The hecklers in the streets, the rotten vegetables pinging against the sides of the house, the splintering of glass from the drawing room. The owner of their rented house would have apoplexy when he returned. It was a good thing he was traveling abroad, or likely they would have been evicted days ago.

Waiting until eight was murderous. Mark had risen a bit after noon only to down a headache tonic and slouch back to bed pleading illness. Sick on gin and wine. She'd heard one of the maids tiptoe into his room, and it was without an ounce of surprise that Marietta walked in a few hours later to discover Mark once more passed out with an empty bottle tipped by his bedside.

The knock, when it came on the eighth strike of the clock, was accompanied by more relief than fear. She needed to do *something*. Anything.

"Good evening, I'm here to see Miss Winters," a smooth, deep voice said.

"And who shall I say is calling?"

Silence met the butler's question, and she walked around the corner in time to see the butler's uneasy expression as Noble continued to stare impassively.

"I can handle things from here, thank you, Yates," she said.

The butler moved back a few spaces, but stayed within hearing distance. She motioned toward the small study at the side of the room, but Noble simply inclined his head and walked back through the door. She hurried after him as he made his way to a carriage parked in front. Darted looks up and down the street showed a blessedly vacant thoroughfare for once.

"Where are you going?" she asked.

A coachman opened the carriage door as they neared. The vehicle was nondescript, sturdy but unremarkable.

"*We* are going for a drive."

He held out his hand and she paused, casting glances in both directions. Seeing no one in the immediate vicinity, and feeling a distinct lack of choice, she gripped his gloved fingers and allowed herself to be helped inside.

The interior of the carriage was quite nice. Rich velvet seats, leather straps, and luxurious pillows. The shades were drawn, even with twilight upon them, and a low gas lamp spread shadows into the corners and crevices.

"You fancy a ride through the park at eight, is that it?"

He closed the door and sat across from her, his face shifting between shadows as he settled. "I fancy not having every sentence of our conversation dissected by your butler and other servants."

Her lips tightened, but it was hard to defend. He spoke nothing but the truth of the matter.

"You doubt my household?"

He peeled off his gloves, a languid, sensual motion where each finger was caressed from root to tip. "Absolutely."

"Quite suspicious of you."

"I am a cautious man. Perhaps I should speak to your brother before we go further in our negotiations."

She knew instantly that it was not Kenny of whom he spoke.

"Mark is indisposed."

He lazily pulled a glove through his fingers. "Pity."

The carriage rocked lightly as they rounded a corner.

"You said that you would decide whether to help my brother by eight." She lifted her chin, clinging to her last remnants of pride. "Have you?"

"You have accepted my terms? Without question?"

Two gleaming eyes reflected in the lamplight under dark lashes and locks, like the devil making a bargain. A fine sheen of perspiration gathered along her hairline. "I have little choice, have I? I would not have sought you out otherwise. And you have given little enough explanation about what you might want from me."

"Dangerous wording, Miss Winters."

"Choice wording, then, Mr. Noble, as I find dealing with you far from safe."

He settled farther into the plush velvet seat. "You may as well call me Gabriel." The corner of his mouth twitched, as if he knew she would do no such thing.

"I prefer Mr. Noble." The words were clipped. Everything else about this situation held her powerless. She would fight until her dying breath to retain some semblance of control.

"And I prefer you call me Gabriel." His taunting tone curled into silk-covered iron. "If we find ourselves in a tavern or on the streets, it's hardly going to do our investigation much good for you to give away the game."

Tavern? Her? We? She bit her lower lip and ignored that portion of his statement for a second. "As if everyone in town knows your name?"

"My name is not unknown to certain elements. It is why you seek to *hire* me, is it not?"

"And your face? Hardly a visage to be forgotten," she said, a part of her surprised at her vitriol; the relief of having someone to help turning into unnecessary combativeness.

"Are you calling me handsome? Why, Marietta Winters, I do believe I am blushing." His voice deepened as he played with his leather gloves, dragging them through his fingers in slow motions.

Her cheeks roasted. "I stand by my statement."

"No need to worry. I usually travel in disguise. Much easier for everyone that way."

He maintained his indolent posture leaning back against the squabs, but a new thread of tension laced through the latticework in the carriage. The gloves dangled from his fingers, forgotten for a moment. Marietta made note of the tension. Though she wasn't sure what it signified, perhaps she could use it to her advantage later.

"And what are we to do while you are off masquerading as Robin the Hood?" Surely, he had been kidding about . . .

"*You* will travel with me, of course." He studied her, and the sides of his mouth curled. "Perhaps as my wench. I find that this case becomes more interesting the more I think on it."

"Pardon me? I believe I heard you incorrectly." She noted his amusement, and relief and irritation surged in response. Terrible man, baiting the desperately starving fish.

"Doubtful. Your hearing seems quite sound. You will accompany me, of course." He twigged the gloves and smirked, but the amusement she had read in his

20

eyes turned to icy watchfulness once more.

"You are serious?" She just stared at him for a second. "You are not simply baiting me?"

"You don't expect me to do all the work, when you're not paying a pence?"

"I'm paying you in favors. Favors that I have not a whit as to what they could entail. I think you are being compensated quite well," she said tightly. Panic and desperation were a poor combination.

"Those who pay me ten thousand pounds have to do nothing more than sit on their hands. You, my dear, will be an active participant. When your favors come due, I need to make sure you are prepared to pay them." His green eyes turned dark and dangerous.

It wasn't that she was opposed to actively participating in freeing Kenny—the thought actually appealed to her overall desire to maintain control. But the thought of what he was implying . . .

"And what types of favors would those be, Mr. *Noble*? Skulking and thieving?"

Prickly, defensive, prideful. Her unmarried state was little mystery at times. She lifted her chin, prepared for a set down.

"I don't recall mentioning anything about thieving, but good on you for taking the initiative, Marietta," he said with mock approval.

"I'll do your three favors, when the time comes— as long as I'm satisfied with your service." She tried to project haughtiness through her gritted teeth and desperate pride. "I suppose you view yourself as some sort of fairy-tale wish granter?"

A faint smile touched his mouth. "If you care to see me

that way, be my guest." He sketched a small bow. "Only I will be asking how *you* can serve *me*. And you *will* give me those favors. I've never left anyone unsatisfied."

His mocking smile turned edged and sensual. She had a strong intuition that he knew exactly what it did to members of the opposite sex. She shivered and drew herself up.

"You think highly of yourself. I will do my part as long as you do yours."

"You suddenly seem much more confident, Miss Winters." Long fingers stroked his well-defined jaw. "I wonder at the change."

"I was nervous. Initially." And desperate—neither emotion had really changed.

"Hardly something I'd admit to a virtual stranger. Who knows what I'll do with that information now?" His voice grew lazy. "And you were nervous before, where you aren't anymore?"

She lifted her chin higher, unable to answer.

His lazy air disappeared as quickly as it had come. He leaned forward, and the air, the tension, coalesced into a sharp point. She pressed into the velvet. He was at least two feet away, but it suddenly seemed more like inches.

"Are you frightened of me, Marietta Winters?" he whispered, his tone somewhere between a threat and a taunt. The interior seemed darker, the shadows longer.

She faked a calmness she didn't feel. "Do I have reason to be?"

His eyes seemed to turn from bright green to black as he leaned past the lamp's light. "Completely."

Her lips parted and her thoughts froze. No. No, she would not be powerless. She threw up a hammer in her mind to break through the ice.

He leaned back, the light catching his eyes and turning them back to that startling green, almost too bright to be real. He continued pulling the supple looking leather through his fingers, as if nothing had occurred.

"There is no one to gainsay you, if you accompany me? Your older brother? What about your society connections? You may be on the fringes, but your family clings tenaciously."

How in heaven's name did he know anything about her family? "Mark will say nothing. As for our social connections . . . they matter little now."

"I've found social connections, especially for the upper class, mean a great deal. Do not think to lie to me so early." His face was smiling, mocking; his eyes were closed and remote.

"With Kenny's arrest and my visit to you I think it safe to say any social connections have already been severed." She looked away, wishing the shade was open so she could blindly stare at the passing sights. "We didn't receive a single invitation today or yesterday. And the day before we received only two—and no doubt that was because they had not heard the early morning news in time to revoke them before they were sent."

"No suitors waiting in the wings?"

"No." It was appalling to admit such to a man like the one across from her.

His eyes weighed her, and she feared he could see deep into her soul. "You could weather this storm,

23

tainted though you'd be. But your working with me may ruin any future offers from your strata."

"I know." The admission didn't come out quite as strongly as she'd hoped.

She longed for a stable home of her own, one where she needn't worry about the next meal or the roof over their heads. But she had learned after her parents' deaths that flights of fancy needed to be buried deep. The type of man she desired was not to be found among her decreasingly small pool of acquaintances, and her sharp tongue had culled the rest of the herd quickly.

Mark had charge of her for another year and was intolerant of the lower classes. He steadfastly refused to let her marry a merchant or businessman . . . not that she knew any. And at this point she doubted even a merchant would want to be saddled with someone so closely related to the Middlesex murderer.

"You could distance yourself from your brother Kenneth."

She shut her eyes tightly and shook her head.

"Yes, I could," she whispered. "But it would show poor character were I to care more for my marital prospects than for my brother's life."

He tilted his head. "We shall see."

She stiffened, and the fear, the despair, once more disappeared behind a cloud of anger. "Must you be such a bear, Mr. Noble? I don't recall having done anything to earn such animosity."

He drew the leather lazily through his fingers as he regarded her, eyes piercing and weighing. "I'll need to see your brother's rooms and go through his belongings."

"As you will. Tomorrow—"

"No. We will go now. You need to gather your possessions, and we have less of a chance of being followed at this time of night." He rapped the trap.

"Gather my possessions? To what do you refer?"

"I'll need you close." He uncurled from the seat as the carriage made a turn. Rising to his full seated height, he looked down at her with his heat-provoking face and cold eyes. "You will need to move into a house of mine. Somewhere we will attract little attention and can come and go as we please."

"Wha-What?" She sputtered. "Stay with you?"

"You just said it wouldn't be a problem, Marietta. Seeing as you aren't worried about your reputation—"

"I didn't say I wasn't worried about it," she hissed. "I'll do what's needed, but what you're asking hardly seems necessary."

He pulled his gloves on, tugging one finger at a time. "So you could leave your home at any time of night without attracting attention? No matter what you are wearing? You could stroll outside and no one would say or notice a thing? Excellent."

She suddenly had a vision of wearing something entirely inappropriate and walking down Golden Square. They had thrown rotten vegetables today and yesterday. What would they throw if she wore something outrageous? "Where is the house located, and who will be with us?"

Fingers worked to straighten each covered digit. "It's close to the East End, where we will be spending more time. There is talk of renaming your brother the

25

Clerkenwell Killer, since two murders have taken place there. We should hunt there first, don't you agree?"

His mocking tone rubbed her. "And what staff do you have in place?"

"Staff? No, no staff. It will be just the two of us."

Her jaw dropped and she tried to say something, but nothing emerged.

"You are in luck. I've just finished a case and can devote myself completely to this task. And it . . . interests me. Now, let's gather your belongings."

"I can't stay in a house with just *you*." An idiotic response, as they had just finished talking about her battered reputation and lack of marital prospects. At least her belligerence survived.

The door opened.

"I assure you that my tastes don't run to waifish brunettes. You have no cause for concern on my account."

He barely spared her a once-over as he exited the carriage, and it stung her vanity, little though she thought she still possessed.

"You are a remarkably rude and awful man," she said as she exited after him and he began to ascend the walk. "I have no idea why I am even listening to you. You have done nothing with which to give me confidence."

He stopped and turned. She expected anger or irritation at the hit to his honor, but was surprised to see amusement instead. "No?"

He stepped forward and circled around her, the cuffs of his shirt brushing against her sleeve, against the material along the dip in her back. "But I could be twice as awful, and though you would complain you would still follow me, would you not?"

His voice was a whisper above her ear.

"Because you have nowhere else to turn and your dear, trusted friend Rockwood said you could trust me. And that's what you are going to do, Marietta, is it not?"

Every hair on her body lifted toward his carnal voice. She gritted her teeth against the sensation. "I don't believe I like you, Mr. Noble."

He laughed softly. She smoothed a hand down the back of her neck to displace the shivers.

"I don't care, Miss Winters." His tone was seductive and low, but there was steel underneath. "As long as you keep your end of the bargain, I don't care in the least. Now get moving."

Chapter 3

Marietta was mildly annoyed when the butler and footman took one glance at Gabriel Noble and allowed him to pass without comment. Probably hoping he was some rich dandy to toss her skirts or who *had* just tossed her skirts. Hoping they might get paid for once, if so. The servants weren't stupid. They knew things were dire.

When meals were restricted to bread and water, and the cook dismissed, it wasn't hard to make the relevant connections. She was surprised the servants had remained with them as long as they had. Mark was a crafty one with his promises and lies.

While the two male servants might be hoping she would toss her skirts for the mysterious man she had entered with, the two maids hovering in the doorway were obviously hoping to toss theirs instead, if their glazed expressions were anything to go by. The butler must have gathered the other three servants in the entrance hall as soon as she left—waiting for the gossip her return might bring.

"Miss?"

The comment was directed to her, but Jeanie's eyes never left Noble.

"Bring my traveling bag please, Jeanie."

"Yes, miss." Glassy eyes stayed on their target. "I look forward to wherever we are traveling."

Marietta watched the other maid, Carla, pin Noble with an avaricious gaze as he visibly scanned the layout of the ground floor. Her eyes took in everything from the tilt of his head to the curve of his backside, and she took what seemed to be an involuntary step in his direction, as if called there by an invisible force.

That decided it for Marietta. She had been thinking about taking one of the maids with her, but she'd rather struggle with all of her fastenings—she'd rather put her dress on *backward*—than have to deal with this again. Besides, neither was loyal to her. The idea of a buffer between Noble had appeal, but not enough to overcome the negatives.

"No, I don't require your presence on the trip. Please retrieve my case."

Noble shot her a knowing look, edged with something that resembled irritation—but for the first time, she didn't think it was directed at her. "Show me your brother's room."

She led the way upstairs. Kenny's room was messy—she had never been able to find a thing in it. She had a feeling that Noble could sympathize with the state, though, judging by his own study.

He poked around, picking up and examining objects, nodding or humming at different things. The humming was a discordant sound in the charged atmosphere.

"I'm going to pack. I trust you will be fine? Don't disturb Mark. He's not . . . pleasant when disturbed after a rough night. Or day."

"Not pleasant?" Noble's sharp eyes held hers, searching for something. He must have found it, because his shoulders relaxed and he waved her away. "I will not pester your disreputable brother."

The two maids, standing attentively in the hall, followed her into her room.

"Who is he, miss?"

Marietta frowned. "Just a man." She took the case from Jeanie, who was holding it. Stunned and dreamy, she didn't look capable of relinquishing it on her own.

Carla, always the more brash of the two, elbowed her way past her stunned compatriot. She was eyeing Marietta with the smug disdain she had taken to displaying after the invitations had dried up and the neighbors had turned their backs. And now Carla—all of the servants—were in a plum spot. Serving out gossip to anyone with a pence.

One part of her could understand it—the servants hadn't been paid in months. Bitter and hungry, they were getting revenge and putting food on the table. The other part of her was angry beyond anything that they were contributing to the fiasco.

"What are you doing with that man?" Carla asked.

"Packing. Are you going to help?" She took an armful of clothing and dropped it in her case. She didn't have much, but without the painstaking care packing required, the dresses took a lot of space.

Carla ran a finger along the edge of the case. "What's his name?"

"His name is mind your manners." Marietta grabbed another handful of undergarments from the linen press—an extra chemise and shift, two pairs of stockings. Jeanie wandered over, still looking dazed, but began helping her fold and place. Carla continued to watch her. Marietta was getting tired of people watching her.

"If you aren't going to help, get out."

Carla smirked and sashayed from the room.

"Sorry, miss, don't know what's been wrong with her," Jeanie said after Carla's skirt disappeared around the door frame.

"Thank you, Jeanie." Marietta looked at the other maid, who had always been sweet. Daft, but sweet. "I appreciate the help."

"Of course, miss. I can pack your essentials, if you'd like."

"Yes, that would be wonderful."

Jeanie went into the connected room where Marietta kept her perfume and pins, her toilette and jewelry.

A sibilant sound from the hallway made her head turn. She walked forward and peeked around the frame. The two male servants were loitering in the hall, trying to look busy.

"Isn't there something you should be doing?"

They gave her varying stares. One smirking, one haughty. Gone was any authority she might have had. The Winters family was in deep trouble in all areas.

She drew herself up. "Go fetch an extra lamp and my parasol."

They both stared at her for a moment and the moment stretched. Finally, they turned and walked down the steps, their eyes promising they would return. Marietta inhaled a shaky breath. Her old life was over. It had been over since her parents died, but now the door was completely shut. She was on par with one of the—*all* of the servants. Or she would be very, very soon.

She placed a hand over her heart, beating as if it would never slow again.

The sibilant sound issued once more. She crept down the hall until she stood just outside Kenny's room.

"It's as I said, sir, I'm here to serve you. I can help with *anything* you need." The emphasis was hard to ignore. Carla lowered her voice, but Marietta could still hear her, as close as she was. "I know where all the treasures be. People paying prime money for the good items. I won't charge you a penny."

The implication of what the maid would give for free wasn't lost on Marietta, nor was the fact that the servants had been searching through and selling Kenny's belongings, as if he was a sideshow. The itch brimming under her skin, a slow anger and irritation, turned into a fire. She knew, *knew*, they were profiting from the scandal, but she had thought it only through gossip, not through thievery. She couldn't pull a thought together out of the flames.

"How many things have you sold? And what were they?" Noble asked, his voice entrancing, coaxing for more.

"Small things, nothing as good as I could give you. A watch, a handkerchief, some cravats. There's a journal hidden. All the deepest thoughts of the Middlesex murderer."

She could feel the wetness on her cheeks, the impotent rage. She wanted to barge in, to grab the maid and shake her, squeeze her until her thieving hands popped off. To demand what right she had to do this.

Some last bit of sense held her in place. She didn't know where Kenny's journal was—barging in now would accomplish nothing. But as soon as the slovenly bitch produced it, she would shake her until there was nothing left to shake.

"I'd be interested in seeing that, and anything else he's hidden. You are certainly a resourceful girl." His voice was melodious and deep. Spellbinding. The words curled around the doorway and wrapped around her. She cut through them with a knife, her anger spilling over to him.

The maid giggled. Marietta could hear her awe and excitement. Could *feel* the way the maid would be leaning toward him, enraptured and ready to do anything for more of his approval.

"It's just over here."

Something scraped across the floor, the night table most likely.

"He hides all of the things here that he doesn't want his nosy sister to find."

Marietta watched the pendulum in the hallway clock as if the continual motion would make things better; make her less likely to sob.

"What does he think of his sister?"

"Probably what we all think. She's plain and poor and sharp-tongued. It's no wonder she's still unmarried."

Something fell and clacked on the floor. She continued to watch the swing of the clock, ticking each plain, sharp second.

"There it is." A swish of a skirt and the solid sound of a book hitting a palm.

What was he going to do with Kenny's journal? Half-formed thoughts of him selling it just like the servants raced through her head. She knew nothing about him. He had given her no reason to think he'd live up to his name. And if her own servants were profiting, what was to stop a complete stranger from doing worse?

"Have you read it?"

She squeezed her eyes closed, the sensation of fainting that had become a constant companion in the past few weeks visiting her once more. She'd given him access to everything. In her desperation she had given him actual material that could be used against her family. What had she done?

"Neh, I can't read. I can do lots of other, better things, though."

"I'm sure that is true. You seem very diligent."

Carla snickered. Marietta thought somewhat viciously that the maid likely had no idea what diligent even meant. There was no sound for a moment, and then Carla moaned, low and breathy. The sound of a woman who had experienced the finest of delicacies. The hairs on Marietta's body rose and her stomach heaved.

"Now be a good girl and collect the other things, will you?"

"Yes, yes, right now."

There were a lot of shuffles and bumps. And Carla kept giggling. It was an awful, grating sound, like a carriage wheel rubbing against its post.

"Ah, yes, this is perfect. And that as well. You are surely a gift from heaven, Carla."

The carriage wheel scraped along a jagged rock. "Anything for you, sir. Anything."

Marietta could stand it no longer. She tiptoed back down the hall, and then stomped back along her path. The maid's grating carriage laugh came to a halt.

She plastered a fake smile on her face and rounded the doorway. "Ah, Carla, there you are. Please help the men downstairs. They are looking for my parasol. It seems to be missing."

Her parasol was in her accessory chest, awaiting packing.

Carla looked furious and opened her mouth, but Noble beat her to it. "A good woman can't be without her parasol." His tone was offhand, but his eyes didn't move from Marietta's—watching her for something.

Carla threw her a look drenched in venom, then turned back to Noble, all sweetness and light. "I will fetch it and return here."

He smiled, that lazy smile that made him look like a well-contented cat. It obviously made women want to stroke him, if Carla's reaction to it was anything to go by. And Marietta had to admit that the image caused her fingers to itch too.

She curled her fingers into her palms with enough force to break the skin.

Carla strode from the room without looking at her, and she could hear the maid's footsteps down the stairs.

"You." She pointed her finger at him, too angry to care that it was shaking.

"Me," he said mockingly. "The man who procured your brother's journal for you." He threw the book at her feet.

She knelt and placed her hand on the leather cover, her anger and anxiety dissipating like steam to be replaced with confusion and uncertainty. "What?"

"Are you going to tell me that you weren't standing outside the door the whole time, Marietta?"

She stared at him, uncomprehending. She was so tired all of a sudden—the last seventy hours collapsing in on her without something solid like anger to hold the cards up. Exhausted. And here was a man who completely unnerved her. Who seemed to carelessly flick cards at random, occasionally taking a swipe at the bottom of the stack, destroying the foundation for everything above.

"Well, do you want it?" Something dark laced his tone. "Or shall I leave it here for your loving maid to sell to the highest bidder?"

He was angry with her? What gave him the right? He was the one using his wiles left and right. Her rage returned full force. "I wouldn't want your efforts to go to waste. Perhaps I should leave you here to sex all the information right out of her."

"Using me for my physical services, I'm aghast." His voice was mocking, but there was a dangerous undercurrent. An eddy that threatened to drag her under.

"You seemed to be doing it well on your own."

"Thank you for your compliment."

"It wasn't a compliment," she said, her lips nearly cracking from the force required to utter the words. "It was an accusation."

"An accusation. How trite. *You* asked for *my* help, Miss Winters."

Her fingernails dug into her left palm. She picked up the journal, shaking it in his direction from the floor. "Were you going to give me this if I hadn't walked in on the two of you?"

"And here I thought you trusted me." His voice was nonchalant.

"I don't trust you at all. A *sin* would be less dangerous."

He was suddenly squatting in front of her, having moved too quickly for her to react. He ran his thumb over the leather top of the journal, the tip brushing her fingers.

"That's a shame, Marietta." His voice held the low hum of an ocean wave at night. "If you don't trust me, your brother is going to hang. And I guarantee that you will still be serving me. Three services. Three tasks. Three nights of sin?"

His fingertips moved along the side of her hand and then lifted. The most dangerous man she'd ever met crouched in front of her. Terrifying in the responses he caused, *created*, in her.

"I want to know if you were going to give me the journal," she whispered, unable to do anything else.

He leaned toward her, his lips mere inches from hers. "And what makes you think I will answer?" he whispered back, a sensual edge to his voice.

Footsteps sounded on the stairs. Frozen, Marietta waited for him to move. And waited. The footsteps grew closer. A foot hit the top of the steps.

His mouth curved, so close she could see the fine lines on his lips. She shoved away from him, standing and clutching the journal in front of her chest.

"We couldn't locate your parasol."

Marietta processed Carla's words without turning. "Bring Mister—bring this—bring this gentleman something to drink, Carla. I'm sure he will appreciate the gesture."

She heard a strangled growl before the footsteps retreated once more.

"Poor Carla. Do you always abuse your staff so?"

She gripped the journal more tightly. His smooth, mocking voice. The arrogant tilt to his head. The way he continued to squat on his heels and stare up at her through the fringe of his hair, green eyes jaded and promising all sorts of things.

"And if I do? I'm sure you will coax her back to a satisfied state. That is what *you* do, is it not?"

"I perform all my jobs well, Marietta." He leaned back on his hands, long legs spread before him. "Were there other services that interest you?"

Sex and mystery coiled, curled, *oozed* from every pore.

"No."

"Pity." He cocked his head to the side, a derisive tilt.

"I thought waifish brunettes weren't your style?"

"They aren't. But adders are something I pride myself in handling."

She stiffened. "Do you get away with this type of behavior?"

He grinned wolfishly. "Always."

"Pity." She turned and walked through the doorway, not trusting herself to stay in a room with him any longer. She'd likely murder him. Or do something worse, like fall prey to his eyes and gestures.

Back in her room, Jeanie had a number of things out for her inspection. Marietta watched her maid look up at her, then past her, Jeanie's eyes glazing over.

"Are you finished packing, then?" that damned voice said behind her, his presence explaining her maid's suddenly slack jaw.

She shoved a jewelry pouch into the corner of her case. "Why don't you bother Carla? She seems quite excited for the attention."

"I'm hurt, Marietta. Truly."

"I'm sure." As if she had the ability to hurt anyone these days. Someone would have to care first. She shut her eyes. Idiot. She was going to have a breakdown if she kept up such pitiful thoughts.

"Is this all you have?"

"If you are going to be obnoxious, I'd prefer for you to wait elsewhere."

He picked up the edge of a black gown, and she slapped his hand away.

He whistled and touched the edge again. "Fashionable. And here I thought little could outdo your current dress."

"I'm in mourning."

"Your parents have been dead for two years."

She glanced up sharply at his display of knowledge once more. "How do you know that?"

"I know many things. Such as when you lie."

That she had stretched her mourning period into a second year was pushing things, but she couldn't afford new dresses, and altering her older, out of fashion garments would only get her so far. Besides, the dark gowns protected her in other ways. Silly, insidious ways where her femininity wasn't threatened. She couldn't be held responsible for her lack of feminine wiles in dresses like *those*.

She shut down that line of thinking. Here she thought Mark the prideful one.

"You know no such thing." She pushed his hand aside and folded the dress.

"Don't spend too much time worrying about which beautiful dress you can't live without."

Mocking words, words that made her want to lash back, but she read the truth in them and the seriousness in his eyes. She turned to her personal effects. Dresses could be replaced. Personal possessions could not.

The servants were untrustworthy, and Mark soon wouldn't be able to keep away the mobs. The streets were calling for revenge. Noble's house, though it chafed her to admit, was a safer place to store her mementos and more precious items. She might not trust him, but deep inside, underneath her tired and irrational anger, she perceived he had a code he would not cross.

The irritating man poked around her room, flashing smiles at the giggling Jeanie and sending Carla on repeated errands downstairs while Marietta gathered the last of her things.

Jeanie disappeared to gather a last box. Noble leaned against a pillow, as if he owned the world. "Did you know they were selling your brother's things before?"

Her lips tightened. "No."

She needed to let her older brother know somehow. She picked up a pen and jotted a note. She crept into Mark's room and tucked it into his hand so the servants would have less of a chance of finding it. For the first time in two years she was glad her brother was passed out. She didn't know if she could deal with him now, and had a strong feeling that he and Noble would not get on well at all.

Mark would be very angry that an outsider was aware of their economic straits. Even to help Kenny, he would not divulge such information. It was why she hadn't talked to him before embarking on her mission.

She walked back and looked around her room. The most important items were packed. She nodded to Noble and they carried her boxes and case into the unmarked carriage they had taken earlier.

She saw three sharp pairs of servants' eyes and one glassy-eyed pair watch them depart. The carriage took a number of turns that seemed unnecessary, as if they were going in circles, and Marietta had to wonder if they were trying to evade followers. But as Noble was up top with the coachman, she had no one to ask. Twenty minutes later the carriage pulled onto a non-descript street.

The street was well-lit with gas lamps, but there was an air of disuse about the lane. There were no lights shining inside the houses. It was as if they were unin-habited—their plain fronts hiding gaping holes inside. Empty boxes stacked side by side.

She watched through the window as Noble leapt down, all insouciant grace and easy movements. He opened the door, picked up the two heaviest boxes, and walked toward the front, leaving her to step down unattended. She followed, fuming in his wake.

The door opened and Marietta was relieved to see a sturdy older woman. She drew close enough to hear Noble ask whether everything was ready.

"Yes, sir, Mr. Noble. I received your urgent note. I've stocked the pantry and larder. There is some of that hearty stew still warm near the stove. Everything is cleaned from last time. I'll come by in the mornings to help the girl."

"Thank you, Mrs. Rosaire." His voice was rich and warm, nothing like the cold, mocking tones he used with her, or the empty sensual ones he had used on her maids.

The woman, who looked to be a no-nonsense type of matriarch, blushed like a schoolgirl. Marietta tapped a foot in general annoyance at her gender.

Mrs. Rosaire gave her a once-over and circled her,

looking at her serviceable shoes, closely inspecting her face.

"She's not a bad one. Not too noticeable. Should be an asset."

"That's what I thought as well. A plain face that can be enhanced when needed or go unnoticed," Noble said, his mouth sleek and satisfied as he smirked at her, deliberately provoking her. Her fingers itched.

"Should I send Clarisse with the usual garments?" Mrs. Rosaire asked.

"Yes, that would be helpful, thank you," he said.

Mrs. Rosaire squinted at her. "She's a bit tall."

"Shall I give you a look at my teeth too?" Marietta bared her fangs.

"And she has a temper." Mrs. Rosaire frowned disapprovingly. "Don't you give Mr. Noble any of your lip, missy. You have no idea what he's done for—"

"Thank you, Mrs. Rosaire. If you could speak with Clarisse, I'd appreciate it." He picked up the boxes from the step where he had deposited them. "Give my regards to Mr. Rosaire."

Mrs. Rosaire patted him on the forearm. "I will, dearie. See you soon." She shot Marietta a warning glare and walked through the front door, shutting it behind her.

The sound echoed in the empty foyer. There were no pot stands or tables, no racks or rugs. Just her boxes, her case, and the two of them.

"Garments? What was she talking about? Who is Clarisse?"

Noble stepped on the first stair. "Clarisse is a seamstress. She will fit you with several outfits. For what we need to do, we can hardly have you walking around in that." He looked pointedly at her dress. "Come."

She maneuvered with her box up the stairs—bare as well—to a sparsely finished room on the first floor. There appeared to be two others farther down.

"This is your room. Mine is down the hall. I'm sure you can find whatever you need." He put the boxes down. "The kitchen is fully stocked. If you need help dressing in the morning, make sure to be up between eight and nine, as Mrs. Rosaire will check in at that time each day to see if you need assistance. Otherwise, I'll be obliged to help you." A rakish smile crossed his face. "Somehow I expect you will be up at eight."

"And that is the only time there will be anyone else around?"

"There are no servants, so you are on your own in the morning. I don't have servants here for the simple reason that the fewer people who know what we are doing, the better. Servants are an invaluable source of information for other people. Something I remember when it comes to my own." He gave her another pointed glance.

"And Mrs. Rosaire?"

"Is not a servant."

"But how do you know she's trustworthy?"

"Because I do. Good night. Oh, and eat some of the stew downstairs before you wither away."

And with that, Gabriel Noble walked through the

door, leaving her with three boxes and a case full of her items in a cold, nearly empty, foreign room. The click of a door closing down the hall echoed in the bare hallway.

Marietta sank onto the bed. It was soft, but the down was little comfort. It was just a nicer version of a lodging house. A rented room. Their dire straits had been leaning in that direction for a while. She had been dreading it, and now it was upon her.

Her stomach growled. Her pride rebelled. She didn't want to go downstairs to the kitchen. He would hear her. He'd be smug.

Her stomach growled again. She'd give it ten minutes. Maybe he would be asleep and she could salvage some pride. In ten minutes and one second, though, pride would be damned.

Her eyes focused on the first box and she opened it. Trinkets and letters, a locket and some pressed flowers.

Her finger grazed the hope medallion she'd made as a little girl. Wishing for a brave and handsome man to come along and solve her troubles. Troubles which then had consisted of sneaking out to the pond and being chastened for skinned hands and muddied hems. Her troubles had turned so much worse when she hadn't been looking. And she no longer could count on some nameless, faceless man to come charging in to save her. She was going to have to save herself.

Her marital prospects had gone the way of their country house. Gone forever. But it would do her little good to worry about that now. She would survive.

She ran a finger over a letter from Kenny. One written his first year at Eton. She pulled the letter against her chest and closed her eyes. She could do this. She would save Kenny.

She clutched the letter and her vow as she tiptoed down to the kitchen. As she ladled the stew into a bowl. As she devoured the heavenly concoction and ignored the tears blurring her eyes.

Chapter 4

The smell of baking bread and fresh herbs greeted her as she entered the kitchen the next morning. She nearly skipped a step in relief. Mrs. Rosaire had helped her dress, and she hoped the woman had cooked again—the stew had been delicious.

She paused in the doorway. Noble paged through papers on the heavily scarred table and sipped a cup of tea. A fine line of steam danced above the rim of his cup and lifted into the air.

She didn't move for a second, once more stunned by the physical presence of the man. She stepped forward, determined not to do anything foolhardy like trip or stare. Without looking up, he gestured to the teapot, and she nodded gratefully at the activity presented. She poured a full cup, the mug warming her hands.

"Interesting reading?" She indicated the stack of papers with her cup. "That looks like quite a brief." She was determined to be congenial this morning.

Noble stopped turning pages and regarded her, a lock of hair falling into one eye. "These are the notes on your brother's case. Mostly legal jargon. But a Mr. Archibald Penner is the one who captured your brother and claimed the reward."

Marietta stiffened and reached for the papers. Surprisingly, he relinquished them to her without protest.

She skimmed the pages until she came upon the last one. Archibald Penner's address was listed. He lived near Clerkenwell.

Noble poured another cup of tea. "Would you like to pay Mr. Penner a visit?" He regarded her over the steaming cup, tendrils twining around his green eyes and dissipating into the air. A demon asking if she'd care to wreak vengeance.

She looked at the page in her hand. All of the other lines blurred so that the address stood starkly against the crisp parchment.

"Yes," she whispered. This was the man who had sent Kenny to prison and whose testimony might send him to his death.

A finger lifted her chin, a dark, too handsome face mere inches from hers. Lips of sin formed words. "Best put revenge from your mind, then, this instant," he said, his finger pulling a line under her chin, his expression going from devilish to steady. "Otherwise you won't step a foot through that door."

She nearly balked, so sure that he had been promising the dark only to rip it away. The tip of her tongue strained, but she swallowed her curt response. The edges of his mouth curled as if he knew exactly what she was thinking, a devil playing her emotions, making it doubly hard to keep silent.

He rose and removed a loaf of bread from the oven, the smell of rosemary and dill wafted through the air. He cut two pieces and slathered a dollop of butter on top of each.

He placed one slice in front of her and rearranged himself back in his chair, tilting back on the hind legs.

"You will become used to it, Marietta." His voice was deep and melodic.

She looked up from the hot, buttery bread to his eyes. "Used to what?"

"Listening to me."

He smirked, and she concentrated on the pat of butter melting into the fluff. "I doubt I will get used to any such thing."

She gently pulled the bread apart and the soft center touched her tongue. She spared a thought for Mrs. Rosaire, a true genius in the kitchen.

"Everyone follows, sooner or later. Much easier for you if you allow it sooner." Noble balanced on the chair legs and tapped a finger against the wooden arm.

She swallowed the pillowy concoction. "You are insufferable."

"And you are nothing short of a delight."

She didn't need to hear the mocking to know the fallacy of that statement. It was obviously a prime sentiment in her household as well, if last night was anything to go by.

"How long have you been taking care of your brothers?"

A crumb fell to the table and she made a production of clearing it away. The topic change wasn't as easy to dismiss.

"I don't know of what you speak."

"I learned a few things from your servants last night. And gathered more this morning. Including reports from a few creditors."

How had he gotten his hands on those already? She silently cursed her servants. They would tell every secret they knew, and there was little she could do about it without a penny to her name. She wondered if Noble had *conversed* with Carla.

Her fingers dug into the sides of her bread. "Everything is under control."

"Yes, your brother Mark seems to have things in fine control." He rocked his chair farther back.

She hoped he tipped. "Mark has had a tough time since our parents died."

And wasn't that the turnabout of the season? She had said the same thing as Noble, in much the same sarcastic tone, but it was different when it came from his mouth. When *he* was attacking her brother.

The front legs of his chair clacked the floor stones. "I don't see you breaking down and drinking yourself into a stupor." His voice was mild as he picked up the other bread slice.

"I don't have the same pressures as Mark."

Something inside her sobbed at the injustice—one she was placing upon herself. She had the exact same pressures. In fact, sometimes she thought hers were worse, because as the female of the family she could do nothing about any of it directly. Powerless.

She straightened her shoulders. She would *not* be powerless.

He eyed her, then finished the buttery slice. "Mmm. You don't have the same pressures. I see. That's good to know."

She nodded tightly, irritated with him and herself.

He watched her for a moment, then cut two more pieces, buttered them and plunked one in front of her and one in front of him.

"Archibald Penner is a regular pub rat, from what I can tell. And a part-time watchmen. Involved in businesses on the east side. Milliners and dress shops, as unlikely as that seems from his description. Clarisse may have gossip concerning him."

Marietta wondered if he procured information from Clarisse in the same manner as from Carla.

A noise at the kitchen door drew her attention. A frazzled looking woman with fuzzy brown hair and kind brown eyes fell through the door, arms full of cloth.

"Mr. Noble, sir! I came as quickly as I could."

"It's not a problem, Clarisse." Again she noted that his voice was richer and warmer than when he had addressed her. He rose to relieve Clarisse of her burden.

She thanked him, then looked at Marietta and bobbed her head. "Good morning, miss."

Marietta murmured a greeting as Noble made the introductions. She couldn't help watching Clarisse as she made morning chitchat with Noble. Her face was friendly, but there was a rather apparent look of worship in her eyes as she spoke with him. Excellent. Another smitten female.

Noble was much more attentive and kind to Clarisse than he had been with her two maids. With Carla, he had maintained a removed look, all the more inviting to her, since Carla thrived on challenges. For Clarisse, he had nothing but friendly smiles.

The smiles transformed his face. Without guile, without sarcasm, he fairly beamed. She swallowed with difficulty and turned away from watching him.

"If you could fit Miss Winters with a few garments? The standard ones should be fine."

Clarisse bobbed her head and followed Noble to the door. Marietta quickly stuffed the rest of her bread in her mouth and quietly followed.

"Are you familiar with a Mr. Archibald Penner?" he asked Clarisse.

"He owns some shops over on the East End. Mostly pleasant. Likes the shopgirls, though he's not a bully. Doesn't have a reputation as a ruffian, but likes his drink well enough."

"Invaluable as always, Clarisse."

Marietta saw the blush stain the girl's cheeks and stifled a sigh.

"Will you be wanting Miss Winters to have the look of a shopgirl?"

"Something like that would do well. And an assistant's outfit. Maybe something that shows a bit of skin around the collar."

Noble left them at the door of Marietta's room and Clarisse got to work.

Marietta watched her curiously. "You work with Mr. Noble often?"

Clarisse nodded and fastened a pin. "Is this the first time you've worked with him? I haven't seen you afore."

"Yes."

"Well, these garments will all work for later tasks too, so long as you don't gain much weight. Not that you couldn't stand to add a stone or two." She looked at her critically and Marietta bit her tongue. "But you are tall. More places for the weight to be distributed when you do," she said in a cheerful manner.

"Mr. Noble likes his victims with a little more flesh, I gather."

Clarisse frowned up at her. Her brow puckered and she looked remarkably confrontational, just as Mrs. Rosaire had, but then her brow smoothed. "I forgot this is your first task. You'll change your tune as soon as Mr. Noble has solved your problem. They all do, whether they want to or not."

Marietta narrowed her eyes. "That is not what I am taken to understand. I have understood there is some uncertainty about his intentions at times. That he is not to be crossed."

"That he isn't." The girl gave her a serious look. "You'd do well to heed him. He can be difficult, but he is infinitely fair. He will do right by you."

Right by her. As if any other man had done so, she was supposed to trust completely that this one would. This man who had twenty different smiles, one to entice each woman. Who exuded nothing less than sex and desire, and knew exactly how to use it to his advantage. And yet, here she was.

"How many women have you dressed like this, Clarisse?"

"A fair few," she said, a bit cagily.

Wonderful. With that face and those smiles, a stream of women had probably trailed through his bedroom doors like an unending Eton parade.

"And the men?" She assumed there were a few on his client list since she had been referred by one. "Do they also get costumed?"

"Oh, yes. My brother is an excellent tailor. Family business. Mr. Noble helped us a few years back. And he pays extremely well, of course."

That answered two of her questions.

Clarisse talked more about the family business and Noble's wonderful, magnificent, perfect presence. It was getting on noon before she finished, but Marietta had two perfectly serviceable servant's garments, a shopgirl's outfit, and two dresses that would provoke a society matron to fits. All were either close to fitting her or pinned in a crafty way to look tailored already. Smart girl, Clarisse.

Marietta followed her back to the kitchen when they were through.

"All done?"

Noble was still sitting at the table, papers spread around him, a small sty of ink-stained linen and parchment.

"Yes, sir. I'll be back later with the last of the garments that need refitting."

He nodded and returned to perusing the documents. Clarisse seemed to think this perfectly normal as she waved to Marietta and let herself out the door.

Marietta waited a moment, but Noble didn't look up

"Clarisse is full of energy," she said.

"Yes. Stew is in the pot." He pointed absently to the stove.

Marietta watched him scratch his chin and make a notation in the corner of a piece of parchment. It seemed so odd to see a man like him so serious and *studious*.

She sighed. Every wandering thought seemed to be about *him*. Maddening. She served herself a bowl. "Would you like a bowl?"

"No, I've already eaten."

She settled back at the table and broke off a piece of bread. "What are you reading?"

He tapped his quill against the paper and looked up through thick lashes. "All of the information about your case. The barrister you've hired—and what he has declared. Your brother will have to answer every question posed by the judge and jury members and deliver his own summary. Barristers do nothing to interrupt or lead, no matter what yours promised. According to this—" He held up the paper. "You've been promised the moon. Right gulled. You'd do well to get your money back."

Her bread dropped into the bowl. "But Mark said—"

"Quite."

She dipped her head and fished her bread from the bowl with trembling fingers. She'd kill him. Mark had assured her that the barrister would solve everything. The barrister had assured her as well. She hadn't had time to research the legal system, not with the work she'd been doing on the side, unnoticed by her brother—small jobs to bring in an extra few pounds here and there. Legal issues had mattered little to her daily life other than to keep them from debtor's prison.

"We will stop there Friday, then find your brother new counsel," he said.

Perhaps she should stop there today.

As if reading her mind, he gave her a sardonic look and said, "My source said your barrister is out of town on business. He'll be back Friday. We'll retrieve your money. I've dealt with his sort before." His brows slashed together as he focused back on the papers before him.

Marietta nodded and determined to read the legislation herself tonight. She shouldn't just take Gabriel Noble's word either.

"A more important matter than the barrister, we need to discover how your brother came to be standing over a dead woman's body. I am working on getting us into Cold Bath Fields, but it may take another day or two."

He checked something off on his page without looking her way. Good thing, as her heart had stopped beating.

"I need you to distract Archibald Penner today, so we can learn as much as possible about that night, at least from an outsider's perspective. I need you saucy, not vengeful, in order to get the information we need. We can get your brother's story later."

Her heart started thumping again. He didn't believe her brother innocent yet, she could tell by the tone of his voice, but if he could get her into Cold Bath Fields to see Kenny, she could forgive him much.

"Thank you."

He looked up and just watched her with those unnaturally bright eyes for a few moments before looking back to his papers. "Just distract Penner."

Archibald Penner answered on the second knock. He was a square man, too square, as if lines had been drawn from shoulder to hip, his body fitting itself to the mold. He had sandy blond hair and brown eyes, which while not especially sharp, held a spark.

"Mr. Penner?" Noble asked, an easy smile on his face, his features somewhat obscured and softened by a low slung cap.

"Yes?"

Noble stuck out a hand. "Nathaniel Upholt, from the *Times.* We'd like to do a piece on your capture of the Middlesex murderer."

Penner's square shoulders puffed back and two spots of color appeared in his cheeks as he vigorously shook the proffered hand. "Come in, come in."

Marietta followed Noble inside. Her first impression of Penner's house was that it was . . . fastidious. Too many perfectly framed pieces, no spare bits of color or style. Geometric. She looked again. Square. Everything was squared away, just like Penner himself.

"This is my assistant, Miss Klein. Don't mind her. She's more for display," Noble whispered in a stage voice.

Marietta didn't know whether to be offended or amused. And what was he thinking? Nathaniel Upholt was a real journalist. Noble didn't seem to understand the importance of that, though, as he calmly retrieved an ink pot, quill, and paper.

Penner gave her a once-over and licked his lips. "Nice, nice."

In her low cut outfit she wasn't surprised she warranted a second look from a man with a taste for shopgirls. Noble had given her cosmetics to apply, and they made her look surprisingly different. They hadn't turned her into a raging beauty, but they had softened her harsh angles and made her look halfway alive again. Her eyes were longer and more almond-shaped, her cheeks and lips brighter, the shadows and pale features covered by the brightness.

"Have me commendation right here." He gave her what she assumed was a coy look. "A real upstanding member of London."

Marietta kept her mouth from falling open. Sure enough, there on the wall of his study was a framed piece of paper with a scrawled commendation from the head of the watch. They really had tried and convicted Kenny without so much as a peep of a trial.

"And the reward bill. Even looks like the brigand."

Marietta looked at the framed handbill with its vague drawing of a man sporting a serious scruff. Nothing like Kenny's baby cheeks. The reward proclaimed the sum of fifty pounds to anyone who apprehended the murderer.

"Planning to use the money to do good works. You can print that." He pointed to Noble's poised quill.

"What type of good works?" Marietta had to ask, despite Noble's warning glance.

"Oh, this and that. Make sure the lads at the pub have a round or two."

Noble gave her a look that promised death should she continue her line of questioning.

"Now, where were you when you realized you had the Middlesex murderer in your grasp?" Noble asked, his tone both flattering and curious.

Penner leaned forward. "I was at me pub. The White Stag. Went out for a bit to clear me head. Been celebrating with the lads. Anyways, I heard a sound. A cry for help. I ran around the corner, ready to help the fair lady, but I was too late." He hung his head. "The bastard had already done her in."

"How do you know?"

"He was hunched over the body! Covered in blood. His eyes met mine. Devil's eyes! I knew immediately 'twas him. I let out a yell and tackled him."

Noble lifted a brow. "You tackled him? Very brave of you."

Penner puffed up some more. "Couldn't let him get away. I'm quite the sportsman. Know how to put a man down. Can handle me fists."

Marietta smiled weakly as Penner gave her another

coy glance. She looked at Penner's form. Tall, lanky Kenneth had probably gone down like a sapling felled by a monstrous axe.

"Did he say anything? Try to proclaim his innocence? Try to run?" Noble asked.

"Blighter looked smacked in the gob. Like he didn't know why I had hit him. As if murdering women were not a sin." Penner closed a fist in disgust.

Marietta exchanged a look with Noble and was gratified to see a thoughtful look in his eyes.

"And then what happened?"

"The watch guards came. We have about five fellas from the Stag that do rounds. One of the men on duty was in the pub."

"The man who arrested K—the brigand—was intoxicated?" she asked.

Noble's lips pinched together as Penner's head swung toward her.

"No more intoxicated than need be. Just what are you implying, miss?"

Noble tapped the feather of his quill against his leg. His expression said, *Talk yourself out of this one.*

"Well, it—it just seems such a dangerous business. You probably needed to double your efforts to keep the murderer subdued if the watchman on duty was below the weather."

It wasn't her best effort at dissembling, but she watched Penner process her words and his slow nod turned more vigorous. "Yes, just doing my duty." He leaned into her space. "I know how to take care of things."

His expression grew coy again. Not quite what

she'd had in mind when she'd lamented her failed charms.

"Lovely."

Noble gave her another warning glance, but was no longer glaring as he turned back to make a few more notes. He asked a few more questions—about Penner's commendation, the White Stag and what had happened after the tackling, but nothing stuck out in Penner's answers. Just a do-gooder who Marietta fervently wished had not "done good" that particular night.

"If you need any more information, send your assistant back. I'll make sure she gets all she needs." He smiled. "I'm a hero."

Marietta forced a smile in return. She had been told she would make a decent mistress once. That her sharp tongue could be put to good use, as disgusting as that had sounded from a man three times her age and size. If she were truly desperate enough to go that route, she would choose someone other than Archibald Penner, the man who ruined Kenny.

They walked from the house, and Marietta held her tongue until they were well away.

"What were you thinking to impersonate Nathaniel Upholt? What is Mr. Penner going to do when he doesn't see his write-up in the paper?"

Noble looked unconcerned. "Oh, the article will appear in the *Times*."

"What? How?"

"I spoke to Nathaniel this morning. He was more than happy to give me the task of interviewing Archibald Penner."

Her jaw dropped. "You spoke to Nathaniel Upholt?"

"By way of courier, yes."

"And you did all of this before I awakened?"

"Not all of us can afford to be layabouts." His arms swung loosely at his sides as he walked. "You upper class types are all the same. Sleep until noon and then fritter your nights away."

She narrowed her eyes. "I do not fritter my nights away."

"Really? And what do you do at night?"

"I go to social events. Parties or galas. Sometimes a musicale. Or a charity event," she tacked on with satisfaction.

"Well, I must retract my frittering comment in that case."

"It's not frittering. It's surviving." She gritted her teeth.

"Oh, yes. Social survival, is it not?"

"Quite."

"That must be very satisfying."

"I find you irritating, Mr. Noble."

"I am most distressed to hear that, of course, Miss Winters."

He tipped his hat to two girls passing on the sidewalk. Marietta looked back to see the girls madly whispering, eyes wide as they watched him, girlish giggles rolling out one after the other.

"Must you do that?"

"Walk?"

"Encourage them."

"I tipped my hat. Are you against politeness?"

"At this time, quite possibly. My irritation borders dangerously close to dislike."

"Yes. I can't say I'm fond of you either."

The lazy grin with which that was delivered made her heart speed up two notches. She was quite irritated by that as well.

Chapter 5

Marietta closed her eyes in awakened bliss, then lazily opened them in the way of a contented cat. The smell of the herbs and feel of the warm steam on her face . . . the colors sharpened, from the tomato red hand towels on the kitchen rack to the daffodil yellow of the sunbeams peeking above the trees. Brought back into a world where color and optimism existed.

She made a last sweep of her bowl with a piece of the rosemary and dill bread that had become her morning staple. Her belly had been full for days and she was finally beginning to fill back out. Her thoughts raced like a well-oiled phaeton instead of the sluggish, rusted hack she'd been. Her temper had improved as well, though Noble seemed determined to push it.

She looked up to see amused eyes watching her. She blinked and the vibrant green was once again shadowed, the gaze arrogant. A picture of masculine confidence and virility, perfection leaning atop the deeply scarred table littered with debris. One long-fingered hand rolled a perfectly formed walnut, hard and brittle, between his thumb and forefinger.

She pulled the overlapping edge of her robe even further together, tightened like a trussed-up nun.

His eyes fell to her robe, and she felt one layer shy of naked. "We are going to Cold Bath Fields today. You'll need to wear servants' garb."

She straightened, her hand still gripping her robe. "We are? Truly?" She felt light-headed. *Kenny*.

"Yes. As soon as you are dressed." He looked her over, his gaze taking in everything from her hair to her robe's sash. "You shouldn't need help changing." His smile turned wolfish, though his eyes remained dark. "Unless you want my help, of course."

"That won't be necessary." That particular gaze did strange things to her. Her skin warmed, a low thrum beat inside her—and her teeth ground together in continued defiance of becoming one of his worshipers.

She didn't respond to his knowledge of her clothing. Clarisse had mentioned creating pieces along the same lines before. No doubt Noble had relieved more than one woman of her clothes in the years that he'd done this type of work. And he was right—one of the dresses was made up of three separate pieces that connected together in the front and on the side. She could handle dressing on her own. Mrs. Rosaire must have come to fix the meal and then been dismissed for the day.

She ran upstairs. She was going to see Kenny.

* * *

Marietta was unsurprised to discover they were walking to Cold Bath, even though it was quite a distance. For the last few days they had walked nearly everywhere. Noble seemed much happier on foot. Or perhaps he thought walking would annoy her. On the contrary, she enjoyed the exercise, but maintained a neutral expression to keep him from guessing her attitude. He seemed to always be watching her, tossing an unbroken walnut in perfect timing to his steps. In a game where he held all of the pieces, she had to get in her digs where she could.

They approached the prison and Marietta shivered. In the otherwise decent neighborhood of cheerful row houses, the sparse, barred windows and spartan trim made the hulking building into a dismal fortress. Some kind soul had planted rows of flowers across the street in an entirely vain attempt to lift the mood.

A stocky, bearded man stood outside on the sidewalk, and upon seeing them, abruptly turned and hobbled inside. She looked to Noble, but he didn't respond to the man's odd behavior. They followed his path into the prison, and she could see the man's dark shirt as he turned a corner.

Noble shadowed the odd little man, and she trailed Noble. Guards and magistrates passed them, chatting or moving prisoners. No one questioned their presence, whether it was due to their purposeful movements or something else, she didn't know.

Two hallways turned to three and the crowds of people dwindled to small groups and then individuals as the wide hallways narrowed to cold paths. She held her breath as they rounded the fourth hall to see the odd, sour-faced man with his hooked nose and bushy brows standing against a massive iron door. No one else was present.

"You can only be here for this half hour when the guards are on rotation." His voice was gruff. "No one should question your presence, as only someone with a key can enter, but if anyone does, I'll take care of it. Three turns right, cell in the center."

The man spoke with a thick accent she couldn't place.

"Thank you, Oscar. That will be the fulfillment of the second favor, then," Gabriel said, his voice smooth and easy.

"Dem right." Marietta blinked at the pugilistic set to the small man's face. "Bertha's all over me backside." He growled. "The sooner the third is over, the better."

"Poor Bertha. Still sore with me over the cat incident?"

The man started muttering, and Marietta heard the words "never forgive" and "nearly ripped me leg off" in the mumbles.

"Tell Bertha that my neighbor has kittens should she want one." Noble's voice and face were filled with barbed amusement.

"Nothing but trouble, you are. Kittens, bah, I'll eat them," he said irritably as he unlocked the door and held it open.

Noble winked—winked!—at her as he walked through. Marietta stared dumbly after him for a moment, then recalled herself and turned to Oscar, whose eyes were narrowed. Judging. The prickly fondness that may have been present for Noble was completely absent now. His lips thinned as he continued to watch her, but he didn't say a word.

"Is something the matter, sir?" Something about the way he was looking at her, like something found under a rock, made her uncomfortable.

"Trouble. I can already see it."

"Pardon me?"

"Go on now." He motioned toward the door, his face set in unfriendly lines. "Thirty minutes is all you get. Not a minute more."

Her feet took her through the door, but she pivoted to ask him about his comment. He closed the door in her face and the lock slammed into place. She blinked.

The sound of a tapping foot made her turn. A perfect brow lifted. "Are you going to tarry all morning, or shall we go find our prey?"

She took a quick step toward him, unnerved by Oscar's actions. "He is not our prey, you horrid man."

He put a hand over his chest and his head bowed. "Your words warm my cold, brittle heart." His hand came back down to rest at his side, the walnut appearing from somewhere and once again rolling between his fingers. He lifted a sardonic brow. "Let's find our prey, princess."

He strode forward and took the first turn. Marietta glanced to the right and left, noticing the cells for the first time, Noble once more having captured her entire attention when he was within the same space, cursed man. Filthy, ragged hands appeared around the bars, followed by ripped sleeves black with dirt. Soulless eyes stared back.

"I'll be your prey, pretty." A clawed hand reached through the bars toward her. Before she could move, something pinged off the iron and the claw disappeared inside the dank cell. A walnut rolled into the corner and wobbled to a stop.

She turned, but Noble was nowhere to be seen. Moving quickly down the hall, she was relieved when she turned the corner and focused on his back once more. She concentrated on him as she walked, the edges of his garments brushing each other as they met in perfect alignment along his shoulders, hips, and legs. Better to look at the cursed man than to see the monstrous conditions of the cells and inmates. To think about what Kenny might look or act like.

They took the last turn and she saw Kenny in an area by himself, as dreary and dark as all the others, but at least empty of the thousand soulless Hecatonchire eyes. He was absently picking at the buckle on his shoe, looking miserable.

"Kenny!"

His head shot up and he sprang forward, gripping the bars, his ripped shirt falling off one shoulder making him look even more gangly and lanky.

"Marietta!" He gripped her firmly as she tried to embrace him through the bars. "Finally! You are here to release me! It's been wretched. I've ruined my shoes. My hair's a mess."

He touched his hair with one hand and maintained his hold on her with the other. "I've a lump on my head that still smarts. Some dilettante hit me!" She tried to say something but words kept falling from his lips, as if he hadn't talked to anyone in a week. "Tackled in the middle of the street. Thank God you are here. Where's the key?"

"Er." She untangled herself from his arms and the bars. "That's a slight problem, Kenny."

"Yes, I know! They've held me here for a week! The food is wretched and there are rats. Rats! I saw one try to steal my bread last night." He sent a glance toward one corner of his cell and edged farther into the bars, gripping them like the other prisoners. "And the Middlesex murderer is somewhere in the prison. What if he murders me in my sleep? The guards mutter about him all the time. They've even forgotten to feed me meals because of him." His stomach rumbled. "About time they nabbed the bastard, though I can't say that I agree with them lessening my rations because of it."

She took a firm look at her brother, who was inhaling deeply after spewing that all out in one breath. He didn't *seem* to be suffering from insanity. "Kenny, you know why you are here, don't you?"

He waved a hand. "They think I killed someone. Ha. As if I can stand the sight of blood." He shuddered. "Knew they'd discover their mistake sooner or later. But it's been a week! Outrageous. Where is the key?"

He looked so expectant that all she could do was blink. A hand came through the bars to grip her arm. "Marietta?"

She didn't know how it happened, but she suddenly found herself disengaged from Kenny, with her brother holding his fingers in pain. Noble's hand fell from her arm before she even realized it was there.

"Ouch. What was that for? Who are you?" Kenny asked, sucking one suspiciously clean finger into his mouth.

"That is of little concern to you. Do you really expect us to believe that you are that clueless as to why you are imprisoned?" Noble asked.

Kenny looked bewildered. Poor boy had never been the brightest tulip. "I've been falsely arrested, and Marietta has come to save me?"

There was so much hope in his face and she hated to be the one to ruin it.

"Yes, your sister has come to save you," Noble said, surprising her. "Little though you seem to deserve it."

Kenny's eyes widened. He had always made friends so easily, unlike her. "I didn't kill that woman. No one can believe I did."

"Not only do they believe you killed her, but they think you killed two other women as well."

Perhaps he wasn't the quickest man, but Kenny wasn't terminally stupid. Comprehension turned to horror. "They think I'm the Middlesex murderer?"

Marietta moved to touch him and noticed Noble shift his position. "Kenny, you are in real trouble. Haven't you noticed?"

He chewed his lip. "I thought they were keeping me away from the others. The guards mostly avoid me. Do they really believe that of me? Does—" his voice lowered. "Does anyone else know?"

Marietta swallowed. "Yes."

"No," he whispered. He obviously read all that she wasn't saying in her one word reply.

Marietta examined her sturdy slippers. "You need

71

to help us, Kenny. It's the only way we can get you released."

"Have you sent for a barrister?"

Her lips compressed. "Yes, but one is of little use in these types of cases."

She had read the laws as she'd promised herself. Noble had been right, damn it.

"But then, what—what is going to—"

"You can answer our questions, for a start." Noble's tone was cold, but he didn't look as completely unapproachable as he had the first night she'd met him. "What were you doing around the White Stag when you were arrested?"

Kenny sent her a questioning glance, his face a mirror of the sharp planes and dark circled brown eyes she had sported before eating Mrs. Rosaire's hearty stews. Though unlike her, his wide eyes made him look comically innocent. Marietta had a vague stirring of hope that a jury would see him that way too. She nodded encouragingly in response.

He ran a hand through his dirty hair and it stood on end. "Mark and Marietta were fighting again. Just had to get out of there."

Marietta bit her lip, the flare of hope quickly firing into guilt.

"I walked for a while. Passed a number of taverns—there wasn't much action in any of them and they lacked friendly faces. Headed east. I had a few pence on me." He looked sheepishly at Marietta. Mark had distributed their "pin" money with the new clothing items they couldn't afford—part of the reason for the fight in the first place.

"There was a raucous tavern. I could see it from a block away. Looked perfect. So I headed for it. Wasn't three strides to enter when I heard a noise. Like the tap of metal against stone. Someone screamed, 'You!' There was this weird sound. Like the screech of a cat."

His eyes pinched together. "I walked around and toward the sound. A woman was lying there. Then everything went black. I woke up in a puddle of blood with a knot the size of a grapefruit on my skull."

"You didn't see anyone with the woman?"

"No. Must have knocked me out. Hurt like the devil when I woke. I couldn't stop moaning. Then I saw the body." He shivered. "Lying there, right next to me."

He paused, his eyes widening. "Dear God." He looked as if someone had just struck him again. "The Middlesex murderer."

"How long do you think you were out?"

"Don't know." He scratched his head, flattening a section and making another stand further on end. "Maybe twenty minutes? Was about ten when I left the house, and I heard a guard say it was half past eleven as they were locking me up."

"And after you saw the body what did you do?" Noble asked.

"I touched her arm. It was so . . . . cold. I didn't know what to do. I just sat there looking down at her. Then this man came barreling down the alley and tackled me. Wouldn't listen to a word I said. He just kept yelling at me. I was here not twenty minutes later. Shoved into this rathole." He kicked a piece of straw. "They think I'm the Middlesex murderer. Unbelievable. And to think, he was right there. Could have done anything to me." He shuddered.

"So far his victims have all been women. I doubt you were quite his style, even with that shirt," Noble said.

Kenny looked down at his overly frilly shirt in bemusement. It was the height of style, at least it *had* been before being dirtied and bloodied and ripped, but Marietta privately agreed with Noble.

"Who are you?" Kenny asked Noble in honest confusion.

"I'm someone your sister hired to help you."

"Hired?" He looked at her. "Marietta?"

"Worry not, Kenny." She smiled brightly. "It's all been taken care of."

She could see the cogs turning. Her brother's face went from stark white to angry red. His fists clenched the bars of his cell. Then he gave Noble a once-over and his indignation turned again to confusion. She wasn't in the same physical class as Noble. It was obvious to anyone with eyes.

"How?"

"Not in the way you are thinking, I assure you," she said, somewhat more tartly than she'd intended. She didn't know if she was more upset with her brother thinking she had sold herself or that he thought there was no way Noble would have purchased her.

She chanced a glance at Noble. His face was arrogant and remote. No change there.

"Well, then how—"

"Your sister answered your question."

Kenny's jaw closed with an audible snap.

Noble watched him through narrowing eyes. "Now, what have you left out of your tale?"

Marietta looked at Kenny, who looked at his shoes. "Kenny?"

He continued to shuffle his feet, buckles clicking against the bars and upending straw.

Noble turned to her. "Marietta, perhaps you should wait around the corner?"

The body. He wanted to ask about the body. She swallowed. "I'll stay. I want to hear everything. I daresay I've seen more blood in the kitchens than Kenny has in his life."

Noble's gaze was narrow and piercing. Probing. "Fine." He turned to her brother. "What did the girl look like?"

"I don't know," he whispered, not looking up.

"What do you mean?"

He shuddered. "She was covered in blood. I couldn't make out her features. She seemed older, though. I don't know what it was that made me think that. Dress? Hair? I don't know."

"There was nothing identifiable about her?"

"No." He took a couple of quick breaths in succession. "She was . . . mangled."

Kitchens or not, Marietta didn't want to imagine the scene. The accounts of the previous victims had assuredly been sanitized in the papers, and even then they had sounded horrific.

She grasped her brother's hands. "I will get you out of here."

75

"Mark?"

She clutched his hands more tightly. "Just hold steady. And don't antagonize the guards."

She could see Noble looking at his pocket watch out of the corner of her eye, but couldn't bring herself to look away from her brother.

"We need to go. It is half past."

Her hands were held in a death grip.

"Marietta?" Kenny said. She didn't know what he was asking.

"We must leave," Noble's smooth, deep voice said.

"Marietta," Kenny whispered, his voice anxious and scared.

"Come." A hand touched her back, and she looked down at her brother's hands joined with hers. She let hers drop and felt the weight of a thousand ships. The hand against her back urged her to move.

She allowed the hand to guide her toward the door, but her eyes were locked with Kenny's.

"Kenny," she whispered.

The look on her brother's face as they rounded the corner etched itself in her mind. Forlorn. Hopeful. Miserable. Innocent.

She followed Noble blindly until they came upon the locked door. Noble knocked and the lock disengaged. Oscar's grumpy visage came into view.

"'Bout time."

They followed him out of the cell area and Noble gave her an unreadable glance. She returned it woodenly, shock and despair coating her emotions.

"We'll head for Coroner's Court," Noble said to her. "See if we can't discover more than your brother could

76

recall." His voice was the tiniest bit warmer than he'd ever used with her before.

Oscar shook his head in front of them. "Won't do you much good. They burned the body," he said over his shoulder.

Noble stopped in the middle of the hall. "They what?"

Oscar turned and nodded grouchily. "They did the examination and then got rid of the body. Fastest I've seen."

Noble's eyes narrowed. "Suspicious."

"Nah, probably just trying to keep the masses pacified."

"From what? It's not like regular folks would see."

"No, but the longer they drag something out, the worse it will be. Clean everything as quickly as you can, and it will pass from the public's memory."

Just as they were trying to do with Kenny's trial.

"Does Frank still work in the same building?"

"Yes. Upstairs from the court. Thought he was done with his tasks?"

"He is. Doesn't mean I can't pay an old friend a visit."

Noble smiled charmingly, but Oscar just mumbled. "Better not pay me any visits once we're done."

The next thing Marietta knew she was outside on the sidewalk, Cold Bath Fields behind her. She was vaguely aware that Noble and Oscar engaged in a brief, coded conversation, but she didn't listen. Couldn't concentrate. Her mind was going again at full speed.

"His groaning," she said suddenly, and Noble peered at her. "Don't you see? It was Kenny who

Penner heard. Not the victim. The victim was long since dead."

Noble was silent a moment. "While I'll agree that it is a good match with what we heard from Penner, something just doesn't make sense. Why leave your brother there?"

She lifted her arms in irritation. "Maybe the murderer needed someone else to take the fall."

"Perhaps."

"You still believe him guilty?"

The seconds ticked by.

"No."

Half the fleet of ships were lifted from her shoulders, leaving only five hundred weighing her down.

"Thank you."

"It is not I who needs to be convinced."

"I beg to differ. You were clearly convinced of his guilt before we came today."

"I was clearly convinced of nothing. I wasn't convinced of his *innocence*. That is what you objected to."

"Was not."

"Don't be petulant," he said, his head tilted.

She gasped. "I'm not petulant."

He tipped his head in the other direction as they continued to walk and another walnut appeared from his pocket. "Maybe he was just after the woman."

"What?" She replayed the conversation. "You think the killer was after her specifically?"

"Your brother heard the woman say, 'You.' That would lead me to believe that perhaps all of the attacks are targeted."

"Instead of random women caught by a crazy man?"

He shrugged, rolling the nut between his fingers. "The watch thinks they are all random attacks. Most of the public does as well. I have been too busy to pay attention these last few weeks."

"But you now think the women targeted?" It made sense. It fit.

He shrugged again. "I don't know what to think, but today has given me much to ponder." He gave her an unreadable look and continued to rub his fingers in a circular pattern.

Marietta didn't know what to say to that, or how to respond to the feeling coiling in her stomach. She paced alongside him as they walked home, gritting her teeth every time they passed a drooling female on the sidewalk.

Chapter 6

Gabriel shuffled another ten pages into his leather satchel. Preparation was rarely a bad thing.

A swish on the boards, a movement in the air. He picked up a quill and with a toss of his head flicked his hair to the side. Part of his early training had given him the ability to hear people before he saw them. To always be on alert.

Later events had ensured he would never forget to stay that way.

She appeared in the doorway looking slightly rumpled. "Good morning," she murmured.

He twirled the quill and returned the greeting, though his voice wasn't quite as smooth as he would've liked and the quill wobbled on its axis. She settled down across from him with her plate of food, and he watched her take a bite. Watched her face transform into the rather passionate expression she always wore when she ate. As if she wasn't sure she would get another meal quite as good.

The first time he had seen that expression he had paused in mid-action—quill suspended in midair, ink dripping onto the papers. Only her eyes lifting toward his had gotten him moving again.

Surprising, really. She was rather plain. Brown hair, brown eyes, and today a brown dress. An average sort of face—one that could be enhanced by cosmetics, color, and lighting, or muted by the same. Good cheekbones, nice lips, pleasant shape to her eyes—passingly pretty, but not beautiful. From the purely physical characteristics, she was perfect for blending in. She was going to be an asset for any tasks he required.

The spirit in her eyes, however, told a different story. It had from the moment he laid eyes on her. She was going to be difficult. Always.

"We will head to the barrister as soon as you are finished eating."

She paused and looked up. "Are we going anywhere afterward? Will this do?" She pinched the plain brown muslin.

"That will be fine. We can always come back to change if needed."

She nodded and resumed eating.

He couldn't help feel some admiration for her spirit, as difficult as it would surely prove. She had taken the past week in as much stride as one of her station could.

Her station. His eyes narrowed and he whipped the quill into another revolution. Even if she was ostracized, her family in disgrace, she was part of society, and there were few people from that strata who could be counted upon. Especially women.

She finished her plate. "I can't wait to tell Mr. Hackenstay exactly what I think of—"

"You will not be speaking with the barrister," he said, his voice even, just as it should be.

Her head drew up sharply. "Pardon me? I have all sorts of things I need to say to that cheat. He swindled us. Took advantage of Kenny's situation. He's a gin-soaked, criminally incompetent, swill-bottled—"

"As lovely as that list is, you will not speak to the barrister."

"I certainly will. No one takes advantage of a Winters and gets away with it." Shoulders pushed back, chin thrust forward.

Even as a woman of society, her loyalty to her brothers was a point in her favor.

"That is certainly a spine-tingling threat—what, with your ready blunt and large network of people to assist you." He twirled the quill again, accomplishing two revolutions in time with his dig.

Color suffused her cheeks. "We can get our revenge other ways. Mark may be insufferable, but he is my brother, and just growing into his maturity. And Kenny is a baby."

"That baby is eighteen."

"He's a baby," she said pointedly.

Having met him, Gabriel decided not to argue. Kenny could grow into a stronger person, he was young, and a strong mentor would make a big difference. But Mark . . .

"You say Mark is growing into his maturity? When exactly will that take place?"

"Soon," she said firmly, her eye twitching only faintly.

"You can't even say that with a straight face. Your brother is older than I am. I can only hope I reach my maturity soon, in that case."

She blinked. He resisted the vain urge to look in a mirror. What, did he look ancient all of a sudden?

He leaned forward and watched her eyes widen, her chest quicken its pace. Male satisfaction surged within him. "I was scraping and scheming at Kenny's age. Backbreaking work, no sleep, risky ventures." Fear and determination his constant companions. "I had to endure more than not being able to afford a new pair of boots. Poor Kenny. Poor Mark," he said scathingly, allowing a rarely given piece of himself into the conversation.

He had little respect for anyone who was not willing to put in the effort required to survive and thrive. Not everyone needed the same driving ambition that had fueled him. That had led him to being possibly the richest man in London without a title in his lineage— all earned in under a decade. That had given him the power to change lives. But a person needed to have the drive to change his *own* life.

Mark Winters was a leech.

Kenny Winters lacked ambition.

Marietta Winters . . . he was still trying to determine who she really was.

"How can you say that? Poor Kenny indeed! He is locked away and most likely will not be given a fair trial."

Her features turned angry, color lighting her cheeks like the first tentative bloom of a rose.

He switched off that portion of his mind. "Which is exactly why we need to sort through this mess with the barrister. And you will allow me to do it."

"But—"

"Do you want to go against my wishes in this?" He mixed sugar with steel and watched her hands grip the edge of the table and the color in her cheeks glow hotter.

Rose was good on her, even with the sides of her lips pinched and stiff. He absently wondered if he annoyed her just to see the color bloom.

"When do we leave?" she bit out.

"Now. It's a thirty-minute walk."

He watched her run a hand over her hair, smoothing it back as she smoothed the expression from her face. She was good, he'd give her that. She had passed most of his tests. She had a sharp mouth, but a sharp mind as well. And he had never been against a woman with some vinegar. It was the sugary sweet ones that raised his hackles. With this woman, you'd always know where you stood, if you knew how to look quickly enough. She showed everything on her face for a split second before masking it.

She might prove to be more trouble than she was worth, but he would continue to watch and see. And test. There was something about her. Her eyes. Both disenchanted and excited—that intrigued him.

They stepped into the bright spring day. It was a great day for walking. The sun was warm, the soft buttery rays caressing his face. A light breeze floated on the air, lifting pollens from the surrounding gardens and suspending them in midair until they caught the drift and surged off.

A passerby sneezed.

"You said that you know men of Mr. Hackenstay's type?" she asked. He saw her grimace as a giggling gaggle of girls walked past.

A slow smile worked its way from the middle of his mouth to his cheekbones. He had no hat to tip, having decided to approach Hackenstay as himself, but he made sure to nod and smile at each passing female. Marietta looked as if she'd sucked a lemon.

"I do. London is littered with them."

"How can there be so many incompetent, swindling barristers?"

"No, not all of them are barristers. Accountants, merchants, peers, *gentry*. The type to take advantage of a situation without regard to others is not limited to one field."

She shot him an angry look from beneath her lashes. It seemed that only she was allowed to refer to her brother Mark as a cheat.

"What did you do for Oscar?"

A sliver of shock ran down his spine. "Why do you ask?"

"He seemed annoyed and crotchety, but at the same time I didn't sense any true antipathy toward you. You hold the favors over my head, but I don't work in any government or secret facility. I don't have connections to help you."

"You are a member of society, you have innumerable connections."

Her eyes turned to gaze at the row houses on their right. "Not anymore."

He knew how society worked. He had been raised

to know everything about it. "Besides, I never said I needed you for your social contacts."

Her head turned abruptly. "Let's be clear on this, Mr. Noble. You don't need me for anything. I am well aware of that."

"Interesting. You seem to have it all figured out, then. You know exactly what I will need you to do."

Annoyance flashed in her eyes. "You know that I do not."

"But you just said that you are well aware that I don't need you for anything."

"Well, I have ruled out the most vile of suggestions. You obviously have a harem ready and willing to serve any time you call." She made a vague motion to their fellow pedestrians. "I highly doubt even with your insinuations that I need to do *that*."

A strange rumbling rippled through his chest. He supposed that he should be outraged over her use of the word vile, his honor scorched, but instead he felt . . . amused? He hadn't been this close to real laughter in the presence of a society lady in a long time.

"I see. I will let my harem know that they need not worry about a possible usurper in their midst."

"It's not amusing."

"No, definitely not."

The rippling bubbled up and he laughed out loud. She stopped, hands on her hips, and glared at him—her expression shifting from horrified to reluctantly amused. Her eyes swung to his left and her glare intensified again. He turned to see a young woman looking up at him, mouth parted. His laughter dried up as quickly as it had come. He tipped his head and started walking again, leaving Marietta to catch up.

It was a minute before he noticed her huffing. He slowed his pace. She never complained about where they walked or the pace at which they did so. He knew she refrained from commenting on purpose—to prove something. And it worked. It explained more than one thing about her character, and none of those things were disappointing.

"So what did you do for Oscar?"

He stayed silent for a minute, trying to discover a way around the question. He could simply ignore it, but found needling her the more appealing option.

Why he wanted to spar with her was another puzzle. He usually wasn't so abrasive, unless the situation called for that response. But then he rarely took cases from upper class women. He hated them so fiercely that it wasn't worth the fortune they could pay, or the contacts he could make.

She continued, taking six steps to his five, even with her long legs. "Did he recently get into a scrape with the watch?"

"What makes you think Oscar needs to avoid the law enforcement? He works in a prison." Either a change of topic or a way to get under her skin was needed.

She shrugged. "Just trying to prod you to talk."

"And what makes you think I helped Oscar recently?"

"Well, he still owes you tasks," she said as if it were the most apparent thing.

He withheld a smile. Perfect. "Do you think I need

to go into Cold Bath Fields every day? Having a large array of options is what makes connections worthwhile. Some favors don't come due for years."

She was suddenly no longer at his side. He kept the smile from his face again with effort, and turned to see her stopped dead on the walk.

"Years?" Her voice sounded as though someone had a grip around her throat. "Are you saying that I might be beholden to you for *years*?"

"Of course. Did you think it would only be a few weeks and you would be rid of me?"

The grip seemed to tighten as unintelligible sounds gurgled from her throat.

He closed the distance between them and leaned down, pleased to see the glaze in her eyes as he paused just an inch too close. Close enough to increase the movement of her chest, to make the pulse at her neck throb.

"No, Marietta. No, no, no," he whispered as he stepped forward another inch, so their toes were brushing. "You will be serving me for a long time to come. But don't worry, I'll have you trained in no time."

He touched her wrist and leaned closer still, concentrating on the throb, watching it jump even more. "I'll save you a prime spot in my harem. Those three nights of sin might take a very *long* time to complete."

He heard her breath catch, saw the way her throat trembled and her lips parted. The reactions drew him closer. He wanted to see what it would take for her to relinquish all control to him. Not that he would allow anything else. A woman ceding control was an absolute, and had been since he was sixteen.

He let the dark cloud envelop him at the unwanted thoughts of his past and twisted them to seduction. He lowered his head, his lips a scant breath away, making her pulse race further just by his proximity and the thoughts of what *could* happen. How he could kiss her. How he could stroke her. How he could do things with his fingers that would make her forget her own name.

Her head tipped back, just an inch.

He could play women like a violin humming a languid lullaby or a furious scherzo. It was his most honed and most hated talent. Most women were easy, needing nothing more than his looks to lure them in. Others required compliments or flattery. Simple as well. The real challenge lay with the ones who required a specific tuning. The turn of a knob, the pluck of the right string, the correct rhythm of the bow.

What would it take for Marietta? A simple kiss? A caress? No. He had a feeling that while she could be lured with the simple things, getting her, *really* getting her under his control would be a challenge.

He stepped away from her, the street and homes coming back into view. The bustle of the traffic—carriage wheels, horse hooves, shouts and curses—mingling with the clop of the pedestrians as they walked past. He saw the knowledge seep into her eyes, the rose creep up her long white throat and into her cheeks. They were in the middle of a crowded neighborhood during one of the high times of the day, and she had completely forgotten where she was.

At sixteen he had vowed to always be in control. It had taken two years, but he'd never failed since.

Challenge or not, she was within his grasp.

* * *

The barrister's office was located in a ramshackle neighborhood near the south docks.

Marietta trailed behind Noble as they entered the building, still completely enraged at what had happened on the sidewalk. She was barely keeping her anger and fire leashed. And he had been smiling at her ire for the past fifteen minutes, which further stoked the flames.

He turned down the hall and she gripped his tailored sleeve underneath the elbow. "His office is that way." She pointed in the opposite direction.

"No. It's this way."

He pushed open the door on his right without knocking and walked inside. This hadn't been where she'd met the barrister previously, but there he was. Hackenstay, with his scrawny frame and heavy mustache, lurched up from behind a misshapen desk. A tin box clattered and fell across the desk, and he hastily pushed a thick stack of fallen notes and loose coins back inside, closing the tin firmly and putting a trembling hand on top.

"You must be Mr. Hackenstay. I'm here on behalf of Mr. Winters and Miss Winters."

Wariness passed through the barrister's eyes, replaced by obsequiousness as he caught sight of Marietta. She hadn't liked him before, gin-soaked little toad, and she didn't like him now.

Noble continued when Hackenstay didn't respond. "I understand that instead of going through a solicitor, they hired you directly. Is it true that you took the sum of two hundred pounds from Mr. Winters and the sum of one hundred from Miss Winters?"

Money that they didn't really have. They had leveraged everything. Used everything. And for once Mark had been lucky at the tables. He'd won a hundred pounds. He would have assuredly lost it the next night if they hadn't used it right away for the barrister. Money never stayed long in the household.

Hackenstay bobbed his head. "For payment."

Marietta opened her mouth, but Noble beat her to it. "Payment of what?"

"Consultation fees and showing up in court with her brother. I plan to help him until the end." He puffed out his chest and rattled off a litany of empty jargon about how he would plead Kenneth's case.

"How much are your usual consultation fees?" Noble looked around the office at the dingy drapes, the faded rug, the ill-placed pictures on the walls. He sent Marietta a glance and a raised brow as if to ask what she'd been thinking to choose this man.

She shook her head and gestured back, trying to convey that she had never been in this office. Hackenstay must have used the main office somewhere else in the building. It had been a long sight better than this one. She'd had second thoughts before, but seeing this office would have given her thirds.

Hackenstay wet his lips nervously. "Do you need another job done?"

"No. I need you to tell me your fee," Noble said, his voice silky and smooth.

"It depends on the job. I rolled the Winters fees all into one price. They still owe me the last two hundred." He sent a softly chiding look her way. The obnoxious lump.

91

"No."

Hackenstay switched his gaze back to Noble, shock edging his features. "No? What do you mean?"

"I'd like to see the work you've done on the case."

He swallowed. "I-I don't have that information at hand."

"How do you expect to help Mr. Kenneth Winters?" Noble idly lifted a folded paper from Hackenstay's desk. The barrister reached out to reclaim it and put it back in its place, squaring it away.

"I will sit in on his trial and plead his case, just as I said."

"With his family watching?" Noble picked up a round glass ball.

Hackenstay tried to snatch the ball back as well, but Noble pretended not to notice as he examined it. The barrister looked irritated, but then switched his gaze to her and shook his head, his lips curling under in mock sympathy beneath his bushy mustache. "Unfortunately, family members may not watch. But I will be sure to relay everything to them after the proceedings." He reached out again for the glass ball and missed grabbing it. "If you could just return my globe?"

Noble tossed it in the air, a short arc of glittering light, and Hackenstay caught it against his chest. He looked more flustered than before.

"I see," Noble said, fingers drifting through papers. "So really, they will have no way of knowing whether you will really help their brother in court."

"I will help him until the end! I will convince the

judge and jury of his innocence." The barrister clutched the globe.

"So you keep saying. Let's be short and frank here." He stopped and turned to Marietta. "Actually, Miss Winters, why don't you explain to Mr. Hackenstay what will happen in the next fifteen minutes."

Surprise stormed through her. What had changed his mind in letting her talk? She didn't give him a chance to take it back. "Your 'contract' is nonsense. As are your promises. You are a terrible man taking advantage of us like that, in our moment of grief and despair. You will return all our money, Mr. Hackenstay. Right now. To the pound."

"I assure you, miss, that you need a retainer for your brother to speak his case." Moisture gathered along his hairline.

Anger, hot and deep, coursed through her. "I've read the laws, Mr. Hackenstay. In felonious cases you cannot do the things you've promised. I'm no longer quite as naive as when I walked through your door last week. Return the money right now or I—*we*—will make sure you regret it."

Noble smiled at her. It wasn't a pleasant smile, but she somehow knew that the unpleasantness wasn't aimed at her. That he approved of what she'd said.

The door opened behind her. She saw Noble tense before his hand brushed his pocket and he turned. She had stopped carrying her pistol around, no longer concerned with keeping safe from the jeering crowds since moving to Noble's. Perhaps that hadn't been a smart decision.

"Here now, what's going on?"

"Mr. Tannett. Thank—" Hackenstay pulled his scrawny frame up to his full height. "These folks are trying to cheat us."

Noble took a step away from her and shot her a look so intense that she stepped back as well.

Tannett's eyes narrowed. "Are they now?"

"Your junior barrister here is trying to swindle the Winters family out of three hundred pounds," Noble said with a rather lazy air, all traces of intensity wiped clean. "Hardly the type that can call someone else a cheat."

Tannett took a step toward Noble. Close to the wall, she was out of the immediate attention of both barristers. She had the feeling that was what Noble had intended by forcing her back.

"I'm not a s-s-swindler!" Hackenstay shouted.

"If you give us back the three hundred pounds, I'll let it go as a miscommunication due to your junior status. The contract is illegal. As a barrister you should know that there is little you can do but to return the money. Otherwise, I'll have a Runner on your case in the blink of an eye."

The side of Tannett's face suddenly turned up. "The Winters family. I see. I think not, Mister . . . ?

Noble just stared at the man without blinking. Tannett's mouth tightened before continuing without Noble's address.

"Mr. Winters is in dire straits. I doubt he will want us broadcasting that to the public, now will he? And with his poor brother in prison, one can only imagine the compounded scandal."

Mark would sooner give up the money than cause further scandal. Marietta bit her lower lip.

"Do I sense a note of blackmail in your voice, Mr. Tannett?" Noble asked, as if only half interested in the response.

Tannett quirked an eye, as if he were especially clever. "You may."

"I see. I think it only fair to tell you that I dislike blackmailers. Actually, I rather hate them, truth to tell." His voice was dark and ominous. He strode forward, and Tannett's hand went to his coat pocket. Noble gripped his wrist before it slid inside the fold. "You might want to tell your junior to remove his hand from that drawer, or else I'm liable to accidentally shoot you."

Marietta blinked to see a pistol in Noble's other hand pressed against Tannett's side.

"Hackenstay." Tannett's voice was high and tight.

"Marietta, be a dear and take Mr. Hackenstay's assuredly shoddy gun from the drawer." She started to step forward, but stopped when Noble's even voice continued. "Oh, and Hackenstay, make a move toward her, and I will put Tannett out of his misery and then start working on you. I won't be quick about it either."

Hackenstay pressed himself as far away from his desk as he could get. She walked around the desk, eyes darting to all the men, and removed the pistol. A quick head jerk from Noble had her back to her corner.

Noble twisted so that Tannett's hand fell from his pocket fold and his arm was wrenched behind him. "I was willing to negotiate with your barrister, Tannett, but now that I see how willing you are to take

95

advantage of innocents like Miss Winters and to use blackmail . . . I have to say that my method of dealing with you seems to have changed its scope."

"I will hunt you down."

"I'm trembling. Really, you should learn from the best first. After a top-notch blackmailer has had his way with you, you'll never be second-rate again."

There was a hesitation in the sentence that was odd, but Marietta had little time to process it.

"Who are you?" Tannett asked between his teeth, obviously in pain.

"That matters little. What should matter to you is what I can do to you." He leaned forward and whispered something in Tannett's ear. The man turned to chalk. "Think that over. We are going to take the three hundred pounds you owe the Winterses. And I'll be back to check on you, Tannett. Rest assured."

Tannett gave a swift nod to Hackenstay. "Make out a draft." When the scrawny man didn't move, he shouted, "Now!"

Hackenstay grabbed the tin box and they waited as he removed a paper with trembling hands and then wrote down the necessary information.

"Marietta, if you please."

She retrieved the draft and stowed it in her reticule. It felt very strange to be carrying three hundred pounds in her bag.

"And with that, gentlemen, we bid you a good afternoon. Perhaps it is time to start a new business or to read through your law texts again."

He motioned to Marietta and she scampered out of the office, her reticule clutched against her chest in a parody of Mr. Hackenstay holding his globe earlier, the man's pistol gripped tightly in her fingertips.

She didn't know how Noble removed himself from the office without leaving himself open to retaliation, but he emerged with a pistol in each hand and nudged her toward the door.

As soon as they stepped onto the sidewalk, he stowed the three pistols and set a brisk pace. He didn't slow until they were three blocks away in two different directions. She could see him looking behind but her mind was frozen. As soon as he shortened his steps, she snapped back to the scene of the bustling streets and the busier areas near the Thames. They stepped onto Blackfriars and a wave of something rocketed through her.

"You just threatened them with a gun. I think *I* just threatened them with a gun. We got the money back. They actually returned it." She took another shaky step. "I feel so . . . vibrant."

His eyes were cynical. "Delayed emotion. Don't do anything stupid because of it."

But not even his words could bring her down. She barely noticed as they cashed the draft and made their way back home. Home. As if she would ever have a real one. But this one at least had rosemary and dill bread, incredible stews and a man who could right her wrongs—and that was well more than she'd had a week past.

Her calves twinged a bit as they made their way to another section of town after a quick stop to eat. She was used to a lot of walking, but they'd been briskly striding across the entire midsection of London today.

She followed Noble into a plain building and down a hall to a door labeled RECORDS. Noble pushed inside and a lanky man with large glasses looked up.

"Mr. Noble!"

"Good afternoon, Anthony. Are you busy?"

Anthony pushed aside his papers and spread his hands. "What can I do for you?"

"I'm looking for information on the Middlesex murderer case."

Anthony's sharp eyes looked to her and then back to Noble. "I see. There's not much. It has boggled the minds of everyone around here. Was a relief to most that they think they have the culprit in custody."

"I figured as much. What do you have? Any previous suspects?"

Anthony motioned to the two chairs in front of his desk and tapped his pen on the oak surface. "There were three. The first victim's husband was a suspect at first, until he was accounted for by twenty different witnesses. Attended some business function during the time of her murder. The blame quickly moved to his business partner, who was not at the function. That thread of inquiry was destroyed, though, by the timing of the next victim. The business partner was in Cornwall—and his story is solid. There were two men in the parish area who were questioned but not held. Joshua Dawkins and a street urchin. Dawkins is one you might want to check out. The Runners have all been leery of him. Described as a suspicious man."

"If there were two people in the area, why did they not get the same treatment as my—as Kenneth Winters?" Marietta couldn't help but ask.

Noble didn't glare at her this time, but she detected something close to a sigh in his expression. Anthony gave her a measuring glance, though his eyes were still friendly. She had the impression of a quick mind hidden behind a nonthreatening air.

"They were much more desperate the third time."

Noble motioned with his hand to continue, and Anthony didn't wait for her response. "The second victim, anonymous, contained no identifiable links to the first. The parish patrollers who found the body quit the next day. I heard it was gruesome."

"Which is why the second victim hasn't been identified?"

Anthony nodded. "There are artist sketches at Coroner's Court of the faces after they were cleaned. May want to have a look and see if you can obtain copies. They have sketches of the first two."

"And the new victim?"

"That one too, I'm sure. I heard they rushed the body through."

"Suspicious."

Anthony tilted his head. "Or frightened."

"Who was the first victim?"

"Mrs. Amanda Sinclair."

Marietta thought the name sounded vaguely familiar. "The Sinclairs? Weren't they just married? It was sudden? Banns barely read in Herefordshire, was it? She was someone from the countryside returned to London?"

"Sounds right. Part of the investigation took place in Herefordshire."

Noble was looking over a paper on Anthony's desk. "Perhaps the link is there. What was her previous name?"

Anthony shook his head. "Easy enough to find out, but I don't know off the top of my head. I'll send a post when I find it."

"Arthur Dresden still assigned to the case?"

Anthony grimaced. "Yes."

"I've not had the pleasure of meeting him yet, though his reputation precedes him."

"Even as the newest Runner, he has wreaked havoc in the ranks. Hungry. Be careful of him, he doesn't get on well with the patrollers or watch. Thinks they are useless."

"Sometimes they are, but it's never a good idea to let them know you think that."

"Which tells you something about Dresden."

"Indeed."

Noble rose and Marietta rose with him. "Thank you, Anthony. Consider this and the victim's name as first payment."

Anthony nodded. "Good luck to you, Miss Winters. I'm sure that Mr. Noble will have your brother out of jail in no time."

Marietta gaped at him. Noble took hold of her elbow and guided her into the hall. He dropped his hand, but she could still feel the imprint.

"How did he know?"

"Anthony is smart. And you weren't being particularly coy. Come."

"You did something for him?"

"Yes."

"Your favors don't seem that bad."

A slow smile spread over his face. "I'm glad you don't think so. But Marietta . . . " He leaned toward her and smoothed a lock of hair behind her ear, leaving tingles everywhere he brushed. "You have no idea what I have in store for you."

Chapter 7

Marietta moaned. She should have been sick of eating soups and stews, but they were so *good*.

There was a knock on the front door, and since Noble looked disinclined to answer it, she did. A young boy stood on the stoop. "Message for Marietta."

Odd that he used her first name, but she appreciated the discretion more than she could express. The last thing she needed was for someone to identify her as living here. She took the sealed paper and rooted in her hanging pocket for a coin, handing it to the boy. He tipped his hat and she closed the door.

She ran a finger over the long sloped handwriting and the eagle seal. She sat at the table to read her brother's note, a tingle of guilt running through her that Mark was in worse straits at the moment—not enjoying delicious food, fending off the crowds. She'd sent him fifty pounds along with her address, hoping he would use the money for food. Knowing that soon she would have to let him know that the remaining two hundred fifty was back in their accounts. She was afraid he'd squander it before they could use it to repay their debts.

Two lines were scrawled on the page. They were moving Kenny's trial up and the barrister's office had been cleaned out with no forwarding address.

She tapped a finger against the paper.

"What is it?" Noble continued writing and didn't look up.

She read him the note. He paused, his pen hovering above his parchment.

"I see that Tannett took my advice. Good. As to your brother—your younger brother—we will need to see if we can hold off the trial."

"How?"

He went back to writing. "I know who to ask. He's holding a masquerade tonight. He loves his masquerades, the more debaucherous, the better. You will need to be dressed appropriately."

He looked up, green eyes surveying her. "Do you have a domino or a mask?"

She clutched the note. "I do, but nothing risqué like you are suggesting."

He waved a hand and went back to his page. "One of the tavern outfits will be more than perfect."

Her jaw dropped. "Are you insane?" she hissed. "Who is your friend?"

"John Alcroft."

She blinked. "I can't attend a party held by John Alcroft dressed like that. People will *know* me there."

"Not if you are a tavern wench wearing a mask, they won't." His pen scritched across the parchment.

"But—"

The scritching halted. "Look, Marietta. No one will notice you or identify you, trust me." His gaze swept her. "You blend in too well."

Her stomach tightened. "I realize I'm plain, but that doesn't mean—"

"You aren't plain. You are mutable." He cocked his head. "Able to look differently depending on the situation and what you are wearing or how your hair is fixed. It's a strength."

She stared at him, her mouth ajar.

He leaned forward, a smile curving his lips to vie with his piercing eyes. "I'll bet before this you wore your hair exactly the same way, every day. And your black or brown dresses? The same. You probably tilted your head the same way to every opening conversation salvo. And the way you glared and stared. The same. Rarely did you smile, I'll bet, and have fun? Not for years."

The only sounds she could hear were the continued simmering of the soup pot and the heavy beat of her heart.

"And from your silence I can see that I would win that bet easily. So tell me, Marietta. If you redo your hair, apply kohl around your eyes, and attach a mask, do you honestly think someone will recognize you?"

The seconds ticked by. She was frozen. He raised a brow then started scritching again.

No, there was no chance that she would be identified. Either as the boring fringe society member she was or the sister of the Middlesex murderer.

She hadn't realized her actions were so . . . predictable. She hadn't liked being out of control since very shortly after their parents' deaths. Perhaps she had gone to the extreme.

There was freedom in going to the masquerade as someone else. She opened her mouth to respond when the back door banged open.

"Lovely day, isn't it?"

A tall man, even taller than Noble, strode into the kitchen, immediately heading for the sideboard without another word. He lifted a bowl and the ladle.

Noble didn't look up, though she had seen him tense right before the door opened. Now he just shook his head, his grip relaxing around the pen.

"Jeremy, what are you doing here?" His voice was exasperated and . . . fond?

Jeremy walked to the table. He couldn't be much older than she—might in fact be younger, it was hard to say. But it was immediately apparent who he was. He had the same cheekbones as her host, though his features were somewhat rounder and more open. Devastatingly attractive as well, but Jeremy was more of a charming, boyish scoundrel, whereas Noble immortalized a dark sexual demon.

Jeremy plunked down so that they formed an off-center triangle and smiled at her—the smile was a little crooked, but all the more charming for it. "Good afternoon. Name's Jeremy Noble."

She smiled back. It would be easy to be captivated by such a man. "Pleasure to meet you, Mr. Jeremy Noble. I'm Marietta Winters."

"The Middlesex murderer Winters?"

Her smile tightened. "One and the same."

Jeremy let out a low whistle and turned to his brother. "Thought you could keep me ignorant of this one, I see."

"No." Noble did not look up. "I thought you should finish Cambridge. Why are you here, Jeremy?"

"Charlie told me you were here working on a new case. Thought I would drop by and see if you needed help."

Noble finally looked up, the same exasperation and fondness in his voice present on his face. He looked . . . transformed. Like a human instead of something otherworldly and untouchable.

"No. Now go back to school."

"We're on break, remember?" He happily cut a piece of bread, his smile never dimming.

"So go bother your friends and get in trouble in Mayfair."

"Done that plenty. I'm here to help you now."

"I don't need your help." His eyes narrowed and he looked more like the Noble she knew. "Go home for break."

Marietta shivered at his frosty tone, but Jeremy just looked amused. He glanced at Marietta. "Do you fall for that? All bark."

He swiped a piece of bread into his soup bowl. "Why would I go home? Much better food here."

"Can't you get Mrs. Rosaire to cook for you there?" she asked, interrupting their banter.

Jeremy blinked at her for a second, then a slow smile crossed his face. It was just like his brother's, but where Noble's devastated her, Jeremy's just made her feel like a co-conspirator. "Is that what—"

Noble made a sharp motion with his free hand and continued writing. Jeremy just looked amused.

"Is that what?" she asked.

Jeremy shook his head. "So, Miss Winters, may I call you Marietta?"

She could feel her eyebrows shoot straight up. But he was so earnest looking and compelling. Yes, these two were both trouble. She shuddered to imagine them together against an opponent. "Yes."

"Excellent. Please call me Jeremy."

"Now that introductions are out of the way, be on yours, Jeremy," Noble said. She wondered what he was writing.

"Oh, no, no. This looks like much too much fun."

Noble gripped his pen a fraction tighter. "We are going to Alcroft's tonight. Another masquerade. You have an invitation. After that I expect only to see you at home."

"I got straight marks this term."

She could see a smile tugging at Noble's mouth, but when he looked up he was impassive. "I expected no less, now be off."

Jeremy smiled and gave her a wave. "I'll see you both tonight."

She waited until Jeremy's footsteps receded. "I didn't know you had a brother."

"Now you do." He continued writing.

"Do you have any other siblings?"

"No."

"Parents?"

"I didn't crawl out of Hell, if that is what you are asking."

"Are they alive?"

He hesitated a moment, the pen scratching to a halt. "Go see if you need anything else for tonight. I'll contact Clarisse, if so."

"Do you ever get tired of ordering everyone around?"

"No."

She sighed and trooped upstairs.

She fit the last feather in place on her mask and slipped it on. Then pivoting slowly in front of the mirror, she analyzed her appearance from all angles. She didn't look like herself. She had transformed into some exotic flower or bird from the head up and a loose woman from the neck down. She wasn't sure both styles went together, but it was the best she could do. And the effect was quite interesting all the same. It would allow her to be two different women if she so desired.

She walked to the kitchen. She found it amusing that Noble chose to work here instead of in the study off the drawing room, spare though it was—just like everything else in the house. The kitchen table was large though and he liked to spread things in every direction.

He looked up at her entrance and his eyes ran down her figure. "Adequate. Are you ready to leave?"

She tapped her hand irritably against her leg. "Yes. Thank you for the brilliant compliment."

His eyes met hers and his mouth opened, then

closed, a peculiar look in his eyes. He pulled himself out of the chair and walked over to her. "Something's missing."

Her hands found their way to her hips. "And what is that?"

"A knowledge in your eyes." His were narrow as they searched hers. "You can wear the clothes, but you have no idea how to carry off the effect."

She tried to keep her anger tapped. "I see."

"Have you ever been kissed, Marietta?"

The anger fled, replaced with confusion and nervousness. "I don't see how that is any of your concern."

"You do realize that we will be carrying off a role in the taverns especially."

"No." She wet her lips, anxiety pulsing through her.

He raised a brow. "I suppose I shouldn't expect you to know what taverns are like, but you will after tonight."

She couldn't bring herself to ask what he meant. He didn't seem to need the cue.

He leaned down. "Have you ever seen two people kiss, Marietta?"

"Yes."

"What did you think?"

His eyes were a darker green, warmer than usual, not with a warmth spawned from fondness, but from the excited heat of a predator.

"It looked . . . perfunctory."

"Ah. No, I meant have you ever seen two people *really* kiss?"

She had seen a maid and footman kiss at a house

party once, when they thought no one else around. The maid had been wrapped around the footman, and he had pressed her against the wall. She thought that was most likely what Noble meant by *real* kissing. It had looked rather real.

"Yes."

He slowly smiled. "Good. We'll start with the basics."

Her mind went blank. "Basics?"

"Of kissing. Most people aren't good at kissing right from the start." He looked her over. "Unless you are a natural."

She blinked stupidly.

His hand reached up and touched her cheek, gently tilting her head. "It's like connecting puzzle pieces when you kiss. Or when you do anything else of a sexual nature." The parts of her brain not already blank blessedly went dark. "You don't want to purse your lips or keep them too slack."

He lifted her wrist and turned it underside up so it hung just below his lips.

"A firm gentle pressure . . . " His lips touched her wrist, the pulse point beating wildly beneath. Her breath caught in her throat. His eyes kept a steady hold on hers, watching. "A light teasing . . . "

Was that a *tongue* that just swiped a swath across her skin? Heat followed the path and bounced in all directions.

"An all-encompassing domination." His warm breath tickled her skin every time he spoke, and then he encased the fire with his mouth. Her head tilted back as he drew her closer and she fell under his will.

"A sweet submission." His lips sucked gently and then released her wrist. "Those all work well depending on the mood and heat."

The kitchen was rather warm.

"Open your lips, Marietta."

Her mouth parted without her express permission.

"I don't think we need to explore the perfunctory types of kisses first, do we?"

"N-No."

He shook his head slowly, agreeing, and she followed the movement with her eyes. She felt as if he had cast a spell over her once again, just as he had in the street on the way to the barrister's office.

His head lowered, his eyes remained fixed on hers. She didn't know what to do, so she stood motionless. His lips brushed hers and the tingling sensation traversed her spine. Her first kiss felt rather nice. He repeated the motion, and she tentatively brushed her lips across his, but instead of continuing the feathery caresses, his mouth closed over hers. An entirely different kind of sensation followed. He had said not to stay still or limp, but not to exert too much pressure either, and she had zero idea what to do. Standing there felt odd, though, as if something was missing. His hand curled around the back of her neck and she was urged closer, his lips opening hers. She started to feel the rhythm, the motion.

She tried opening and closing her lips around his, and it was awkward. Embarrassment ran through her. She started to feel light-headed.

He pulled back and she saw the amusement in his eyes. "Remember to breathe, Marietta."

"How can I breathe when your lips are covering mine?"

He tapped her nose, an entirely inappropriate gesture, as was all of this. "Through your nose. Or take in a little air with your mouth when we separate."

Separate? They had been joined at the lip.

"Let's try it again."

"I dislike you."

"I know." His eyes said he didn't believe her one bit. "Put that to use in kissing me. Try to get your revenge."

His eyes twinkled in challenge, the darkness lurking just behind. He lowered his head again and when his lips met hers she wasn't shocked this time and it felt even better. More natural. She tested breathing through her nose and wanted to kick him in the shin when she felt his laughter against her mouth.

"Mmmm . . . " he said against her lips. "I can't remember the last time teaching someone to kiss was this fun."

The tremors from his words, his mouth, vibrated against hers. "Do you do this often?" she asked against his lips, the movement of her mouth against his suddenly making her grasp what he was trying to teach.

"No, not often," he murmured. His mouth closed around hers, and this time she followed his lead, responding in kind, warmth flowing through her like a fresh hot brick under her blankets. She had no delusions that she was doing this kissing thing well, but it felt more natural, and he seemed to be responding. The kiss deepened further and she found her body inching closer to his, brushing against him, seeking further contact.

All sorts of strange feelings flowed through her. A coiling in her belly, as if all the butterflies which had been fluttering there before had been captured in a net and secured—their wings beating furiously in one tight package.

Her body was feeling more languid and relaxed, where at first she had been taut and strung tight. Her embarrassment was a haze above her, not as apparent as it had been previously. Her fingers moved to touch him, and only with strong will did she keep them at her sides, clutched in her tavern dress.

"You can touch me, Marietta," he whispered. "But then, of course, the opposite is true as well."

She jerked back, not breaking their contact above but removing all the places that they were touching below the neck. She felt him chuckle again, then his hand at her nape tugged her closer and his other hand wrapped around her waist, bringing her flush against him so they touched *everywhere*. His mouth *seared* hers, the kisses turning from languid and exploratory to dominating and overpowering.

Her hands reached up to clutch his sleeves as he more forcefully opened her lips. Her body leaned in for more. His tongue slipped between her teeth and the shock was absorbed by the bigger shock of feeling something hard pressed against her lower body. His tongue pressed against hers and his fingers stroked her nape, urging her to respond in kind. She tentatively pressed her tongue back against his. It was a strange sensation and she started to feel hot and out of sorts—the rubbing of their bodies doing strange things to all parts of hers.

She should push away from him right now.

She held on tightly instead, her fingers crushing his linen sleeves.

Did all men kiss this way? She suddenly had the dawning comprehension of how women lost their virtue—and how they became pregnant out of wedlock. Of why it happened. Perfunctory kisses didn't lead to that state. Kisses like this . . .

She pulled back, breathing hard. Gabriel Noble smiled and let the hand holding her neck trail along her throat, fingertips scorching her skin before dropping to his side. Her hand pressed against her chest, to the exposed skin above her bodice, which felt overly hot. His eyes searched hers and satisfaction appeared.

"Now we are ready to go." He turned on his heel, and she followed him out, still feeling dazed and out of sorts.

The carriage pulled in front of a lavish row house in Hanover Square.

Guests were walking through the door and light blazed from the windows.

Noble helped her down from the carriage this time and placed her hand on top of his sleeve. She knew from earlier that the silky feel of his jacket was expensive and fine, and she was glad to have her gloves between them. She didn't need any more stimulation from that quarter.

A man dressed in black, similarly to Noble,

approached them as they walked through the door. "I just spoke with your brother and he said you were bringing a lovely guest."

Noble smiled, his cheekbones nudging his mask. "Good evening, Alcroft. May I introduce you to my partner for the evening, Miss Rose. John Alcroft."

Blue eyes speculatively swung her way. "Enchanted, Miss Rose. Long has it been since Gabriel has brought a partner to one of my humble gatherings."

She didn't know what to say to that, so she just echoed his greeting. She had met their host, John Alcroft, before, briefly, but didn't know much about him personally.

"I need to speak with you later," Noble said to him.

Alcroft inclined his head. "I can slip away around eleven. Will that do?"

"Yes, thank you."

"Of course. Enjoy the evening, Gabriel, Miss Rose. Until eleven."

Alcroft moved past them to greet more guests, and Noble guided her farther inside. The party was in full swing. People were dancing and chatting, a freer atmosphere than a strict ton gathering, yet she saw more than one person she knew. More than one person who could identify her.

Noble's hand ran down her back. "Don't think about them. They won't recognize you."

She felt the tensed muscles in her back relax. She knew it was true. She hadn't even recognized herself in the mirror. "I've never seen you at a gathering, even though you seem comfortable enough here. Do you dance?"

He smiled suddenly, roguishly, and held out his hand. "I do."

He pulled her onto the dance floor, straight into the middle of an already formed set. Bad form, but he somehow seemed above the censure.

And that reason was that he could *move*. There were three types of men in the ton. The ones who were forced to dance, the ones who seemed to enjoy it and were always available to dance, and the ones who made it an art form. Gabriel Noble was definitely one of the latter.

It was like dancing with liquid. Like *being* liquid. Every sweep and curl executed with precision and flair. Never had she had a partner who could move like this. Never had she been twisted and handled and shown off on the floor.

Never had she met a man like Gabriel Noble.

Was he lacking in anything? Besides some of his personal skills, of course—he was quite a bear most of the time. Although past the first few days, he had mellowed slightly toward her—not counting the barbs that he tossed every so often. But the affection he displayed for his brother and the people with whom he worked told a different story.

And even with the animosity, every time she had been in a situation where someone could have harmed her—her brother (not that he would have), the other prisoners, or the barristers—he had taken definitive action.

If you were in Noble's circle, you were obviously under his protection.

He smiled as he showed her off in a turn. She knew she looked like a wonderful dancer at that moment, and even though she was passably good, *he* made her look great.

He brought her close again and she could see something in his green eyes, unhidden behind the mask. They had carried that same look earlier when he had been about to kiss her. Heat swept through her, but he simply turned her again.

"You didn't answer my question."

"Which one was that?" His body touched hers.

"Do you attend these functions often?"

"No." He twirled her. "Just Alcroft's. And his masquerades are the best. Sometimes I think he holds them so often because he knows I will attend."

"You are good friends? I thought you disliked anyone to the manor born?"

She felt his muscles tense beneath her glove, beneath his jacket. "Alcroft and I have been friends a long time. And I don't dislike everyone in the upper classes."

"If you say so."

He spun her and her breath caught. Her feet barely touched the floor when she danced with him. "I do."

"Where did you learn to dance like this?"

"Down by the docks."

She tried to look down her nose at him at the same time she held onto him. She had a feeling the heat she could feel in her cheeks and the excitement from dancing showed on her face and negated any glare.

"My mother, if you must know."

"You danced like this with your mother?"

"I was required to stand in at dance lessons at one time in my life. It was easy enough to apply what I had learned before."

"Dance lessons, where?"

He pulled her against him again as they turned and his green eyes turned smoky as he lowered his head. Her breath caught and she had the inane thought that this kissing activity really required practicing right now.

The music stopped and he switched his arm from about her waist to underneath her hand. Before she knew what was happening he was escorting her from the floor.

She caught the admiring glances sent their way. More than one woman was eyeing Noble with an avaricious gaze. She had a feeling that most of the people there knew who he was. Apart from the standard masquerade wear, he hadn't attempted to disguise himself tonight. And even if he had, after that turn about the dance floor, his identity was assuredly obvious to all those who knew him.

They stopped by the refreshment area.

"Noble," a voice purred, a woman in a fashionable royal blue dress slinking to his side. "I haven't seen you in a double fortnight. Been keeping away from us?"

"Mrs. Dalworth. I've been busy. How is your husband?"

She waved a hand. "Away, as usual."

"I see. This is Miss Rose. Mrs. Dalworth."

The woman barely spared her a look and a baring of teeth. "Charming. I wanted to extend the invitation to meet with the ladies at tea. We are interested in sponsoring your foundation. A formal note will be sent tomorrow too, of course, but I wanted to let you know in person. I stopped by your residence today but your butler said you were out."

"Excellent. I will respond posthaste. What good sense you ladies have." He smiled charmingly and Mrs. Dalworth preened. Marietta wondered why she didn't see the hard light in the back of his eyes, the edge behind his charming smile. Mrs. Dalworth seemed only to be taken in with his sweet guile. Perhaps she only saw what she wished to see.

Or what he wished her to see. He manipulated women as easily as making a deft turn on the dance floor. She had to remember that.

"I will see you soon, then. I hope you two enjoy yourselves this evening. I have found patience never lets me down." Her voice lilted at the end as she sashayed off.

The woman wasn't even trying to be ambiguous. She had a fine figure, and Marietta knew the features beneath her mask were fine as well. But she didn't have a chance with Noble. Couldn't she tell?

"No, she never can. What is intriguing is how you can tell?"

She looked up to see Noble watching her, eyes calculating. She realized with a dawning sense of horror that she had said that last bit out loud.

"Your eyes," she replied.

They immediately shuttered and she cursed herself. She had just begun to be able to read him and she had given her advantage away.

The shutters fell just as suddenly as they'd been erected. She could see amusement there and interest. "Mmmm. I'm interested to see if you continue to guess correctly. Most see only what they wish to see."

119

She didn't comment on his part in that equation—that of providing that vision for them. She didn't think herself so different from most. She too liked to see what she wished. But desperate times required rationality and attention, and the last few years had made her look more deeply.

"A game?"

"A challenge. Come, Marietta, take my challenge." His voice was husky and deep, sexual and mysterious. She saw the truth in his eyes, though, which were watchful and keen.

"I accept."

Pleasure and increased interest joined the watchfulness. "Not everything is singular, though, remember that. There is nothing wrong with discovery alongside a challenge. It is all in how you approach it."

His hand slid along her back, dipping to touch her natural waist. "I hope you give in to the desire I discovered in you earlier." He turned her and pulled her against him. Her buttocks nestled in the juncture of his legs. Heat shot straight up her spine.

They had attracted some attention. She tried to calm herself by repeating that no one knew who she was. She was just some woman who had arrived with a too attractive man.

"I want to see my brother released. That is how I'm approaching it."

She felt his lips brush the back of her ear and she forgot to breathe. "If we are lucky tonight, Alcroft will know of a way to delay the trial. What will you do for the weeks that we might be searching?"

She pushed away from him and turned to face

him, an angry retort on her lips. His smile was lazy and rakish, but his eyes . . . were watchful, calculating. Damn. He was going to give her a permanent headache.

"You are testing me."

He inclined his head, watching her. "Perhaps."

"Well, stop. I am perfectly capable of following through on my tasks, I've already told you that."

He bowed toward her so his face was level with hers, his arms clasped behind his back. "You have yet to be truly tested, Marietta. You may think me poking fun about the kissing earlier, but you will need to carry off your disguise when we leave tonight for the tavern. Your brother depends upon it."

She lifted her chin. "I will do whatever it takes."

He smiled that rakish smile again, and this time it was echoed in his eyes. "Perfect."

At eleven they slipped from the festivities and Marietta followed Noble into a well-appointed study. Bookshelves lined the rooms and everything was very neat. Spartan even. The complete opposite of Noble's messy desk.

Alcroft was standing in a corner, pouring from a decanter, the liquid falling into three crystal glasses in turn.

"Miss Winters, I presume?"

Marietta jumped. Alcroft had the same way about him as Noble. He didn't turn around, just expected everything to be as he wanted it. His shoulders tensed *just so* in anticipation that they might not.

"How did you know?" She looked at Noble. He

nodded in affirmation at her unasked question.

For all that she was supposed to be in disguise, a surprising number of people seemed to know or recognize her after only a few brief comments. Anthony, Jeremy, now Alcroft.

"Gabriel told me." He balanced the glasses and put them on the desktop, waving a hand to the two chairs on the other side. "Please."

Noble made himself comfortable, removing his mask, as Alcroft already had. Marietta perched on the chair and kept her mask in place.

"What specifically did you need?" he asked.

Noble lifted a glass and leaned back. "A way to hold off the trial. We need more time."

Alcroft nodded and sat back in his chair as well, steepling his fingers in front of him. "You'll need someone from Parliament to place pressure. Lords would be better at the moment, though someone in the Commons would do if you have a power player."

Noble shook his head. "I have a couple of very big favors owed me by power players in both. I could call one in, but it wouldn't be commensurate with the request. And creating a debt is out of the question."

Alcroft smiled. "Always wanting the upper hand, never wanting to be the one to owe. Nothing changes. I do have a favor I can bring due with the Home Office head, Casenton. Do you want it?"

Noble nodded and relaxed a bit more into his chair, swirling the Madeira. "That would be perfect. Is it enough of a recompense for the favor owed?"

"Yes. And I was wondering if it was ever going to

be used. He doesn't deal in the horses I love, and a favor from him is by far closer to your area than mine. Frankly, I will be well rid of the tie to him. He is keeping it hidden well, but his creditors are knocking. He will be more than willing to pay a debt without having to draw a draft."

"I suppose you want the Newmarket favor?"

Alcroft tapped his fingers together. "You know I do."

"Excellent. I was going to gift it to you the next holiday anyway. As if I care about the races."

"You bastard."

"Yes. Wonderful, isn't it?" Noble gave a cheeky grin, which Alcroft returned. Marietta felt as if she had stepped into another country where she didn't speak the language.

"You will let me know what Casenton says?"

"Of course."

"The quirks and quillets will be out for this one."

"Yes." Alcroft shot Marietta a speculative glance. "It should prove entertaining at the very least."

She didn't see anything entertaining about the situation, and it must have shown on her face.

"No offense meant to you or your brother, Miss Winters. I refer to the game of manipulating the law and enforcers of such until such time that Gabriel can absolve your brother." He tilted his head. "Gabriel always finishes the tasks set before him. Do not despair."

She looked between them. "How long have the two of you known each other?" Alcroft was part of society, and though Noble seemed able to hold his own, he hadn't been born to it, that much was obvious. It

123

seemed likely they had met through business, no matter the easy friendship between them.

"Oh, we have known each other for what now, twenty years?"

Noble agreed to her right, but she didn't look his way. Alcroft seemed amused, and she couldn't understand why.

"Quite the puzzle, is it not, Miss Winters? I will leave you to suss it out."

She looked to her right. Noble seemed equally amused, but there was a fine line of tension about him.

Alcroft's eyes changed. Noble tensed even further. She hungered to know what was behind that look. "Did I ever tell you that I begged Lord Dentry to allow you to attend Eton?"

Noble snorted. "I'm sure that was a scene you'd like to re-create."

"No, no I would not."

Noble looked to the long case clock at the side, tension visibly strumming through him. "We've kept you too long." He rose and started retying the strings on his mask. "Let me know about Casenton. We are staying on the row."

Alcroft rose too and rounded the desk, bowing to Marietta and shaking Noble's hand, his mask held loosely between his other fingers. "I will. Perhaps I'll drop by sometime this week as well. I admit that Jeremy has infected me with his excitement about the case. I will send a note first. But there might be something further I can do."

Noble nodded and they exited the room, leaving Alcroft behind.

Noble slipped his hand around her waist as they walked down the hall, bypassing the ballroom and heading straight for the door.

"And now, my dear, it is time for you to become my wench."

Chapter 8

Marietta removed her mask in the carriage. Utilizing the light from the gas lamps and her small pocket mirror, she attempted to smooth away the smudges beneath her eyes.

"The extra kohl is perfect. You look smoky and sensual." Noble leaned languidly against the back of the seat across from her.

Her cheeks warmed. She had never been called smoky or sensual—not that it would have been at all appropriate. But she found that it suited her sensibilities just fine. She smoothed her fingers down the low-cut dress and watched the man across from her.

Noble had changed into an outfit fit for a laborer. It was too big for him, hanging from his defined edges, but she had a feeling it was that way on purpose. He had another cap on, this one set at a jaunty angle. It would allow him to hide his eye color mostly in the shadows. His cheekbones appeared flatter. She hadn't been paying close attention, but he'd done something with the kohl. He was still going to turn women's heads, but in the guise of a rakish longshoreman instead.

He looked like the kind of man ladies had strict orders never to talk to.

The carriage turned a corner. They had to be close. "Remember that we are just here to soak up information and to see which patrollers and night watchmen are friendly and which are not. If the chance comes to ask questions, or the topic of the murderer is broached by someone else, you have to be enamored with everything about the murders and murderer. Like one of the women who attend every execution and then touches herself on the spot."

Her hand holding the mirror dropped into her lap as she stared at him. "Pardon me?"

He waved her off. "Just be enamored and try not to act too bright. I know it will be difficult for you."

She held her tongue at his obvious amusement and stowed the mirror without looking at him. She decided to change the subject. "Does Alcroft owe you favors as well?"

"No. We trade them as a matter of course, but I've never done a job for Alcroft in the way I'm doing this one for you. Alcroft's jobs are free."

"So once you become friends with someone, you are free to hire?"

"Are you looking to become my friend, Marietta?" He looked amused. He didn't give her a chance to answer. "Alcroft enjoys intrigue and gossip. So does Jeremy. Those two will try to get under foot. Shoo them away if they bother you. They know how I work and will push as much as they can to be included, like toddlers trying to find their limits, even though they know better."

They pulled up on a street one over from Greville Street and the White Stag. They couldn't very well exit an expensive carriage in front of the pub looking as they were currently dressed. Noble spoke with his driver for a minute.

Marietta took a deep breath.

He slipped an arm around her shoulder and she leaned against him as they walked around the corner toward the pub. The pub where Kenny had been arrested. She suddenly had a horrible thought.

"What if Mr. Penner is here tonight?"

"I made him an appointment to receive a certificate of merit from a group in Windsor today. Festivities to last through the night. He'll never make it back in time to visit the pub this eve."

Relief rushed through her, and she had to admire Noble's forethought. She wondered again why he was doing this. Why he took cases like hers where he wouldn't get paid. Unpaid cases where he would have a toehold into a future spot ripe for favors, she could understand. Hers, she couldn't.

They entered the pub and Marietta was surprised to see the number of people inside. She didn't realize so many people could fit in one space. No wonder Kenny had been drawn here. She was jostled and Noble pulled her more securely against his side, fitting her under his warm arm.

Sheer luck found them next to a table that was abandoned just as they walked by it. It wasn't situated in the best spot in the room, out in front as it was, but it was a place to hunker down and see how the different groups interacted in the pub. Thankfully, even though it was far from a corner, it was against a wall. Noble pulled one chair next to the other so they were both sitting side by side facing outward.

He leaned toward her and tipped her chin up. "Are you ready, Marietta?"

She swallowed. Kenny. She was doing this for Kenny. No one would recognize her here. She had no future to preserve now. The cacophony of the pub blurred into the steady beat of her heart. She had expected it to be racing, but it was just beat, beat, beating in expectation.

She gave a jerky nod.

"Give me a smile." His fingers traced a line from her jaw to the back of her neck and down around her collarbone. His fingertips were light and comforting, and at the same time they made her body lean into his for more.

She could almost find it laughable that he had called her smoky and sensual when it was obvious those were qualities *he* exuded. His eyes pinned hers and the only things she could think about were more S words like stunning, sexual and sinful, strong and steadfast. The last one would have provoked more thought from her if Noble hadn't all of a sudden laughed lightly.

His eyes changed to a more roguish bent. "I'm forgetting myself. These aren't the actions I'm supposed to be taking dressed as I am."

His hand abruptly switched to her thigh and started

stroking her leg. He caught her body's jump beneath his fingertips and held her in place.

"Come now, luv, we are playing a part remember?"

Her smile strained as his fingers traced a pattern up and down her thigh, working her dress up as he went. Her mind rebelled as her ankles came into view. Her calves. The bottoms of her knees. His fingertips dipped under the material and between her knees, and she slapped his hand in instinctive reaction, then pushed her dress back down.

He gave a raucous laugh, the sound foreign to her ears and entirely unnatural on him, then pulled her in for a hard kiss that left her dazed. Instead of the subtle surrender of his earlier sensual domination, this one was brusque, harsher, and lacking in any type of subtlety. But even though he was obviously doing this as a way to create a character, his actions still sent her heart racing and her cheeks warming. She thought it might be distinctly impossible for the man to kiss badly. Not that she had much experience, but sometimes intuition never lied.

There were parts of this role that were really not difficult to participate in at all.

When she looked up, a waitress stood across the table. Marietta was impressed with how fast she had gotten through the mob. The woman wore an outfit similar to her own, her body packed tightly into it, her ample bosom pushing out the bodice, but her face was hard, the lines around her eyes and mouth strictly set.

"What can I get ya?"

"Two ales, please. Whichever you recommend,

darlin'." Noble had a cocky expression on his face and was looking at the woman through his lashes.

The waitress raised a brow, though her eyes softened a bit, as if he was just the type of character that made her compliant. "Right away, dearie." She gave him a wink and barely spared Marietta a glance.

He leaned back in his chair and splayed out with his arm across the back of hers. He shot her a hot glance beneath his lashes. It made her skin heat and her toes curl, even though she knew it was for show. Noble had said in the carriage, *I'm going to be the worker who is trying to worm up the pretty tavern girl's dress. I'm wooing you, after a fashion. After we have a drink or two, who knows what position you'll find yourself in outside in the alley.*

She could only imagine.

He leaned closer to her, so that they were touching at the shoulder, his head dipped toward hers. He wasn't going to try that again, was he? She felt exposed and uncomfortable, and was horrified to be the slightest bit excited. From the corner of her eye she watched some of the patrons give them a look.

"What are you doing?" she hissed. "Didn't we just establish ourselves?"

"I'm making us invisible to the rest of the pub, except to those lechers that get off on this kind of thing."

"I beg your pardon?"

He nodded to the corner. Through the shifting bodies she could see a man and a woman writhing against one another, their mouths fused and their hands in motion. No one was paying them any attention.

"We are not doing that."

He had the temerity to laugh, a warm, rich sound this time.

Soon they had their drinks. Marietta thought she hadn't tasted anything quite as awful as the ale in front of her, but she forced herself to take small sips.

Noble and she whispered back and forth as they sipped their ale and watched the regulars. Every so often he pulled her into a mind-drugging kiss, if they'd gone too long without one.

His strategy seemed to be working. They had passed the initial inspection and were now mostly ignored.

The hierarchy in the pub became obvious. The men around the bar area were clustered around a few central figures—the leaders—while a few men by their sides—the main lackeys—held their chins aloft. The other men vied for attention or listened attentively.

The men seated at the tables looked to be a bit more democratic in their groupings. Still, the main cluster at the bar held the power. That was where they would find their information without asking direct questions, as those men looked as if an audience was their most desired commodity.

She hadn't even needed Noble's subtle finger pointing to tell her that. And when another bunch of men squeezed into the bar area looking similar to the band of men already there, it was like seeing two sides square off for a prize.

Noble leaned into her and nuzzled her neck. He captured her hand in his when she jumped. "Just relax, Marietta. Watch the two men near the edge of the bar. The ones who lead their groups. Don't make it obvious. Tip your head back. That's right." The side of his face rubbed along her throat, his lips dropping kisses as he mapped the area. She couldn't think while he was doing this. He clamped his lips around her pulse point and the men wavered in her vision. "No," he whispered. "Don't close your eyes. Tell me what you see. Softly."

"The man in green is—" Her breath caught. "—arguing with the man in blue."

The conversation filtered a bit their way. The bodies shifted and the noise dimmed, as if everyone else in the pub wanted to be privy to what was happening too.

"I don't care what you *think* you can do, magistrate, we handle that area."

"Who said that?" Noble whispered into her ear as his hand worked up her side and one thumb grazed her breast.

"Green," she choked out.

"—as if you can handle your own district, watchman."

Noble's thumb began a slow circle around her breast through the dress, stays, and chemise. Thin protection against his warm, moving fingers, his hot palms. "Blue." The word got strangled in her throat as he brushed the tip.

"Shhh, shhhh." He whispered against the skin under her ear. "I've got it. Just relax and watch. I'll listen."

She didn't think that was possible. Any outrage and maidenly virtue had flown right through the pub's doors. Her body was undulating, sinking into his, like the charmed snake she had seen at a sideshow. Her eyes fought to remain open as his lips moved against her throat, under her ear, beneath her chin, and his hands spiraled a coil of heat that kept spreading further outward.

"Marietta, stay with me." His hand moved down along her breast and brushed between her legs. Her eyes flew open. He rested his hand on her thigh, which at this point was about the most innocent placement she was likely to receive.

"Damn magistrates thinking they can run things. Stay in Holborn where you belong."

"Listen to them whine, Sam, you'd think the poor watchmen didn't need help with their street fights." She could barely concentrate enough to see the leader in blue say that to a crony over his shoulder.

The leader in green visibly bristled, his shoulders coming up and flaring out. He took a step forward. "As if you helped in that scuffle. You were in the way. Davey and the boys had it under control. You just made it worse."

The other man stepped closer as well, putting their noses inches apart. "Dangerously close to Holborn territory. You know that's our jurisdiction."

"As if we'd forget, what with you whining about it all the time, as if you miss your mummy and she's nesting on the line." A nasty smirk appeared.

"You keep believing you are capable and we'll keep being amused." The sentence was delivered calmly, but the man's knotted fists said otherwise.

"Problem?" A new voice entered the fray, and Marietta got a reprieve as Noble's lips moved from her neck. A lock of his hair tickled her chin as he stole a glance at the newcomer.

The man was of average height, but the way he carried himself made him seem taller. He stood next to a few of the more hulking men, and even though he was shorter, there was something distinctive about him. Not something necessarily nice, but dignified all the same.

"Here we go," the man in green groaned, lifting his pint and tapping it against the side of a fellow watchman's.

"No wonder the crime in Middlesex is so high. Too busy drinking your pints to patrol," the new man said.

"Here now, the murderer's been caught. And by one of our own. Didn't see you catching him, and wasn't that your job, Runner? Didn't see you collecting the reward." The green watchman leaned back, physically taunting the man as well.

Marietta tightened her grip on Noble's hand and he gave her a comforting squeeze back. They were in the midst of a tavern filled with watchmen, magistrate appointed patrollers, and a Bow Street Runner. And all of them were jockeying for position.

Noble moved so he was near her ear again. "This is exactly what we want. Relax."

"He was lucky. If Penner hadn't needed to piss himself so badly, he never would have found him."

"Call it luck all you want, Runner. But it's not you that gets the glory. And the patrollers have to continue licking the magistrates' ballocks just a few days more."

The man in blue and his fellow patrollers bristled.

"You think that stopping one man, one murderer,

is enough to put you on top? To stop the might of Bow Street?"

The Runner had dignity, yes. But it was a *forced* dignity. Like that of a competent man who always felt the need to prove himself.

"Oh, la, la. The might of Bow Street. Hear that patrolman Joe? We are facing the might of Bow Street." The watchman in green smirked at his counterpart in blue.

"I'm shaking in me boots."

"You would be wise not to incur our wrath." The Runner was either an idiot or dangerous. She wasn't sure which yet.

"Always a *pleasure* to have such an educated gentleman in our midst, eh, boys?"

The tide had turned from the two groups fighting one another to showing a united front. She would bet a pound though that as soon as the Runner left, they would be back at each others' throats.

"Look around Runner. These are pleasures you'll never have. A fine ale, a fine woman." She saw the man point to the couple in the corner and then straight to them.

The Runner locked eyes with her, and his narrowed. Noble hooked his fingers around her thigh, brushing against her again at the same time he pulled her earlobe in between his lips.

She arched back and gasped. The Runner's lip curled and he turned away.

"You can have your weak drink and pox-ridden prostitutes."

Marietta felt a slice of outrage pierce her haze. She was neither a prostitute nor pox-ridden. The green man with his comment of "a fine woman" rose through the roof in her esteem, while the Runner buried himself six feet below.

The Runner sneered at the serving gal, and all hell broke loose.

"Don't you sneer at Betsy!"

She felt Noble chuckle against her throat, warm puffs of air hitting her skin and then skittering away. He looked up and sat back to watch the fray. She grabbed her ale and took a few quick gulps.

"Betsy, is it?" The Runner looked their waitress up and down, his eyes communicating that he found her wanting.

Betsy narrowed her hard, lined eyes. "Rumor whispers you have the cock of a worm. Hard to catch the pox with such wee bait."

Marietta spewed her beer forward. Noble patted her on the back as the pub roared with laughter at Betsy's response.

"Just what I expect from a *lady* in this pub." The Runner moved to the back and settled into a seat. His eyes scanned the room, assessing everyone and watching their movements. Marietta grew increasingly uncomfortable.

With the arrival of the patrolmen's group and the Runner, pubgoers had been forced to spill outside.

"Come." Noble pressed closely to her ear. He nudged her up and they made way through the crowded pub. Their table was swallowed up immediately behind them.

Marietta caught a last sight of the Runner's eyes following them as they stepped through the door.

They spoke with people of all types as they exited the pub and milled around the street—pickpockets, patrollers, prostitutes. Most of them had seen nothing. Some had seen the arrest. It wasn't until nearly one in the morning that they found treasure.

The gap-toothed prostitute, smelling of gin and sex, looked Noble up and down. "I seen another man, yea. He was standing over both of 'em—the girl that got herself killed and the boy they arrested."

Marietta froze, her arm still wrapped in Noble's as it had been the entire night.

"What did he look like?" Noble's tone was curious, but she could feel the tension vibrating through him as well.

"Hard to tell, yea. But dark hair. His clothes was dark too."

"Could you recognize him, were you to see him again?"

The prostitute smiled, the spaces between her teeth wafting a smell in Marietta's direction that was anything but pleasant.

"Prolly not. Coulda been you for all I seen."

"Why didn't you tell the watch what you'd seen?" Marietta asked.

The prostitute looked at her for the first time, and her eyes narrowed. "Cor, you sound a right high, your highness." She laughed at her own joke, slapping her thigh. "Best get those airs gone. Though I s'pose some men might toss for it."

She eyed Noble again. "Maybe should get me an air."

Noble squeezed Marietta's arm. Her crisp speech had not helped, though the prostitute seemed too far in her cups to care. Marietta tried again in a more moderated tone. "Why didn't you tell the watch?"

"That ol' Daise had seen something else?" She laughed riotously. "Got to get back to me corner, unless you want somethin' besides talk?"

Noble gave her a coin—well more than he had given the others, who were more mentally fit—and Daise shuffled away.

"Why don't we have her tell the watch? They'll have to let Kenny go, or at least submit it at his trial."

He looked back at her from where he had been watching Daise walk. "Don't be silly. They would no more believe her than they would believe us were we to walk inside and declare him innocent."

"Well why not? Her story matches Kenny's and—"

He released her arm from his and turned to lift her chin. He tilted her head gently as he searched her eyes. "It does you credit to say that she is a valid source of information, even if it is only to get your brother released. But most people would not trust a drunken prostitute like Daise. Would you have two weeks ago?"

She blinked at him. "I don't know." She hadn't even thought about prostitutes, drunken or not, two weeks ago. "That could be me on the corner were things different." She swallowed. "Or if they go differently, it still could. I would want someone to believe me."

His eyes were shaded with the fall of the gaslight and she couldn't read them. "Marietta, you—"

"Isn't this touching. A broker and his *lady* together on the street."

They both turned to see the Runner standing at the corner. Daise must have beaten a hasty retreat. She felt Noble stiffen.

The Runner's eyes ran over them, back and forth. "I've been watching the both of you all night. Stirring up trouble about the murderer? Should I arrest you for harassment or try and discover your larger scheme?"

"You have nothing with which to arrest us." Noble tipped his head so his eyes were in shadow.

The Runner strode forward. "I don't need much."

"Even a Bow Street Runner needs evidence, and it seems that you might need more than most. Little trouble with your last case, I'm taken to understand."

The Runner stopped a few feet away and his eyes narrowed. "I thoroughly document every case. There is never anything wrong with my evidence."

"More than five hundred captures to your name even though you are fresh to the hire, isn't that so?"

The Runner's eyes sharpened and Marietta felt a twinge of real fear. What was Noble doing? He might be as wealthy as Croesus, but Bow Street Runners could cause real trouble.

"You seem to have an advantage over me," the Runner said. "What is your name?"

"Terrence Jones, not at your service." Noble made a mock bow.

"A smart one, I see," the Runner said distastefully. "Why are you interested in the Middlesex murders?"

"My lady has an interest. I make sure to sate all of her curiosities."

Marietta dredged up a smile. The Runner gave her a disgusted look and turned away, but his head whipped back and he studied her.

"And what is her name?"

Obnoxious toad. Not even asking her the question, as if as a woman she didn't have two solid thoughts between her ears.

"Cornelia Jones. No relation." Noble smiled in the character of an obnoxious rake with his lazy posture and sly look.

The Runner continued to assess her, eyes narrowed and piercing. "I don't think that is her name. But I don't plan on seeing either of you again, do you understand?"

"Of course not, dear honorable sir."

The Runner stiffened, but turned and left.

Marietta let out a breath. "I think he might have recognized me. I don't know how. But there was something in his eyes."

Noble had dropped his pretense and straightened to his full height, eyes narrowed. "Yes. It is just our luck to have Arthur Dresden still interested in the case. I thought he had moved on, but it must be true that he can't let things go when he doesn't solve it himself. This makes our task more difficult."

Marietta had heard of Dresden even before Anthony had mentioned him. He was known for his tenacity. Like a terrier that wouldn't let go. Always trying to bring peace and justice—at any cost. Although he was reported to be a by-the-book investigator, he had been reprimanded more than once for his tactics in extracting information. As long as the bad men were punished and the good people saved, he was reputed not to care if the means justified the ends.

He was not the kind of man one wanted to be noticed by.

But then neither was Noble. For all that Dresden looked like he wanted to toss them in the nearest cell for just existing below his moral code, Noble was far more dangerous in other ways.

He abruptly cocked his head.

"What are you doing?" she asked.

"I thought I heard something." He shook his head. "As to what are *we* doing, I do remember saying something about what position you might find yourself in at the end of the night."

Tingles on top of her skin overlapped the increased pace of her heart beneath.

One long finger touched her cheek. "Over a pub table? Up against an alley wall? In a carriage, the windows open, the wind blowing through as we race down the streets and you ride me to the end?"

She swallowed, then swallowed again.

"Yes, I think I like all of those images. I can see your head thrown back and that long, smooth neck exposed to me in all of them." His finger trailed down the side of her throat. "Your eyes are becoming even more smoky and sensual, Marietta. From the inside out now, rather than the outside in. Shall we see what happens when the knowledge blooming there becomes a large petaled rose?"

A muffled cry shook the night and he pulled her behind him. The sound seemed to be emanating from a darkened street. With her still behind him, flat to his back, he walked forward. It wasn't until they came to a connecting alley that they saw who had made the sound.

A man, reedy with menace, hit a woman. It was obviously not the first strike—the right side of her face was swollen and cracked in the faint gaslight.

She felt Noble move. A sickening crunch echoed in the alley, and the reedy man howled.

Noble stood to the side, wiping his hands on his trousers as if the mere touch to the other man's arm had left him with the plague. "Shame about that arm."

The man charged him.

Marietta winced as another crack sounded, unnatural and loud.

"Do try that again. It would be a pleasure to watch you eat without the use of your hands for the next three months." He leaned down to the man, not close enough to be struck, but enough so the man shrunk toward the wall. "I will find your address and happily *feed* you every bite."

The man gripped his arm and stumbled from the alley. His beating footsteps retreated, leaving the lane in silence.

"You shouldn't have done that," the woman said. "Eugene will be real mad once he stops being piss scared." Her chin trembled.

Noble flicked out two fingers holding a card. "Go here. Ask for Peg. She will help you."

The woman grabbed the card, eyes weighing, no trust in sight, then turned and disappeared the same way the man had gone.

"Will she go?" Marietta asked, shock still holding her immobile but something in the woman's eyes prompting the question.

"Perhaps. Some do, some don't. One has to want to be helped. Come."

Gabriel Noble stretched out a hand to her. She took it.

Chapter 9

He stared challengingly at her across the table a week later.

"I don't trust you with it," she said.

"I'm hurt. Really, you don't think I can do this simple task after all we've done together. After all of the places I've opened that you thought could never be unlocked?"

They had spent another week visiting Clerkenwell and the surrounding areas. Questioning people. Calling in favors. Making another visit to Cold Bath and Kenny.

Her brother had looked even worse than before, despair turning down his eyes and sagging his jaw.

Casenton, Alcroft's contact and favor, had come through and the trial had been delayed two weeks. They had one week remaining. Time was dwindling.

"Gaining us access to Cold Bath is one thing," she said. "This is something entirely different."

She was pleased to see the amusement in his eyes. He hadn't been nearly so jovial earlier when they'd run into Arthur Dresden, the Runner, again. "How do you think I get by without servants, Marietta?"

"Well, *Gabriel*." It seemed silly to keep calling him Noble after having her lips locked to his for most of the previous nights this week when they were out and in costume. "I think you get by because your dear Clarisse and Mrs. Rosaire organize things so that you can."

"Is that so?"

"Yes, it is."

He leaned back in his chair and smiled lazily. "Would you like to make a bet, then?"

The challenge was too good. And she desperately needed to continue the lighthearted banter after their trying day. After seeing Kenny looking so poorly. "Yes, I suddenly find myself curious to see what you can burn over the fire."

"Burn? I see."

"Come now," she scoffed. "You eat terribly. I've seen you ingest pints of tea and that awful coffee you enjoy instead of having a full, hearty meal. If it weren't for Mrs. Rosaire's soups and stews, delicious as they are, I think you might have withered away to a coffee bean by now."

"Is that so?"

"Yes." She nodded emphatically. "Perhaps I should start cooking regular meals."

"My manly heart is enraptured."

"You need to keep up your strength if you are to serve me."

Gabriel's chair legs smacked the kitchen floor. He leaned forward, nearly touching her. "If you needed me to serve you, Marietta, you should have just said so."

Her cheeks flamed under his intense stare, his one-sided grin. "Serve Kenny."

"Well, that I am most unwilling to do. It's you or no one." He tipped the chair back again.

She snorted. "I highly doubt that."

"I am in demand, it is true."

His tone was nonchalant. She wondered about him once more. He used the female attention whenever he needed, but intuition told her that he didn't *like* the attention. Strange. She'd met popinjays in the ton, more than one cock of the walk, a score of libertines, Corinthians and dandies, and all of them seemed to revel in female attention. Or at the outside be arrogant concerning it. Gabriel Noble was arrogant about it, yes, but it covered something else. Something deeper.

"Then it is decided," she said. "You will try your hand at this meal, and when that doesn't work, I will start cooking regular meals and we can stop relying on Mrs. Rosaire for everything, though her delicious soups and stews would be nice to continue." They were just too good. From the amount of food he partook in her presence, though, Gabriel didn't eat enough. "And perhaps I will need to clean up after you as well."

She really should watch her tongue. Her cooking was average at best. But Noble was just too good at most things. This was going to be amusing.

Unless he was a run of the mill cook as well. Then she would just have to outdo him at being average.

"You are allowing me to cook tonight, then? You aren't going to bemoan my sending Mrs. Rosaire away?" There was something in his eyes as he made the last remark. Something that cautioned her to be wary. She ignored it, too high on their banter after a trying day.

"Go ahead, Noble. Give it a go."

He unfolded himself from his chair. "What would you like to eat?"

She clasped her hands together on top of the table. "I'll leave it to you."

"Salmon with wine sauce?"

She blinked as he turned and walked to the sideboard. He pulled two slabs of fish from underneath and deftly tossed an onion from one hand to the other.

"Pardon?"

"Is salmon with wine sauce to your taste?"

She met his eyes and saw the glimmer there. The high was still upon her, but suddenly she wasn't sure she was going to be celebrating his defeat after all. "Are you sure you should try something like that? I will settle for something much less." Let it not be said that she lacked stubbornness.

"Oh, no. No, no, no, Marietta. I can't have you settling." He smirked and grabbed a large butcher knife, tossed it into the air, then cut and boned the fillets. He gathered vegetables and dry ingredients, laying them out across the high cooking table.

Her feet moved of their own volition when he started chopping things as if born to the knife. She stood next to him, one hand along the high table edge.

"There is a reason you don't eat as much at the table, isn't there?" A cook was always sampling as he went.

"There is."

"Mrs. Rosaire doesn't make the soup, does she?" she asked, her voice barely above a whisper.

"She does not."

She closed her eyes at the confirmation. Of course. That was why Jeremy had almost corrected her.

"You must have taken a nice laugh at my expense."

He looked at her out of the side of his eye, through the hanging locks. "No. It's just something I don't share with people."

"But Jeremy assumed I knew."

"Jeremy is usually away at school where he should be."

She tilted her head to study him as he crushed the garlic clove, minced the shallots, and washed, trimmed, and quartered the mushrooms, forgoing for the moment the interesting bit of information that he didn't share his cooking abilities with others and yet was fully doing so with her.

"You never attended school, did you? You speak as if you did. You carry yourself as a graduate of the finest when you want to. But Alcroft said something about wanting you to go to Eton."

"I had the best teacher possible. But no, I didn't attend Eton or Harrow or Charterhouse. Nor Oxford or Cambridge."

"But Jeremy has."

"Yes. And that is why he will finish."

"Because you never had a chance to go?"

"Because he will have opportunities I never had."

She looked around the kitchen and at his fine clothes, sleeves rolled up and baring his forearms. "You haven't done so poorly."

He owned a house in one of the finest addresses in the city, and if her assumption was correct, an entire street here. She hadn't seen a single person enter or leave any of the other properties surrounding them. She had a feeling Noble owned them all. In a city where land was considered king, he had a kingdom.

He didn't respond.

She picked up a knife and quartered the carrots, trying to make herself useful. The challenge was completely moot. If he was the one making the soups and stews—and bread—that she had been devouring every day, there was no competition. The Rockwoods' celebrated chef wasn't half as good.

"What do you do with the ten thousand pounds you collect from the paid cases?" she asked as she sliced another carrot.

"Slightly personal, don't you think?" He dropped his ingredients into the pot and then picked up her carrots and dropped them in as well.

"I could go back to asking you about schooling."

"I could ask you why you've never married."

"You could," she said as lightly as she could manage.

"Good. Why have you never married?"

"The mart was dry during my years. Not much to choose from." She kept her voice light. "And neither was I much of a prize."

"Mmmm."

"My tongue does have a rather funny way of saying things that are not particularly docile and genteel. My parents weren't as concerned with the graces while we were growing up. When they died, we went into mourning. Things were . . . different when it was time to come back out."

"Your parents spent too much time at the races."

Her hand tightened around the knife. "And at the tables and in the gentlemanly sports wagers. How did you know?"

"I know much about you, Marietta. And your recalcitrant brothers." He was nonchalant as he stirred the pot.

"I must make sure to delve into your past as well."

"You can try. You might even succeed. If I've ever met someone as industrious as you, I'm not sure I know of it."

She stopped fiddling with the garlic nub. "That sounds quite close to a compliment."

"My old aunt Tilly wasn't half as industrious, though she never found herself in dire straits." He stirred the pot and looked at her slyly from the corner of his eye. "We called her the old battle-axe."

Her jaw dropped. "You—You—"

He chuckled and winked at her. Her ire evaporated like the steam from the pot—coiling and disappearing into the air. When he used his wiles on her, he was tantalizing. With that purely happy look on his face he was devastating.

"You do realize that I will have my revenge?" she said calmly, though her heart was racing.

"I could hope for no less." He flashed her a grin, and she gripped the side of the table to keep from moving closer.

"I dislike you."

"Always a comfort to know." He looked at the kitchen clock, a small mantel piece positioned precariously on a shelf. "Right on time for the night."

She blinked. She supposed it was something of a nightly ritual. "Wouldn't want to disappoint you, your highness."

"Your majesty, if you will."

"But of course, your majesty. Can I bring you anything?"

"A bottle and glass of red wine would be lovely." He pointed to a cabinet.

Marietta retrieved a bottle and two glasses.

They were on to their second glass of Burgundy wine by the time Gabriel was placing the fillets in a shallow serving dish and sprinkling them with fresh parsley.

The meal was excellent. Moan inducing. The fish melted in her mouth, the sauce just the perfect balance for letting the flavor come through and hinting at something further, something deeper—teasing her to take one bite and then another.

She paused in between bites and took a sip of wine. Gabriel lifted a brow, though she read the pleasure in his eyes and it pleased her in return. "Where did you learn to cook?"

"I learned from one of the best French chefs that upper class money can buy."

That hadn't been what she expected him to say. "You hired a chef to teach you how to cook?"

"I thought you knew better, Marietta. I am purely merchant class, no matter my wealth." He lifted his glass and watched her over the rim.

"Some noblewoman purchased a chef for you to learn?"

She immediately knew it was the wrong thing to say, even with a teasing tone of voice, as she watched his fingers tighten around the stem.

His smile was slow and sensual, and though it did funny things to her stomach like always, his eyes were emerald hard. "Of course. Isn't that what would make sense, after all? Very perceptive of you, Marietta."

And unlike his earlier teasing compliment, this one held contempt.

"I meant only to tease you." She looked at her plate, not wanting to see the hard look and mocking, sensual smile. "I suppose it is getting more and more apparent why I am headed firmly for the shelf." She tried to laugh, but it came out forced.

Her thought had been an easy assumption to make, what with his obvious ease in gaining favor from women and his tricks to manipulate them. But the language in his eyes—it always said differently, and she had chosen to discount it in lieu of being witty.

The silence stayed unbroken in the kitchen for twenty ticks of the mantel clock.

"I've always liked the kitchens." His voice was more reserved, and she already missed the extra note of affection that he had begun to use with her. "They are warm and hidden. Owners and guests rarely enter them. A chef took me under his wing when I used to run about under foot. Put me to work."

She bit her lip as he continued.

"It was a good place for me. I thought about becoming a chef, but events led to other things."

"What types of other things?"

"This and that. Favors exchanged. New favors to use." His gaze washed over her. His voice warmer. "I do believe I won our bet. Unfortunately for you, you did not specify the terms." The look in his eyes made her butterflies move in an abstracted pattern.

"The loser cleans the dishes, of course," she said lightly, pushing the butterflies down.

He raised a brow, heat still sparking from his eyes beneath. "I will make sure to set the terms myself next time, but this once I'll let you off easily."

He moved to clear the dishes and cutlery and she moved to the basin. She washed each item and stuck them into a rack to drain. He pulled a cloth out to dry and they worked in a charged but comfortable silence until she placed the last dish in the rack.

"Where are we headed tonight?" She found herself on edge in anticipation of his answer. Of what they might find. Or what they might need to do in the interim.

"One would think you enjoy the forays into the underbelly of the city."

"Hardly the underbelly. We've barely stepped foot in the East End."

"For someone like you, the East End would be farther than your worst nightmare. The areas outside of Mayfair are the underbelly for someone of your station."

"Says the man with the enormous house in Mayfair."

"Says the man who didn't always have that house. You, on the other hand, are used to the genteel aspects of life."

"I worked and went to various unsavory parts of the city to pay our bills." She lifted her chin.

"Perhaps." His eyes were keen. "But they were probably positions at the same level as the barristers', correct?"

"Yes."

"Not in the same level as the true East End." He nudged her aside and washed a cup that he had found somewhere in the kitchen—one of his many coffee cups, to be sure—and placed it in the rack to dry. "Where did you work?"

"I sewed for a seamstress near the Strand. And did some knitting and assembly at shops nearby."

"Industrious of you."

She gave him a look that said how much she appreciated being called a battle-axe once again. She picked up the drying towel and his cup from the rack—the last item inside. "You didn't answer my question. Where are we going tonight?"

"Nowhere."

Disappointment rushed through her. "Oh."

"Are you disappointed because we won't be furthering your brother's case or because you won't get to kiss me?"

She nearly dropped the cup. She put it back in the cupboard. "Because we won't be furthering my brother's case. Don't be silly."

"You realize you can kiss me anytime."

Her heart picked up speed. "Don't be silly."

He leaned against the high table. "Don't be coy."

"Why would you even want me to kiss you?"

"You don't find kissing pleasurable just in and of itself?"

"Yes. No!" She was like a child's string, tied in knots and being pulled willy-nilly.

"You have me confused. Which is it?"

"Kissing is fine. Not too wet or slimy."

"Mmmm. Sometimes wet is excellent. Slimy, though, I'll give you that. I'm happy that our kisses haven't been too slimy for you."

She tried to ignore his taunting. "But they are only for show. For getting the information we need. For helping Kenny."

"I see. So you are only interested in kissing to help Kenny? Is that why you are so keen to go out? Because you can only kiss me if it's in the line of furthering the case?"

"Yes. No! I just think we need more information."

"We've been to the White Stag three nights this week. They are going to start thinking us regulars. And Dresden is no doubt well aware of our presence. I'm sure he has more than one informant in the pub."

"Then we should go elsewhere."

"We've been to every pub in the general vicinity of the murders. We've traipsed all over Middlesex. Our clues are somewhere else for the moment. Which for some reason—" He tapped her chin. "—reminds me of a conversation we had earlier today about beginning new avenues in the morning. Funny that you seem not to recall it."

She stubbornly refused to recall a thing. "We have to have missed something."

"Yes, you've missed that the only reason you want to go traipsing around tonight is so you can kiss me."

She lifted her chin. "I do not want to kiss you."

"Fine. Shall we leave?"

She was taken aback for a second. "Leave? Where are we going?"

"You just said we must have missed something. That we need to revisit our haunts. Let's do that."

"Y-Yes." She smoothed her hair. He was wrong about all those things. She didn't want to kiss him.

"I have something to show you before we leave, though."

His mouth met hers before she knew what was happening. A gentle pull, a soft caress. She was surprised for a second. *She didn't want to kiss him.*

She melted into his body and called herself ten kinds of fool.

This was a new type of kiss. Exploring and questioning. It wasn't instructional, or claiming, or for show. It asked a question. She wasn't sure of the response. So she returned the kiss in the same way. Exploring and questioning. What did he want from her? What type of game was he playing? And did she care? Or was she so caught up in playing it too that she wasn't thinking of the future?

Her future was muddled and dark. Like the sky before a storm. She wasn't sure what it would look like come the metaphorical morning. Or if she would still be standing. But this was her chance to taste and explore. To break free from her cage. To be in control of her own destiny, even if for a small amount of time.

His lips ran down her chin. Down her throat. He'd discovered a weak spot at her pulse and had been exploiting it all week. His mouth captured the spot and she arched against him, the air escaping her lungs. He pressed her against the table and scooted her up so she was sitting on the edge. Both hands reached into her hair and he drew her forth to kiss her again. His legs nudged between hers and he brushed against the spot where the heat always traveled.

His hands moved down her arms and wrapped around her knees, tugging her closer and wrapping her legs around his waist. It brought them flush together and inflamed the lovely aching.

"Do you still wish to leave, Marietta?"

He rocked against her and pleasure jolted up her spine.

"No," she moaned as his lips clamped the spot on her neck.

"You have this lovely dress on, though." His breath whispered across her neck. "We could travel to some pub and I could devour you in front of the masses. It could be part of the disguise. You wouldn't have to choose a thing. You wouldn't have to say that you want this."

His hand moved up her thigh.

"Wouldn't have to be in control."

His fingers moved over her hip and waist and under her arm.

"You could pretend that this is all happening because you are unsure of what to do. That you are martyred for the cause."

His thumb pressed against her breast and made a deep circle on her nipple. The heat rushed through her body, spreading.

"But I would know that you really wanted this. That you were more than happy to see what lay beneath my shirt. Farther below. To feel your back pressed against this table. For me to bend your knees and bury myself in your heat."

He didn't allow her to speak, taking her mouth in another kiss, this one drugging and dominant. His words caused pictures to appear in her head. Things she'd thought of continuously this past week.

"I think you would like being taken, Marietta. And I would more than enjoy taking you."

She wasn't sure *being taken* sounded pleasant. But then again most anything Gabriel did to her ended up being pleasant, even if it was preceded by taunting words or challenging eyes.

"Would you like being made love to on a table? Perhaps not the first time. But after we get that pesky little problem out of the way, shall we try it here?"

Pesky little problem. As if her virginity, so highly prized in her world, was little more than an annoyance. Then again, her lack of a virginal state wasn't likely to be an issue these days.

He was dangerous and arrogant, but he was also

a protector. Oh, he would undoubtedly leave her at the end of an affair and send her on her way, but intuitively she didn't think he would hurt her. As long as she didn't expect anything more from him. Or heaven forbid fall in love with him.

"Should I take your silence as assent?" He kissed her lips, lingering on her lower one and pulling it between his before releasing it with a pop. "I won't, you know. You'll have to vocalize your desire. Just once, and I'll do the rest."

Her head dipped back as he kissed along her neck. Devilish kisses, seductive words.

He leaned back and met her eyes, his dark and beguiling. "You want to learn the art. I can see it in your eyes. Every time I kiss you, I can see it burning in your gaze. You hide all that passion behind the prickers you wear so proudly. It makes it all the more of a challenge to uncover the soft, velvet center."

He touched her breast again, fingers pulling and lifting to the peak. Her head dipped farther as the muscles in her neck gave way.

"And I will teach you all you wish to know."

"Do you do this for everyone?" she whispered, eyes hazed as she tried to focus.

She felt him stiffen, but he immediately resumed his ministrations. "No. You aren't the only one who wears your prickers proudly."

"Why me?" She pulled her neck upward. She had looked in a mirror. She wasn't blind, and neither was he.

"Because I want to," he whispered against her exposed throat, fingers lazily circling. "Tell me yes, and I will continue. Tell me no, and I will withdraw."

It was true. All of what he said. She was curious. So very, very curious. She wanted to learn everything. Wanted the power he had over her for her own. Never before had she felt this way about a man, and such a man as this . . . one who seemed to know her body better than she did . . .

"What is your pleasure, Marietta?"

"Yes." The choice was very simple in the end.

His eyes were fierce and triumphant.

He led her to his room and laid her on the coverlet of the bed. Her skin was on fire but her brain was frozen and panicky. "Remember what I said about kissing? About how to respond and feel the response given back? Use that the same way."

He kissed her gently, his fingers working at the fastenings on her dress, the latches of her stays. She kissed him back, pushing her nervousness into her response, trying to overcome her fear by kissing him as intensely as he kissed her. The feedback became stronger as her fierce kisses turned into more demanding ones from him.

He pulled away slowly, softly kissing her lips. Somehow he'd managed to get her untied, unlatched, and freed. Only her chemise remained. He tugged her upright and shimmied the material up and over her head. She immediately crossed her arms to hide her nakedness.

Here was a perfect specimen of male beauty sitting in front of her, while she, so bony and gangly, was exposed before him.

He raised a brow at her action and tugged one arm down. Her arm immediately rose again. She looked down at herself and grabbed for her chemise.

"What are you doing, Marietta?"

"I—I've changed my mind."

He stopped her from putting the garment back on. "Because you are truly having second thoughts, or because you dislike your body?"

Her chin lifted. "What difference does it make?"

"A great deal of difference." He lowered her arm and tugged the garment from her. "You are skin and bones, it's true. Nothing that a few more weeks of regular food won't cure. But that doesn't matter. You could stay this skinny or be three times your weight and what would really matter was the spark. How you respond. The passion you allow to be unleashed."

He stroked her arm and she shivered.

"The physical shell is nothing without what is inside. I could be with what the masses consider the most beautiful woman, and if I wanted to pretend there was something deeper there, I could. I could delude myself as to the connection between. But why would I settle for a substitute if I could feel a real spark? And you have one in you, Marietta. I can taste it. It's not what you look like, Marietta, it's what you choose to show."

His fingers combed through the hair at her nape, pulling her head back.

"Show me that spark. Feel it and return it. That's what matters."

The heat that had cooled pumped again. "And if it is disappointing?"

"Then we will be disappointing together. Would you be happier to know that you are not the only one with uncertainties?" He nipped her ear and laid her back out. "Know then that I'm scared witless."

Somehow she couldn't believe him as he took her mouth against his own, as his hands moved down her body and soothed the tremors.

"I will have you, Marietta. I've known it since we first kissed. Since you first released that passion. I'll coax every drop out of you, if I have to."

His words, his hands—she was the snake and he the charmer. "Good." She released it on a moan as something hard pressed against her, right where she needed it most. He rocked against her and she rocked back, wanting the pressure, the heat. Her body was restless, agitated, needing something she couldn't name.

"That's right. Don't hold back any of your responses." His voice was soft and deep. "There's no one here. Just the two of us. And I want you wet and burning all over these sheets."

She didn't understand, but her body seemed to. It kept trying to press closer to his, and the heat was turning damp. He had his shirt undone and tossed to the side. A well-formed chest, a sprinkling of hair and lean muscles, crouched over her.

"Show me what you feel, Marietta."

Her head tipped back and her mouth opened in a silent scream as he tugged her nipple into his mouth and gave a strong suck. Licking and sucking over and over. The heat became uncomfortable, the dampness grew.

He moved to her other breast and she arched into him, trying to make full contact again, as he'd moved up to change position. Her nipple appeared with a pop and he smiled dangerously at her. Green eyes rakish and daring. Hair mussed and charming.

He stood and undid his trousers. A perfectly formed Greek statue, looking at her with a hungry stare. She knew without a doubt that she had never felt this powerful before.

He pulled back the covers and she scooted underneath. Curiosity, fear, and power coursed through her. Here was what all the ladies tittered or dithered about. He scooted in next to her. "Have you ever touched yourself, Marietta?"

His fingers caressed her stomach and ran farther south.

"Here." His fingers stroked over the hair between her legs, one touching the skin beneath. She jumped. Shifted. The heat was calling her there.

His fingers parted her and lightly teased the top. She froze. The feelings were pleasurable, but there was something altogether odd and intrusive.

He turned her toward him, so they were lying on their sides, facing each other. "Watch what I'm doing. I'm getting you ready. Preparing you so that everything feels good, nothing feels bad." One finger dipped and caressed just inside the edge. "To make us slide together."

She watched the top part of his finger disappear. Her breath caught as it moved *inside* of her an inch. He pressed closer to her. "Music to my ears. You don't know how much I wish that finger was a different part of my body right now."

She looked between their bodies at the portion of him that was much larger than a finger. She hesitantly reached out to touch him. Silky, but hard. His finger curled inside her and something rocketed through her. She gripped him tightly.

He laughed, somewhat less steadily. "The feedback between us. Exactly. Keep exploring, Marietta. Don't hesitate to touch whatever fascinates you."

She stroked him, watched as he strained to her hand. He touched her fingers and placed them on top of his. His finger dipped inside of her—more than an inch. Her eyes closed and he kissed her, quick and hard.

"Look and feel."

She looked at her fingers on top of his. His middle finger joining his first as he delved inside of her, the hard pads of his fingers stroking the soft interior, increasing the heat. The tip of her finger touched her curls, the skin beneath, as he delved more deeply. His other hand took her fingers in his and touched them to her. Moving them down and around his. Her fingers skimmed something that made her body twitch.

He wrapped her fingers back around him and touched her with his thumb, stroking over the same spot. Heat shot through her. She arched toward him, pulling along his length.

"Shhh." His voice was heavy and strained. "I know. Just a little more."

His fingers had disappeared *inside* her. They were doing something, some dance from within, twisting and scissoring. The heat wanted to explode, needed to explode.

He was an exceptional dancer. The inane thought leapt through her mind.

His mouth returned to her breasts. She arched forward, into his mouth, into his fingers. The butterflies beat a mad staccato. His fingers withdrew and he framed her face with his hands.

"I'm going to have you now, Marietta."

She leaned forward and kissed him, her body naturally arcing into his. The fear that she might have possessed, *had* possessed, gone, obliterated by the trust she now placed in him. That he had engendered with his slow movements and running dialogue.

He wouldn't hurt her.

She felt a nudge against her curls, even though his hands were still touching her cheeks as they lay on their sides, face-to-face. "Rest your knee on top of mine."

She did as he suggested, opening a vee between her legs. She looked down and saw him pushing back toward her, and heat swirled again. The tip of him pushed against her, just as his fingers had, and the sounds returned.

"Just a little bit at a time. I want you to push against me every time you feel able."

She gave a little push and felt some resistance. She paused. He kissed her.

"Sweet and slippery. Your body needs to adjust," he whispered against her lips.

He touched her nipple with his free hand, lightly pulling the tip between his fingers. She arched toward him, the heat below demanding satisfaction. Another inch inside.

"Shhh. Just hold yourself there for a second." He continued to play with her breast, and she gritted her teeth to keep from moving. He pulled out a bit and then pushed back in. A wave of heaviness passed over her head. Anxiety to move. To reach something.

"Halfway, love. Which—"

She grabbed his head and pulled him toward her, kissing him hard. Breaking his touch on her breast and dragging him inside. His eyes were bright green and triumphant when he pulled away.

He flipped them so he was lying on top of her, his hands braced on either side of her head. He pulled out and gave a short thrust and then another, the promised slide materializing as he pushed farther in. Her feet scrambled on the bed, trying to find purchase to push up, to reach that heat that everything to this point had promised.

"Keep pushing, that's right. Wrap your legs around me. Follow everything your body tells you and let go of the rest."

He pulled out and thrust all the way inside her. Her head fell back, the feeling too much, and she moaned, deep and loud. She was too far gone to feel embarrassment. She just wanted relief.

"Don't forget to breathe, Marietta. Deep breaths. Moaning is good. That's right."

He thrust in again, the long length of him spearing her and lifting her an inch off the bed. Her legs, wrapped around him, pushing forward, to touch the place that he had just rubbed. He pulled back, and when he thrust this time she lifted her hips to meet him. The edge of her vision went hazy. Sparks of flint ignited, she could feel her mouth caught in a silent scream.

"Sweet and lovely. Let go, love."

He thrust again and again and she barely could lift her hips as she followed his direction and let go of everything. Moaning and gasping against his shoulder, she burst apart in his arms, butterflies scattering to the four corners of the room.

Chapter 10

Gabriel awakened abruptly to a vigorous knock on the front door. He glanced at the clock to see the hands lethargically indicating a hair past five in the morning. He hadn't planned on rising for thirty more minutes. Sixty if he was feeling lazy.

A lock of brown hair slid along his arm. He was definitely feeling lazy. Perhaps he would stay in bed all day. He looked over to see the brown head buried into a pillow at his side. He lifted a hand to lightly touch her back. He had never invited a woman to his bed, choosing other locations instead, but she looked natural there.

A heavy knock fell again, and he suddenly realized where he was, with no butler to answer the door. Off his game again.

He threw back the covers on his side and grabbed a dressing robe. As his brain started reasserting itself, he hoped whoever was at the door realized their days were numbered. He saw Marietta's body shift in his peripheral vision as he stormed from the room. The knocking continued.

He opened the front door to see one of his footmen, Billy, standing on the stoop looking apoplectic. Gabriel motioned him inside and counted to ten.

"Mr. Charlie sent me, sir. He said to give this to you immediately."

Gabriel took the missive and opened it. "Why didn't you just come inside and awaken me?"

"Forgot the key in my rush. Mr. Charlie said it was of the utmost importance that I get this to you immediately. Sorry, sir. Won't do it again, sir."

Gabriel started to mutter something suitably terrifying, which would even have cowed Charlie, his giant butler, when his brain caught up to the realization that Marietta had been in bed with him and the whole thing might have been *awkward*. Billy was looking terrified already, and Gabriel decided to rib him instead, until his eyes caught the first paragraph.

The paper crinkled in his fingers. "Did you bring the carriage?"

"Yes sir, out front, it is."

"Good, stay here."

Gabriel took the steps two at a time. Another murder. All remnants of sleep cleared from his head, as he'd been taught to do in his youth. They would have to free Marietta's brother now. That was the good news. That the real killer was still running around, and Marietta would be leaving him, was the bad.

He paused at the top of the steps. Should he awaken her or let her sleep? The scene would be gruesome. She didn't need to see it. He aligned his steps so they were silent on the floor.

His silence didn't matter. She was sitting up in bed, looking rumpled and delicious, the sheets pulled around her.

"What is happening?" Her voice was husky but alert.

He hesitated.

"Gabriel?"

"There's been another murder. I'm going there. Go back to sleep and I will return by the time you rise."

"Another murder? Like the others?" Her hand dropped from the sheet and exposed part of her breast to his lovely view. "Go back to sleep? No, I'm coming with you."

He wasn't surprised. Her grit was one of his favorite qualities. Still . . . "It won't be pretty. Think of what your brother described."

He saw her shiver, but she shook her head. Her eyes were clear, her expression determined. "I'm coming."

He nodded. "Get dressed. Call if you need help. We are leaving in ten minutes."

They left in eight.

The streets were foggy and dark. The early morning shadows from the gaslights cast odd shapes against the buildings and stones.

Gabriel watched Marietta stare through the window at the passing streets. Last night had been . . . interesting. He had taunted and seduced her and found himself falling into his own trap.

She was . . . interesting.

She made him laugh.

She didn't hold her tongue around him. Most

women bent over backward to please him. Oh, there had been a few who hadn't in the past, but none of them had produced a pull, a desire to continue a liaison for the pure joy of it. And even if her face went moon-eyed with want like so many others, he *wanted* to see the expression on her.

Strange.

His driver pulled up to the curb. There were a lot of people milling around the area, and the watchmen were trying to keep them away from the corner, a daunting task with the two streets converging and four directions to watch. Dresden was roaming the crowd, sharp eyes taking in each face.

"Dresden is here." He tapped a finger against the window. "If we exit, he will know who you are without a doubt."

"You said he probably already does."

"He will hunt you." He thought about confining her to the carriage.

Her shoulders straightened. "Kenny is going to be exonerated. He will have nothing to hunt me for."

Gabriel wondered what she would do after her brother was freed. Try to get back into society? Retire to the country? Find some young man to marry who didn't mind her tongue or the fact that she would try to be the strong one in the relationship?

He wondered if he could continue a liaison with her. He was strangely unwilling to let her go.

He had worked with scores of women over the years. He had even been interested in a few. But the attraction ultimately fizzled. Every time.

This one was still going strong. He had known it

before taking her to bed too. Had scared him witless for a moment.

What was it about her that kept his attention? He watched her clutch her hands as she looked out to the crowd, nervous and excited to see her brother freed. She wasn't the prettiest. She wasn't the smartest or the tallest or the bravest. But she was all of those things wrapped together in a package that just seemed to fit *him*. How utterly terrifying.

He had never imagined Marietta Winters walking in and blowing a hole in his well-planned life.

He pushed open the door. He would see what happened. And if she didn't come to him . . . he would *bring* her to him.

He helped her down from the carriage and they walked toward the scene. Dresden's eyes focused on them immediately and narrowed. Gabriel snapped his fingers for Billy to follow. The young footman jumped down from his spot on top with the driver.

Pushing through the crowd, Gabriel saw the outline of blood on the ground, but no body.

"Cor. Where's the gal? Anyone know her name?"

He sent a silent thanks to the older woman hovering nearby for asking the questions he wanted answered.

"Moved to Coroner's Court already. Heard she was broken and unrecognizable."

"Like the others. They caught the wrong man!"

A murmur went through the crowd, and he saw the relief in Marietta's stance. The Runner clapped his hands. "Actually, that is not entirely true."

Marietta stiffened and Gabriel fought from doing the same.

173

"It looks like an internal maneuver, and we are bringing in the Middlesex murderer's brother for questioning." He looked directly at Marietta. "The whole family is suspect."

Gabriel tamped his shock. Dresden was no fool. He knew that cutting off the pleas of innocence and giving the crowd an alternative that would make them feel as if the problem were under control would stave the tide. And if the savage look Dresden had leveled in their direction was anything to go by, now that he had an acknowledgment of who they were, he was taking their actions personally. Gabriel turned and gave Billy swift instructions. The boy darted through the crowd, and Gabriel pulled Marietta closer.

"Mark."

"Shhh. Let's get to Coroner's Court."

He didn't look away from Dresden. The Runner's dark smile across the crowd boded ill. "In fact, the sister of—"

Gabriel signaled abruptly to his driver, and the edges of the crowd screamed as the horses went wild and the carriage careened off. His driver would be receiving an increased wage soon.

He pulled Marietta through the back of the crowd as everyone was distracted and running about. She didn't say anything as he pulled her around the corner. Her eyes were empty and unfocused. He reached down and gripped her hand as they rounded another corner, turning back and moving parallel to the scene they'd just left. His carriage was waiting at the end of the street in response to his clockwise signal.

174

He lifted her into the carriage and motioned to the driver. "Coroner's Court. Quickly. We have about twenty minutes to keep ahead."

He was barely seated when the carriage took off.

"Mark," Marietta whispered.

"He will be fine. Billy will get him out of your house, if possible. Focus." He snapped his fingers in front of her glazed eyes. "I am going to run into the court to see what I can find."

A bit of spirit returned to her eyes. "I'm coming with you."

"Fine." Frankly, he would have been worried if she hadn't argued. "We need to be quick, though. I have a contact in the building who has already been alerted. We can work from there."

She was standing much taller when they entered the building. Not like a woman who might lose both brothers to mob madness.

They walked into the court. A crowd of people were positioned around a body in the corner.

"Sorry, sir, but you aren't allowed in here."

He flashed a smile at the guard. "Assistant to Nathaniel Upholt. Rory Carney." He shook the bemused guard's hand. "He sent me ahead to gather the initial information. I see that you are doing a fine job maintaining order."

The guard puffed up a bit. "We try our best, sir."

"Do you think we might have a look before the mob appears? It would be very helpful." The man looked to be above a bribe, but there was a tattered edge to his trousers. Taking a chance, Gabriel palmed a note and shook the man's hand again.

175

The guard's hand closed around the note, and he looked undecided for a second.

"We will be out of the way. Five minutes is all."

The guard looked around and nodded. "Five minutes."

Gabriel flashed another smile. "Thank you, my good man."

He walked over to the milling crowd, Marietta pressed behind him. Members of the court, patrolmen, and watchmen all gathered together talking. He recognized a few from their recent excursions and his previous case encounters, so he kept his head bent.

There was soaked blood on most of the cloth covering the body. He tucked Marietta farther behind him. She could look if she wanted, but he wasn't going to force her to stare if she didn't.

A man was cleaning the woman's bloody face, which was bared above the cloth. Another man was making notes, and they were talking back and forth.

"Bruising on her wrists. Matches the second victim. The other two were without. Blow to the head. Slit throat. Open at the midsection . . . "

Gabriel let the words wash over him. The wet cloth was moving along the victim's cheek and something was stirring inside him. A sliver of fear.

The cheekbones of the woman were both bruised, but there was something very familiar about her. Her brown hair was matted, but he could see a pearl comb hanging from a tangled lock of hair.

"Interesting cuts along her necklace—"

No.

"—emeralds, do you think? Someone with money."

It couldn't be.

"As if someone was outlining it. Taunting? Her money? Maybe a gift from a lover?"

A gift from her rich father. Flaunted and taunted. The report from his investigator had said she'd never parted with it even after the family money had dwindled away.

A forehead was uncovered, a pointed chin. The sheet slipped to the side and he could see the emerald and gold necklace heavy and dull at her throat. Covered by blood and set on a crusted red riverbed.

He heard a crash and looked to see the small table at his side on the floor, felled like an uprooted tree.

He had to get out of here.

He stumbled out of the room, barely registering Marietta at his side asking him if he was sick.

"Poor bloke. Some men can't handle the sight, 'tis true enough," someone said.

One of many faces he had hoped never to see again. Not that he particularly cared that she was dead. He hated her. Hated them all. But he had separated himself from his past long ago. What the devil was going on?

"Gabriel?" Marietta whispered.

Her voice came from far away, though there was a hand on his arm and another around his waist. He forced his eyes closed, then opened them again slowly as he'd been trained to do. To show no emotion. To show no affect.

He straightened, the hallway stretched in front of

him toward the staircase. "Upstairs." Better to keep communications short until he could truly take hold of his tangled thoughts.

Where was his father? When had Jeremy's break begun? Where had his investigator gone? He hadn't received a report in almost . . . almost a month. No.

No.

This could be a coincidence. Could be a nightmare. He had to see the sketches from the other murders.

He pounded against the door that read FRANKLIN LEWIS. It opened and a surprised Frank stepped aside. "Mr. Noble. I received your note. Are you unwell, sir?"

"I'm not unwell, Frank. I need a favor. I can pay."

"'Course you won't pay! My last favor didn't pay my due. What can I do for you?"

"Can you obtain sketches from Coroner's Court?" He tried to keep the desperation, the abject terror, from his voice.

Frank looked thoughtful. "For how long will you need them?"

"Ten minutes, that's all."

"Then, of course. That shouldn't be a problem. I can have them here and back before anyone notices. And there's a bloke who owes me in case I can't. Now's the best time, while everyone is in a tizzy. I'll be back in a few minutes."

Frank exited the room, leaving him alone with Marietta.

"What happened downstairs? I couldn't see around your shoulder very well. What I did see was gruesome, though." She shuddered. "Nightmare inducing."

"Yes," he said absently, thoughts coiling and refusing to connect.

"Gabriel?" She touched his chin and turned his face toward her. "We can leave. I'm sure we can come back later."

A fierce surge of something passed through him. "I'm fine. We need to get through here before Dresden puts a halt on our ability to move freely."

Dear God. What was he going to do if his ugly suspicions bore fruit?

Frank huffed into the room. "Darn circus down there. I think ten minutes is about all we can spare."

Gabriel nodded and took the sketches from him. Cold fear coiled in his gut as he looked at the first one. Yes, with what he knew now, this woman was familiar. Older, but he could fit her features on his memories, his nightmares. He flipped the page. Fear turned to ice. He fiddled with the edge of the paper. He didn't want to flip to the last page. To confirm.

From the corner of his eye he saw Marietta look at him.

He flipped the page. The paper wavered in his view, and he placed the pages on the desk before his shaking hands could scatter them to the floor.

A woman with a different name. The one identified victim. Anthony would surely be sending him a note any day with her original name. Amanda Forester. A rushed wedding, Marietta had said. He should have received a note from the man who was paid to keep track of the women for him. To let him know that one of them had changed her name. What would he have done had he known the victim's original name earlier? Before the investigation had begun?

"I see." He forced a smile. "Thank you, Frank. This was very helpful."

Helpful in the way that someone helped you dig a grave in a cemetery plot that just happened to have your name on the headstone.

"Come." He turned to Marietta. "We must be out before Dresden appears." He turned back to Frank and shook his hand, forcing the steady calm he had mastered to deal with any situation involving *them*. "Thank you. Please let me know if there is anything I can help you with."

Frank smiled and gathered the papers. "It was no problem, Mr. Noble. I'm always available to help with your cases. Especially the ones like mine. I appreciate all you do to help us. The 'Protector,' we call you."

Protector. Would he still retain that goodwill if his past were to become common knowledge—especially now with four dead women from it lying in the coroner's office either on a table or in a sketch?

He forced his lips into a smile. "Miss Rose here will be forced to tease me from my arrogance for a week now."

Frank smiled at Marietta. "Good luck to you, miss. I'm sure that whatever you need help with will be resolved soon. Problems always are when Mr. Noble is involved."

Such faith. He had developed a network to make sure that those who sought help would not find themselves in the same position he had once found himself. Helpless. He shuddered, covering the involuntary action by gripping the door handle. Everything was coming full circle.

He strode from the room.

Marietta followed behind. "What did you learn from the sketches?"

And Marietta. Completely in the dark. Trusting him like they all trusted him. Not knowing that she could be the first one to whom he might betray that trust.

"I was looking for age, physical characteristics, anything that might tie them together." It wasn't a lie, it just wasn't the full truth.

"And?"

"They mostly look to be the same age. I will see if I can get someone to copy and circulate the pictures to discover more about them."

He wasn't sure he was going to do any such thing. He didn't want anyone to recognize the victims. He couldn't believe no one had yet, even though, at the same time, he would have been hard pressed to identify them himself if he hadn't been presented with pictures of the matched set. He wondered if it was the murderer's intention to make them unrecognizable.

Why hadn't anyone claimed them missing? He'd have to see where the hell his investigator was and what he had to say. The man was well paid to keep track of them. He should have received word concerning Amanda's marriage *weeks* ago.

He balled his fists. The man was paid exorbitantly to keep track of their whereabouts so that Gabriel could forget all about them—unless one was up to her

181

old tricks. He dealt with any of those tricks swiftly and financially. That was definitely one reason a few of them wouldn't have been missed yet—tossed from society and penniless as they were.

He was so wrapped up in his thoughts that he never saw the man step in front of them until he stepped on his foot.

He cursed when the man's face came into view and moved to sidestep him.

"Going somewhere, Mr. Noble?"

Arthur Dresden's face was set in lines somewhere between satisfied and comically enraged.

"Finally figured it out, eh, Dresden? Congratulations. Now, if you'll pardon us." He reached a hand behind to Marietta and tried to step around. The main door and freedom were only twenty paces away.

The Runner stepped in his path again. "Going so soon? I don't think so. I have questions, you see."

"How extraordinary for you. But you can't detain us here. We'll be on our way."

"You think I cannot?"

"I know you cannot, Runner." Some people might be scared by a Bow Street Runner and the tactics they used, but Gabriel had read all their codes. All the laws concerning them. Unfortunately for the man in front of him.

Dresden's eyes were scorching. "I've heard all about you. Using the law as you desire. Bribing people to do your *justice*. It's outrageous. The law is not to be trifled with. I will be watching you, Noble, make no mistake."

"I'm touched by your interest. Now if you wouldn't mind moving out of our way?"

Dresden turned to Marietta. "You are trying to free your brother. Admirable as that *sentiment* may be to some, how does it feel to obstruct the workings of the law, Miss Winters? It is rather apparent that you were the one, Mr. Noble, to orchestrate the bid for the trial to be repositioned to a later date."

"Your detective skills are keen, I must say. How anyone is denied justice in a land where you make arrests is baffling."

"Laugh all you want, Noble. The truly pernicious thing is that you believe yourself to be helping others. To skirt the laws, to obfuscate justice to your own demands."

"The truly pernicious thing is that you believe in your own world of hypocrisy, Dresden."

It was obviously the wrong thing to say, if he cared about such a matter, as Dresden's color changed from white to red. "If I can lay any of this at your door, I will, Noble. As for you, Miss Winters, your older brother will be keeping your younger brother company very soon."

Her hand tightened on Gabriel's and a tingle of rage ran through him at Dresden's bullying tactic.

Dresden leaned toward Marietta. "If you weren't a woman, you would join them posthaste."

The Runner obviously didn't think much of women. A monumental mistake to underestimate them.

"How terribly insightful." Gabriel started walking, and this time when Dresden got in the way, Gabriel shoved him to the side and kept moving. The sound of a body hitting the floor behind him was terribly satisfying.

Dresden roared his name.

Gabriel pushed through the doors and hurried down the steps, Marietta held firmly in his wake as he strode through the crowd, paving a path. More people were filling in the area around the court, onlookers trying to discover advanced news they could pass on to their neighbors. Any morsel of gossip.

They finally made it through and vaulted back to darkened safety. He was never so glad to be in a carriage as he was now. He leaned back against the seat and closed his eyes. What a disastrous morning. Perhaps he would awaken and discover Billy's knock and all the subsequent discoveries to be merely a horrendous nightmare.

A sound across from him had his eyes opening back up. Marietta's lips were pinched together and her hands were clutched in her dress. He reached over and tugged her onto his seat, tucking her head under his chin. He could feel her silent sobs.

"Shhh. Your brother will be fine."

"They won't release Kenny."

He didn't have anything to say to that. He wondered if Dresden was solely responsible for putting the new spin on the murders. A joint project between the brothers, or one brother copying the other in an attempt to free him. It didn't matter. If public opinion went against them, they were in trouble. The jury would be influenced, and the judge would guide the questioning.

"We will start a campaign to free your brother."

The problem was that if his footman had been successful at hiding Mark, it would merely lend credence to Dresden's tale. It would look as if Mark were hiding to escape the murder charge. They were cuffed. Marietta could lose both brothers.

And if his awful suspicion, his awful fear, proved true . . . could he sacrifice his family in order to save Marietta hers?

The puzzle turned sharply. Gone were the faint sides and rounded corners. Sharp spines and fanged teeth decorated the edges now. That he was working *this* particular case . . . He didn't believe in coincidence. Men like him made their own coincidences and returned them onto others. What was happening?

"And if they capture Mark?"

He hugged her closer. She was innocent. In all of this madness, she was innocent. And that needed salvaging. "The murderer has shown himself to be unwilling to accept the gift that your brother's arrest presented. He will likely kill again. If Mark is caught before that happens, then they will have nothing to show against both your brothers."

Unless they then tried to pin it on Marietta. Or on him, acting as her agent. If the authorities started to dig around in his background . . . they could pin the whole thing on him. Or on his family—which would hurt immeasurably more. The smart thing to do would be to drop the case flat. To turn Marietta out and try and salvage his own stake.

His eyes closed tightly. Surely all of the people he had helped and the network he had designed was enough? He had paid his penance and didn't need to pay one more.

"So you are going to let Mark get caught?"

"No. We will take our chance that the case against Kenny is lessened by this. But if your other brother is caught, take comfort in my previous statement. The killer is still out there."

Marietta clutched his collar, her face pressed against his neck. A tear wound down his throat and into the fabric beneath. He stroked her hair, his thoughts colliding as to what he should do—about her, about the situation.

And if he did the wrong thing, would one more sin damn him? He was already a ruined man.

He had been since he was sixteen.

Chapter 11

M arietta read the note that Gabriel had handed her as she paced back and forth in the kitchen. Mark was in a house hidden in London. Safe. At least for the moment. Mark was liable to do any number of stupid things like leaving the house because he became bored or didn't see the seriousness of the matter.

But perhaps he did finally. He had looked shaken when they'd met at a little spot in Hyde Park off the beaten paths—minutes before he disappeared with Gabriel's men.

Gabriel had been strangely silent since Coroner's Court. No quips or barbs had come her way. He had held her and comforted her, but his gaze had been strange and unfocused. It still was. And if she had thought him diligent and hardworking before, there was a new zeal to his work. He was buried in tomes and treatises, laws and pamphlets. And his notes fluttered everywhere. Time lines and dates, initials and locations. She'd tried to read a few of them, but if they'd been incomprehensible before, his shorthand was now completely cryptic.

And they hadn't discussed a thing about last night, though with the events of the morning, there hadn't been time for tiptoeing discomfort or declarations.

"Marietta?"

She turned to see him watching her from where he was hunched over the table. That was another thing. Gabriel had never *hunched* before. He'd always held himself as if he were two steps away from seduction, that at any time he could rise or move from wherever he was and have her begging for another kiss. He still looked kissworthy, with his hair falling over his forehead, his green eyes intent on hers, and his lips parted on the question of her name.

"Yes?"

"Stop pacing."

It was a relief that some things didn't change. She dropped into the seat across from him. "I need to do something. If you could just tell me what you are researching, I could help."

He looked down at the spread of books and papers. "Why don't you visit Mark? Make sure he is settled and knows not to leave." His voice was casual. The hairs on the back of her neck rose. "I'll have the carriage take you. It will be a very roundabout way, just in case, so you may want to tear your way out of the vehicle by the time you get there. You will be back by dinner."

It all sounded so reasonable, and perfect. Nothing worked like that for her. "And you?"

His lower lip slid between his teeth. "I'm going to sit

here and pore over legal documents. Nothing exciting."

"Oh."

Something about that statement was not right. But as he'd gone right back to the documents, there wasn't much to be said. And she did want to speak with Mark. To make sure he stayed safe.

Besides, she trusted Noble, didn't she?

"Find out from your brother where he was last night. Also, here are the dates of the other murders." He handed her a piece of paper, his voice still bland and not at all like him. "See if he can remember where he was. If not, I will have to send someone to your house to gather the correspondence to help his memory."

"What about the servants?"

He tapped his forefinger against the scarred table. "I had Billy pay them and turn them out with the proper papers."

She supposed she ought to be displeased that he had assumed the action without asking, but she couldn't.

"Thank you."

His shoulders relaxed slightly, but she realized how tense he still looked. Nothing like the arrogant, supremely confident man she'd first met. Oh, it was still there, waiting to be unleashed, but something had muted him.

He looked at her through his hanging locks. "I thought you might be angry."

"I might. But there is little doubt nothing in the house would still be there if you hadn't taken action. There still mightn't."

She was once again glad she'd moved her important items, and Kenny's as well.

"The locks will be changed as soon as the locksmith can do so."

"Thank you."

His eyes followed her mouth as she formed the words. She ran her fingers over her lips. Confusing thoughts to want his lips on hers and to be scared at the same time that everything in her life was falling apart. Comfort and desire.

"The carriage driver is in the next house on the right. He knows where to go. For your safety, you won't. Tell him to come talk to me and I will send you on your way."

Gabriel waited no more than a few minutes after the carriage wheels clicked down the street to grab his top hat and set off. He arrived at Alcroft's house half an hour later.

Alcroft's face lit in surprise as he greeted him in the drawing room. "Gabriel." He looked him over. "You look terrible."

"Why, thank you, John. I appreciate that."

Alcroft motioned him toward his study and closed the door behind them. "I take it you don't want the servants overhearing."

"Even servants as well behaved as yours have ears and mouths."

Alcroft leaned forward. "What has happened? I heard there was another murder."

"The first victim of the Middlesex murderer was Amanda Forester."

Alcroft blinked. "Lady Dentry's old crony?"

"Yes. And the second victim was Celeste Fomme."

His friend did nothing for a second, and then looked at his desk. "She was a tyrant, but dead? And in that . . . way?"

"Yes. I'm sorry."

Alcroft moved a piece of paper across the surface and then another, as if trying to find the answers in the parchment. "You have more to tell."

"I saw the sketches of the other two victims. With those two identified, the third was Jane Moreton. Abigail Winstead was murdered last night."

Alcroft looked up. "No."

"Yes."

His friend looked at a portrait on the wall. "I spoke to Abigail recently, you know. She thought she was being stalked. I didn't believe her."

This was news to Gabriel. "You spoke with her? Has anyone reported her missing?"

"Doubtful. I thought she had already left. She said she was leaving for the country. That the city wasn't safe. I thought she had gone. We are hardly friends. She came to me because she thought I could help." He crushed a paper beneath his fist. "I ran a report for her, but I didn't believe her. I should have done something."

Gabriel kept his tongue. Ladies like Abigail were overly dramatic and given to fits. It was hardly surprising that Alcroft hadn't taken her seriously. That wouldn't make his friend feel much better, though. He knew that firsthand. "Did she say anything? Any idea who was stalking her?"

"Some Dentry servant." He shoved his fingers through his hair, and Gabriel was glad the action took his eyes away from him, or else Alcroft would have seen his stiffening, the fear in his eyes that he quickly masked.

"Did she say whom?"

"Yes. John, Joseph, Jacob—Jacob! Jacob . . . " His lips pinched together. "I have the report synopsis. Worley? Yes, I think that was it. A footman."

Relief so enormous that it was painful crashed through him.

"Gabriel?"

He feigned a cough and gathered himself. "Forgive me, go on."

"Said he had shown up outside her rented house more than once. He'd just stare at her from across the street. Right creepy, she said." Alcroft pushed his pen. "Dead. All of them?"

"Yes," he said tightly, their goading faces floating in his memories.

Alcroft looked up, and Gabriel could have sworn a look of sympathy crossed his face. He *knew*. Cold crept down his spine.

"What do you know, John?"

His friend looked taken aback for a second. "Only that they had their ladies' club and they would torture some of the boys in the household by making promises and pretending interest."

If only. If only that had been the extent of it.

"The footman probably caught a lure and became obsessed." Alcroft shuddered. "Can you imagine what would lead to something like that?"

Being obsessed with something? Yes. Killing women? No.

"But this is good news too, no?" Alcroft said. "You will get Miss Winters's brother out of prison."

"Unfortunately, the Runner on the case is proving difficult. They are now after Miss Winters's older brother as an accomplice and murderer."

Alcroft's face mirrored deep shock. "How did they determine that?"

"Idiocy and hoping to keep the public from panicking. Unfortunately for the public panic, Mark Winters has now gone missing."

Alcroft's eyes were shrewd. "How unfortunate indeed. I must commend you."

"Do you still have the report on the servant?"

"Yes. The report was on the servant's state and movements. I had an investigator do it. You were working on the other cases, and I wouldn't have brought this to you." He ran his hand along his neck. "I didn't want to bother you with it."

Gabriel said nothing.

"The investigator didn't find much, and I had him send the reports to Abigail. I do know, though, that he was trailing the servant when the first murder happened. I was at the Plakens' rout when the news came that a gruesome murder had just occurred in Clerkenwell, and I remember thinking about the investigator. I have an address for Abigail; perhaps you can locate the brief." He paged through his papers, organized and neat as they were. "Here it is."

Gabriel took the paper. "Thank you, John."

He was thanking him for more than just the address, and Alcroft seemed to know it. He nodded solemnly. "I know you'll find the bastard."

Gabriel ran those words through his head as he walked home.

He also repeated Alcroft's later words: *Are you going to tell Marietta?*

No.

It had to be this man, this nearly faceless servant. It wouldn't be someone from his family, someone he knew or loved. It wouldn't be someone from Marietta's family. They would both be pleased at the end. Free to do whatever they both wanted.

If only he could convince himself of that. If only he could keep his mind from churning over escape routes and alternative plans. They kept forming and solidifying in his brain.

He forced himself to think of Jacob Worley. Of the man that he would catch, the man who would confess to everything.

And with that thinking, there was cause to celebrate tonight. To take back the control that had slipped from his fingertips this morning.

With every step he convinced himself more and more. He recognized the irony that he was deluding himself, but forced that section of his mind to lie dormant. He had always been a realist. A disgusting survivor. He hated the weakness. The fear. He had thought them stamped out long ago.

Anger surged through him. He was going to catch the servant and bury his weak emotions six feet down where they belonged.

They were going to hunt Jacob Worley.

He had to brush up on his hunting skills. And that—he smiled wickedly, ignoring a passing girl's gasp—was a task he could enjoy tonight.

Marietta sat in the kitchen, absently pawing through papers and fuming. She was back earlier than she'd thought she would be—Mark had vacillated between raving and staring. She hadn't been able to deal with his mood swings for long. She'd told him to behave like a grown man and read him the list of rules before leaving in disgust.

She was also obviously earlier than Noble had thought she'd be. He had said he wasn't going anywhere. She'd known he looked shifty earlier. Was he investigating without her? What if he met Dresden and she wasn't there to save him?

She read a note from Anthony that said the first victim's former name had been Amanda Forester. The name was vaguely familiar in the way fringe society names were. She wished she had kept more abreast of the gossip instead of focusing on keeping them fed. Silly thoughts.

The front door opened and banged shut. Measured footsteps clicked down the hall, and Noble came into view, hair mussed and windblown, eyes dark and predatory. The image of a hunter who had finally found his prize.

She sprung up from her chair. "I thought you said you weren't leaving? Where did you go? Why didn't you tell me?"

He strode forward and kicked her chair out of the way. She didn't have a moment to be nervous before she found herself flat on her back on top of the table, papers crinkling beneath her.

"What—"

She barely took another breath before he tossed up

her skirts and pushed her legs up and out. His mouth pressed against her. Dear. God.

Something gurgled from the bottom of her throat and out between her lips. She bucked against him as he licked a broad stroke up. And then another. She didn't have time to ask him what he was doing, to be mortified at what he was doing, as all thoughts centered right where his mouth was and she found herself bunching papers beneath her fists and arching her head so far back that her shoulders weren't touching the surface of the wood.

His arms hooked beneath her legs and he buried himself between. His tongue thrust inside and his lips pressed over the sensitive surface of *that* place and one of his fingers circled her and *ohdeargod* she was flying and dying as her hips bucked upward and papers tore beneath her hands.

She panted on top of the table, legs shaking and forehead damp. What in heaven's name had just happened to her? What was *that*?

He pulled her forward and took her lips in a kiss that was demanding and passionate. Drugged and sated, she could only hold on tight, legs splayed, as he kissed the spirit right out of her and then refilled her with more.

He tasted like *her*. It was a strange thought, but she couldn't be unnerved by it while the absolutely clever things he was doing to her blocked all thought.

"You are going to let me have you, aren't you, Marietta?"

The wobbling of her head must have said yes, because a triumphant light lit his eyes.

"I thought of tossing your skirts up all the way home. Today has dealt quite the emotional upheaval. I found some interesting information. Do you want me to tell you about it?"

"Yes." Her brain started to right itself.

"How should I tell you? A little bit of information between kisses?"

He sucked her bottom lip between his and his hands moved to cup her rear against the table.

"Only the pertinent items as I'm filling you?"

Her mind crossed as he pulled her against him, the place that he had just devoured pressed tightly to a thickening area of his trousers.

"Or is it morbid to talk about these types of things while making love? Most likely. But we are closer now, Marietta. Soon we'll have your brothers released and there will be no more family worries."

She thought that was a strange comment. Phrased oddly.

He was back to the seducer. A man in control. Whatever had ailed him had been switched to the background. She could see the shadows lurking behind his eyes, but the bright green was whispering all sorts of promises.

"What did you just do to me?"

Of all the things vying for her to ask, that was the one that emerged.

"I tasted you, Marietta. I'm not displeased to say that you taste exactly as I thought you might. Strong and sweet."

Flabbergasted and hot, the clutched butterflies that had been trapped in her stomach since she met him, the ones that had returned fuller and brighter after being scattered to pieces last night, beat more furiously against their binds.

"That was a quick taste, though. Furious. Should we slow it down and try again? I wouldn't want to disappoint."

"No, you wouldn't," she said faintly. She was trying to read his eyes, which always told the truth, but they were hazy behind the film in front of her own. She blinked to clear them, and though his words were the practiced ones of an extraordinary rake, his eyes were hot. The cynicism in them tempered by real passion.

She wasn't ashamed to admit that his practiced words would have done the trick alone. It was hard to believe that even the most stalwart of women wouldn't want to believe herself special enough to cause that type of attention, false as it would likely prove, from this type of man. But the look in his eyes made his words pale in comparison. Her chest, her throat, her cheeks were on fire. Scorching heat that seemed to jump right from his green eyes into her skin.

"Good." He unbuttoned her dress, unlatched it and let the top pieces hang as he laid her back on the table, her dress spreading out on the surface with her lying in the center.

He touched the exposed skin as he circled the table. He leaned over the side and licked a stripe over the material covering her right breast.

"I haven't had dinner yet. This looks like the most marvelous feast I've ever seen."

The rational part of her mind said she was far too

bony and gangly to be particularly attractive. The rest of her took a blacksmith's hammer and beat that part of her mind into submission as his warm breath coasted over her skin.

"I don't know where to start. Everything looks so delicious."

He drew a finger down her breast. She followed his finger's path, the rise and fall of her chest in continuous motion. "Your dress, your stays, your chemise. The layers of cloth rubbing together. Does the silk rub your skin? Does the linen perk your nipples? Do they become taut and peaked and grasping for touch?"

So sensitive. And on fire. The poor butterflies had been burned to cinders, now kindling in her flames. Her body arched up unconsciously, following his fingers as he stroked from the outside of her breast to the peak through the remaining cloth.

"What do you wish, Marietta? For me to remove your stays? Your chemise?" he whispered in her ear. His fingers moved to her other breast. "To take your nipples, one by one, between my lips and feast?"

Whatever had happened to her before was coming back. She was hot, her body languid and sleek.

"If I—"

Her hands moved of their own volition, touching his cheeks, framing his face, interrupting him. "Yes, Gabriel. Anything."

Her hands lovingly smoothed the skin of his cheeks, the feel of silk with just a hint of bite.

She arched into him and it took her a moment to realize he was standing stock still against her. His fingers frozen in place. His eyes shuttered. The look on his face foreign and strange.

"Gabriel?"

He recalled a rakish smile, but it didn't reach his eyes, which were glued to hers.

"I—"

His eyes shut. Pinched together.

"I—"

His eyes opened and darkened to jade. Leashed control. As if he had lost it for just a moment and harnessed it back with all his might.

"I will make you beg for the want of it."

His fingers drew circles on her stomach, then moved down her skirt and underneath. Intent and purposeful. Seeking and demanding. He gave a little hum of pleasure and his eyes darkened further.

His fingers curled into her warmth, into the place where everything coalesced.

"It's like pure liquid gold."

Before last night she would have wondered if such a thing were possible. She crushed a paper in her hand. It obviously was. His thumb grazed *that* spot and her hips jolted up. She couldn't stop a moan.

"That's right, Marietta. Show me what makes you moan."

She was a marionette on a set of strings, and he was pulling every one. She didn't even need to vocalize her begging, as her body's language was simple to understand, her noises uncontrollable. And though it might make her nervous later, right now she couldn't dredge up the outrage.

His thumb grazed her again and one of his fingers

dragged along something inside of her. She moaned again and started to pant breaths. The heat was too intense. It was everywhere. And unlike before when she'd been taken by surprise, this was a buildup. To that lovely feeling. But it wasn't a lovely feeling now. It was frustrating and jaw-clenching. Like a carriage that would not go fast enough, or a dream where she couldn't run.

She felt his mouth, saw the top locks of his head bowed between her legs, her skirt obscenely bunched around her waist, her knobby knees bare to the air. Felt him do something, and she exploded. Her stomach clenched as the top half of her body half rose from the table and then flopped back down. Tremors wracked her, and he continued touching her as she rode the lovely feeling. The end of the frustration.

She settled one hand on her stomach, breathing deeply. The second time was somewhat different from the first, which had been different from last night, but it was lovely all the same. An even more languid feeling took over her body. She was exhausted.

She saw him watching her from between her bent knees. There was something dark and dangerous in his eyes.

"You are now mine, Marietta Winters."

Chapter 12

"**E**xplain to me again about this odd man?" she asked.

He should have reveled in the fact that she was still flushed and slightly breathless, but his heart was beating much too quickly. He had lost control for a moment there. The world tilted oddly on end. He couldn't let that happen again. He had needed to switch his plan to take her against the table to simply pleasuring her again instead. He was afraid of what might have happened had he done the former. Would she have entangled a piece of his soul?

"He was seen lurking around the last victim more than once. We need to track him down," he said.

He shoved the fear away. He was in perfect control. He always was. Nothing had changed. Nothing *would* change.

"How did you discover this?" she demanded.

"Luck. There was a notice about a necklace matching the one the woman had on. An inquiry into the necklace gave me a name and an address, along with the information that a strange man had inquired after it and was always following the victim around."

Spun tales in his direct power.

"And the middle two victims?"

"Still no word on them." There hadn't been. He didn't count that he already knew their names.

"Shall we tell the Runner?"

Cold sweat broke out on his forehead and he surreptitiously wiped the side of his hand across it. "Not yet. We need to establish something first. He'll never believe us otherwise."

She looked disappointed. He wanted to shout. There was no way he was telling Dresden a thing. Just a little bit of investigating on Dresden's side and . . . No. He wasn't even sure why he was telling her this part. Better for him to secrete her with her brother and carry this on himself.

He tried to say that exact thing. His mouth opened but nothing emerged. He tried again. She looked expectant.

"Yes?"

"Nothing."

It wasn't healthy, this want, this need, to keep her around. Why? Because she seemed able to read him more than any other female of his quite large acquaintance? Because he liked sparring with her? Because of that damned spark that wasn't going away?

What the devil was it about her?

She wasn't that attractive.

His mind was already conjuring up plenty of pictures of her face in wanton lust. How she responded to him. He had never seen anything more beautiful than her response.

She was too opinionated.

He hated doormats. He liked her spark.

She wanted control.

The voice in his head was silent.

"Gabriel?"

"Yes?"

"You haven't said a word for an entire minute. And you are looking at me as if I'm a summer roach."

He quickly wiped his face of expression.

"You really think it's this man? This renegade footman?"

"I think we should search the address I was given and see what we can find. Perhaps we find nothing on the footman. But if she did think he was stalking her, perhaps we will."

He had spun a fast tale. He had left Alcroft out of it, and anything to do with either him or his family as well, of course.

He'd protected Jeremy all his life. He would take the fall before Jeremy, if it came down to it. There was no question in his mind. It was purely fact. His brother would be protected over everything.

He gazed into Marietta's eyes. Was it any wonder, after all, that she had sparked something in him from the first? Concern for her brother outstripping everything, including self-preservation.

"When are we going to search her house?"

"In the morning. We can use the daylight instead of having to rely on lamps and lights. The neighbors might notice."

"And how are we going to get inside?"

"Leave that to me."

Marietta looked around a bit frantically as Gabriel did something to the door of number six. No one seemed to be paying them any mind, but she felt as if there was a news caller on the corner shouting, "Illegal tampering," and pointing right at them.

Relief swept through her as the door clicked open and Gabriel walked inside. She hurried after him and he pushed the door shut.

"Where did you learn to do that?"

"A good ser—" He fiddled with the tool he had used, closing it. "A good sir always knows how to pick a lock."

"That makes not a whit of sense."

He smiled wolfishly. "That it doesn't."

She had no reply for that and followed him as he poked around the front hall. There was a table stand with unopened mail and a ring of keys on top.

"What do you suppose happened to the servants?"

"Let go, perhaps?" He lifted the ring. "An odd thing for a butler to leave the house keys behind. I can try the servant network and see if anyone knows anything."

Not one to question the value of servants' gossip, Marietta pawed through the invitations, recognizing a few of them. "Abigail Winstead was a member of society. Not an outstanding member from the invitations, but she had a few connections."

She fingered a gold filigreed invitation in disgust. "The Shossers didn't see fit to extend us an invitation a week ago."

"It is surprising that society hasn't wanted the gossip directly."

"Oh, they did, at first. We had a number of callers the first two days." She threw the invitation down. "But no one wants us to grace their doors now. At least not yet. I wouldn't be surprised if when Kenny goes to trial we receive a few—to judge our state, mind you."

"Cynicism is such a lovely trait to possess."

"Realism. You should know the difference."

He hummed in agreement and poked through more of the unopened mail. "Shall we see if we can find her writing desk?"

The victim's writing desk was in her sitting room. A lovely mahogany box with mother of pearl inlay. Marietta opened it and found a jumble of papers, as if someone had collected the lot and thrown them inside. She touched the edge of a book and unearthed a leather-bound journal from the mess.

"What did you find?" Gabriel was searching the table, where papers were neatly stacked.

"A journal."

Gabriel's head shot up. "A personal journal?"

The initials engraved on the cover seemed to indicate it as such. "Seems to be."

"Let me see it."

She pulled it out of his range and opened the front cover.

January 2nd, 1813. L.D., C.F., J.M., A.F., T.R., and I have taken it upon ourselves to indulge in some fun. We have formed a club. It will have the utmost discretion. We—

The journal was torn from her hands. She gasped. "How rude. Give it back."

He held it out of her reach and flipped through. Something flitted past his eyes. He seemed to be looking for something.

"Gabriel!"

Page after page flipped, as she inelegantly reached for it, even going so far as to use the chair to stand higher. He simply moved away from her.

She sat in the chair and crossed her arms. It seemed an eternity later that he stopped flipping pages.

"It's just a silly personal journal. Nothing is written since 1815. We need to find out if she kept any correspondence about her fears."

Marietta held out her hand for the journal. He paused a moment, then tossed it to her. She sniffed and tucked the book into her bag. She wasn't sure why, but she wanted to read it later. She began paging through the loose sheets. Gabriel sat next to her and grabbed a handful as well. His warmth seeped into her side as they rummaged and sorted bills from letters from notes. She leaned into him.

If only Kenny weren't in prison, and women weren't being murdered, the whole thing would feel like some grand adventure.

"She owed a lot of creditors." Marietta looked around the room. "From these notes I would think her in dire straits, but the house is well-appointed."

"Living beyond her means. Your brother is quite familiar with the state."

She gave him a haughty stare and returned to the papers.

Butler needs replacing. Hardly knows what to do with himself. In the old days, I would have had him under my heel and begging like a dog to serve.

"She seems quite . . . scathing."

"Do you mean comments like this, 'Maid a twit. Frame her for jewelry theft next week.'"

Marietta stared at him and then pushed the side of the note in his hand down so she could read it. "Does it really say that?"

"No."

The note said to purchase legumes from the grocer. She whacked him in the leg. "I almost believed you too. I've read more than a few in that vein."

"How do you think I came up with that one?"

"Twit."

"Gull." He smiled. Warmth spread through her and she leaned in a little closer as they continued to read.

He made a triumphant noise. "There's an address listed for the footman, Jacob Worley. She hired an investigator." He flipped through the pages in his hand. "There are a number of observation pages here."

Marietta held up the page she had just been skimming that had an account of the footman's activity on a Wednesday two weeks past. "You are right. Here are a few more. Seemed the footman really was following her around. Right scary that must have been."

He bumped her shoulder in a companionable fashion. "Gather all the correspondence. We'll take it with us."

"What if someone notices?"

"I'll return it when we get through it all. The

208

servants are gone. Shouldn't be too difficult. I saw a lease agreement. The house is rented through the month."

Marietta nodded and grabbed the haphazard stack, shoving it into her bag.

"I want to look around, see if we can find anything else."

Looking around only seemed to show that Abigail Winstead was fastidious and odd. Her strict sense of order with everything else in the house made it even stranger that her writing case would be so messy.

A peek into an armoire drawer showed a few things that a straitlaced woman would not possess. Various sized implements of different dimensions were nestled into clothing that a lady would never wear. Ladies that weren't trying to free their brothers, she amended.

"If you want one of those 'tools,' I can find you one. But you are assuredly not taking hers," his low voice whispered in her ear.

"I don't even know what they are for."

He turned her around and pulled her against him, her body connecting pleasurably with his. "We can easily change that." He looked around and there was a dark light in his eyes. "But not here."

"Well, that answers my question about what they might be used for. Are sexual pursuits always on your mind?" She whispered, though she didn't know why. They were completely alone.

"Oh, most definitely." He grinned darkly.

There was little else of consequence in the house. The overorganized feel was somehow more threatening than the spartan feel of their temporary house. Marietta was happy to leave. Gabriel picked up the key ring and the invitations and locked the door behind them. The birds were chirping discordantly as they walked down the path and back up the street.

"What do you think of Abigail Winstead?" he asked.

"I don't know." She looked at him. "What do you?"

He stayed silent for a minute as they walked past brownstones and lovely brick facades, colorful flowers trailing from their pots and troughs.

"Single-minded."

She tipped her shopgirl's bonnet. "Yes, I think I agree. So she would have likely been single-minded about the man who was following her."

"Yes."

"Do you think she might have gone after him?"

"Perhaps. But she was murdered on a corner far from her house. Far from this address as well." He tapped the bag containing the papers they'd collected. "Why?"

She shook her head. "Perhaps we will find some clue in her papers."

Marietta settled in with Abigail's journal after dinner in the small drawing room on the first floor. Unlike the other rooms, it had a cozier feel, with two armchairs and a plush settee. Gabriel had stepped out, but she expected him back any minute. She'd had to retrieve the journal from his room. How it had ended up there, she didn't know. She knew he thought the journal silly, but she couldn't help seeking it out.

The journal unfolded like a story. Her eyes were glued to the elegant writing. It was fascinating and horrifying.

We have a new one. He is so delightful. We call him our little avenger. He is more prickly than our last, full of spirit—seems to think we are blackmailers! I laughed, for it is nothing but the truth. And yet we have so much to teach him. I see the way L.D. looks at him. How they all do. He is beautiful. A crown jewel.

A hand touched her shoulder, then drew along her throat, up under her chin to her cheek. She hadn't even heard him walk up the stairs, she was so absorbed. She leaned into the touch, as she had for the past two days, and turned the page to the next entry, dated a week later.

He is more beautiful than anything we've seen. And defiant. I have never seen a more defiant servant. Must be his mother putting ideas in his head. Or the way the other servants dote on him. He acts above his station.

But there is something quite seductive in that. I doubt our little avenger would be as near to our hearts were he a beautiful face on a bland, eager package. There are so many of those and they can't keep our interest for long. They don't respond to the toys as well and their disgusting eagerness shows their breeding—like dogs.

Not like our little avenger. And the sweetest part is the look in his eyes. When reminded of his place and what will happen to his family if he doesn't comply, they always so blazingly speak of retribution. Banked fire and eternal damnation. I find it amusing that he thinks he might hold the key to our downfall. That he would try to beat us at our own game.

The hand along her cheek stopped its movement. "What are you reading?" She was left staring at her hands as he plucked the book from her grasp. "Abigail Winstead's *journal*? Where did you get this?"

"From the stand inside *your* room. Speaking of which, I put that in my bag! How did *you* get it?"

"You put all of the documents in your bag. I started going through them."

"Well you already dismissed the journal." She waved her hand. "Hand it here."

"There is no reason to read this tripe." He shook the book, his eyes a dark jade.

"I beg to differ. It gives a terrible insight into the deceased woman."

"Here is an insight—she's dead. This book is ten years old. Go through the more recent documents."

"But the book has a whole host of reasons why someone would want to murder her."

Gabriel paused in his movement, and she took it as a sign to continue.

"They were debauched, this circle of six women." She lowered her voice and leaned forward, as if spilling a dark secret. "I think they used men, younger boys, to do as they would. She hasn't spelled it out yet, but it becomes more apparent in every sentence." She lowered her voice further. "I think they had male sex slaves."

"Sex slaves? Quite a bawdy opinion for a woman who has just recently experienced the pleasure of sex herself."

"Stop poking fun. This is serious. They were using young men for ill deeds."

"Using them?" He seemed amused, but there was something in his eyes that made her shift in her seat. "I would think most men would be thrilled to have six—is that how many you said?—women *use* them."

Marietta bit her lip and looked back down at the book. "I don't know. It sounds like some of the victims were willing, but there are a few they forced—"

"Victims?" He gave a harsh laugh. "Most would scoff at your use. How old were these boys?"

She mentally flipped back through. "Sixteen to twenty."

"A normal sixteen-year-old boy wouldn't have known what hit him if six women pounced on him."

"I can't believe that. You are saying that a man would have no regard for being taken advantage of?"

"By six willing women?"

"It doesn't matter if the women are willing, if they are the ones doing the abuse!"

"Are they ugly, wretched hags?"

"It sounds like they were not. What difference does that make?"

"Then the *normal* sixteen-year-old would have been best pleased, would he not?"

She crossed her arms. "You are horrible."

"I am saying what most men would tell you."

"I don't care." She reached out and grabbed the journal. "It sounds like this boy right here didn't want to participate, and they *made* him." She flipped through it. "They called him a pet name because he stood defiant—their aven—"

Gabriel plucked the book from her grasp and tossed it on the far side of the room, where it landed with a *thwack* against the hardwood floor. "Stop reading that."

"No!"

His hand slipped to the back of her neck and gave it a gentle caress. Her eyes connected with his and he leaned forward. She leaned in as well, his lips met hers and she savored the feel—soft and strong.

Her body was already responding—warmth rising, tingles flowing. He would have her. She would let him. It would be so easy to give in. Did that say she had no measure of resistance?

She pushed away slowly. "I want to finish reading that book."

"No."

"No?" Testing herself turned to indignation. "You can't tell me no."

"Can I not?" Green eyes full of challenge pinned her to her seat. "I seem to remember from the very first night of this little exercise telling you that I could, if you wanted my help."

"For matters that required it for the case." She bit her lip as she stretched the truth. She clearly remembered the conversation and he was correct. But she'd been afraid of him then. How different the feeling of security made one act.

"Desperation breeds strong capitulation, and you capitulated, my dear." He tipped her chin up and ran his fingers down her throat. "With your stained dress and gaunt frame. Your desperate eyes." His hand moved against her nape.

"You were already strong and fierce. But food, comfort, and security have given you even more. Hopefully it didn't clear your memory." His fingers worked into her hair, cradling her head as it tipped back. "I said that you will do exactly as I say throughout the task. *Everything* I say. You agreed, if I recall."

Her memory was perfectly intact. Security gave her the nerve to keep arguing. "You aren't being reasonable. This is my brother we are talking about. Both of my brothers. You think I would willy-nilly my time away on some mad woman's journal if I didn't think it was pertinent?"

Strong lips captured the *ent* in pertinent. It was a scorching kiss, and she moved further into him. He was right. She didn't deny it. Along with the food there'd been comfort and a sense of security. A strong sense. It made her feel powerful, not powerless, for once.

She'd never felt quite as safe as she did when he was close to her. And wasn't that a scary thought? To entrust those feelings to a man who already held all the power. Even when they were arguing about a silly journal—

She pulled away, pushing into the chair's back. Every thought purged from her head by a few skillful kisses. Manipulated. *He manipulates women with little effort.* When had she forgotten that the statement applied to her as well? A burgeoning friendship with the devil himself? "Whenever you don't want me to do something, you seduce me!"

"As if it is that easy. The snap of my fingers and you are seduced?" His face was a mixture of irritation and something else. Guilt?

"With your kisses! With your proximity and searing looks." The thoughts started to roll out faster and faster. "You are trying to *control* me. My God. Could my emotions have confused things that badly? I thought I was *safe*."

She was feeling a little hysterical as one thought crashed into another and her safety net ripped like a web dashed from its bindings.

His eyes were hooded, his face dark. "You know little of what you are talking about."

"I know exactly what I am talking about. You are good, fantastic at it, I'll give you that. How many women have told you no? Very few, I'll bet!" Hysteria built. Sharp and uncontrollable. "And to a one, I'm sure they were very happy with their choice. But I won't allow myself to be controlled by you!"

"Interesting." He circled her. "So you will deny yourself the pleasure because you want to be the dominant one?"

"There you go again with your games and dominance." Frustration surged into her hysteria and she craned her neck to see him as he passed behind her. "I don't know what you are on about, but why can't you just be *normal*?"

A lopsided, broken smile lifted his mouth, reflected in his eyes as he stopped in front of her. There was something in that smile, in the self-loathing gaze, that made her want to snatch back her words, even though she was so light-headed she felt close to passing out, erratic energy coursing through her.

"Yes, why can't I be normal? It's an excellent question. One I ask myself frequently."

He turned. "Until the morning." It was clipped, polite, informal. Like a butler to the mistress of the house.

It wasn't until she heard his door click closed down the hall, sealing her out, that she realized he had taken the journal with him.

Chapter 13

Marietta looked straight ahead while she walked, trying not to sneak glances at Gabriel. Her shop girl skirt snapped as she tried to keep pace with him.

She disguised a look at him by pretending to watch a carriage click past. The sun was on a downward pitch and the rays caught his profile, setting half of his features in the light and half in shadow.

The cityscape changed to a dingy gray as they entered the edges of the East End. Gabriel was dressed again as a longshoreman, but the cocky walk he had adopted previously was clipped and edged.

He had retreated into the cold man he'd been when they'd first met. She fought to keep from rubbing her eyes. The night had been wretched. And alone. Muddled and confused thoughts vying with irritation and betrayal. Why had she suddenly thought he would be different from every other man?

And was she being unfair? The last thought had

made her toss and turn. Just remembering the look in his eyes before he left the room had left her numb. But he had to give her *something*, allow her to understand what he was thinking, or else she was going to continue to feel used. After they finished their business here, she was going to work up the courage to face his stoicism and ask.

The numbers along the street increased until they were standing before a drab three-story building that matched the address written in Abigail's note.

The walk-up was dirty. Papers and food littered the cracks and crevices in the stairs and against the rail. She followed behind Gabriel as he strode up the steps. His fist rose to knock on the door, but before his knuckles made contact with the wood, the door opened.

A man with a long scar beneath his chin stood in the frame, obviously on his way out. He opened his mouth to say something, perhaps "Pardon me" or "Good day" or some equivalent. Gabriel cocked his head to the side to receive the comment and his body moved fractionally to allow the man to pass.

Then their eyes met.

The moment suspended.

The hair on the back of her neck shot straight out, trying to balance her on the suddenly thin beam on which the tableau stood.

The man moved first, bolting back inside, the door crashing into the wall behind him. Gabriel went from a dead start to a sprint as he raced after the man. Stunned, the feeling that had coursed through her during the encounter with the barristers revived and poured through her again. Marietta hiked her skirts and ran as fast as she could in their wake. She rounded a corner in time to see the fleeing man toss himself through an open window, and she gasped as Gabriel dove through too. She looked to the right, then left. A closed door innocuously stood to one side.

She used precious seconds gripping the knob and forcing it open. She could see both men picking themselves off the ground, the stranger in the lead, Gabriel going from a somersault into a full-on sprint once more. Rubbish bins overturned and laundry ripped from its pins. A Yorkshire terrier gave chase and its little legs pumped after the two men, who were in no danger of being caught by the small bundle of fur.

Marietta rushed after them, but she was about as useful as the Yorkie, trailing and yapping at their heels. Gabriel threw a hand out, and she followed the movement. The street formed a U. They would come right back to her. The men disappeared behind the buildings blocking the U of the street. She frantically searched the area and picked up the heaviest thing she could find—a misshapen rock near an upright bin.

There was no place to hide. She just had to hope she looked docile enough for the man to pass. They curved back around and she could see Gabriel gaining on him. But the man was surprisingly agile. Then again, most footmen were. He headed straight for her, veering off the street. Her eyes went wide and she quickly backed up, cocking the rock back in her hand. He barreled straight for her. She let the rock loose. He dodged it and caught her in the midsection. She hit the ground and . . . nothing happened. No sounds, no smells, the image was static in front of her. Then it wavered. Gabriel's face appeared in front of hers. His lips moved.

Whoosh. She gasped, deep gaping breaths. She could feel his fingers tighten around her arm and then he was off again. She pressed one hand against her stomach. She thought rather inanely that all the butterflies may finally have been crushed for good.

Gabriel returned a minute later, swearing. He crouched in front of her and moved her hand. A quick press around her ribs had her gasping. He prodded and pushed against her chest, her stomach, and under her arms. She was too dazed to say a word, only answering the questions he asked.

"You will be fine. Bruising, definitely, the bastard. But nothing looks broken. Thank God."

He picked her up and set her on her feet. The coldness was gone from his eyes, replaced by something wild. "Come. Let's investigate Worley's room. Maybe he'll have a lapse of judgment and return. We won't get another chance if we leave."

He tucked her against him and led the way back to the building.

Worley's door was locked, but Gabriel made quick work of it. A few of the other boarders wandered by, but no one said anything. Nice neighbors.

The room was dark. He took her arm and led her inside. She didn't know what to think of his care in touching her again. Gabriel shut the door and opened the curtains. Marietta examined the decor. The bedroom was pretty average, if dingy. Nothing too exciting.

There was a stack of parchment on the desk that was pushed up against the wall with some charcoal on top. She walked over and saw a partially completed sketch of a woman. She looked very similar to one of the women in the coroner's sketches.

"Gabriel. Look at this." She moved the picture aside, but the rest of the papers were clean. There were charcoal marks on the wood of the desk and a few smudges on the wall in front.

He didn't respond.

"Gabriel, I think Worley drew a picture of one of the victims." She turned.

He was just standing there, knuckles white around the cupboard handle, staring inside. "I think you are correct," he finally said.

She hurried over and looked around his shoulder. The window allowed just enough light to see sketches plastered all over the three walls. Women's faces stared back. Handbills, notes, newspaper clippings. MIDDLE-SEX MURDERER CAPTURED! There were dates and times. Lists of names and places. Candle stubs clustered around the floor. A mad type of makeshift shrine.

"Oh my."

"Quite."

There were handkerchiefs and scraps of lace pinned to the wall in between the other items.

"What are these?"

"Pieces from the victims? I don't know."

She didn't know what to say to that. It all seemed too grotesque.

"Let's light the candles. Do you see any—ah, there we go."

Soon there was an eerie blaze on the floor, casting wicked shadows on the sketches. The sketches were quite lifelike—even the one of the mysterious woman with a veil—making them appear more bizarre. The women's eyes appeared to be looking down on them, and Marietta felt a shiver. It was as if she was in Abigail's journal and these women were sitting in judgment. There was a yellowish tinge to Gabriel's face, an odd effect of the lighting. Marietta took a quick look behind her; the last thing she wanted was for Worley to wander in while their backs were turned.

She looked at the sketches. Most of them consisted of eyes, some of other body parts, a few of profiles or full faces draped with fabric or animals to partially hide the view. "There are four or five different women sketched here. Maybe more. And one looks considerably older than the rest. His mother, maybe?"

"I don't know." Gabriel's tone was gruff. "Perhaps."

"This one looks familiar." Marietta touched a picture of a woman in profile. "Is there another picture of her from the front? Do you see one?"

He crouched down. "I don't know. Probably some woman on the street," he said dismissively. "Do you see anything resembling a weapon? They never found one on any of the women. Leads me to believe the murderer is using the same weapon on each victim. A souvenir, perhaps?"

Marietta went back to check the drawers in the desk and to search under the bed and under the pillow. She wiped her hands against her skirt. She felt dirty touching anything in the room. "I don't see anything."

Gabriel was still staring in the cupboard.

"What is it?" she asked.

He turned to look at her. "Nothing."

"What should we do?"

His eyes were focused on the open window. He didn't respond.

"I know you don't want to involve Dresden, but he will have to acknowledge at the very *least* that there are other suspects besides Kenny and Mark."

He continued his silence, not looking at her.

"We need Dresden in order to get Kenny released."

His eyes met hers. She was surprised to see anger there. Why would he be angry? And the emotion seemed focused on her. What had she done?

"Do you disagree?" she asked tentatively.

He looked back to the window. "We could take all of this with us, though it won't look good if we are found with the lot." He sounded as if he were talking to himself.

"Take it with us? Before showing it to Dresden? That seems like it will just point the finger more firmly to my family. Dresden needs to see it here."

"He will start horning in on our investigation."

"He thinks we are horning in on *his* already. Gabriel, we need Dresden. You know this better than I."

He watched her for what felt like the longest minute in her life. He was going to say no. He wasn't going to bring Dresden here. She could read it in his eyes, in how he held himself.

Despair shot through her. Dresden would hold her or arrest her eventually without Gabriel's help. Both of her brothers would be tried and found guilty.

His eyes shuttered. "We will bring Dresden here."

She was too stunned to speak for a second. A crazy torrent of relief spilled through her. Of course they would. It only made sense. Why would she think he would consider not doing so? And yet, she would swear that had been his intention a few seconds past.

"Might make a difference, might not. But he will be forced to at least look at the evidence. That *this* is the man who most likely committed the crimes."

"You think Dresden might still think we are lying?"

"Yes." He fiddled with his cuff. She had a feeling he had no idea he was doing it. "But it may go a small way toward helping your brother."

Even with this evidence, Dresden might not believe them. She stared blankly inside the cupboard.

He walked over and touched her chin, lifting it. "We will take the chance," he said grudgingly, as if making a major concession to her instead of just doing what made sense. "Let's track down the Runner."

Gabriel paid an exorbitant amount of money to two men with strict instructions not to let anyone inside the room until he returned—at which time he would double their money. Marietta had little doubt they would return to find the room intact. Furthermore, he gave them an incentive that if they saw and held the man who lived there, he would double again the sum.

They hailed a hack out front and set off for Bow Street.

Dresden's eyebrows shot halfway up his forehead when they walked in. She was surprised when, after he heard their story, he followed them to the boarding-house with little fanfare. However, after the numerous weighing looks he sent in Gabriel's direction during the ride, she was less surprised. He was keeping his enemy close.

For all of the Runner's stubbornness, she was grati-fied to see the serious expression on his face as he examined the room and cupboard at the boarding-house. He cataloged everything with his eyes. Expres-sions ranging from grimness to irritation crossed his features.

"Could have been you two all along, setting this up," he said gruffly.

"Could have been. Up to you to ask the folks around here and discover the truth," Gabriel pronounced with an unapproachable look on his face.

"I don't like people mucking around in my investigation."

Gabriel tipped his cap and turned. "I leave it to you to solve."

"Noble, I will catch up with you eventually."

"I'm sure you will."

Gabriel led her out of the house and beyond the cu-rious eyes of the boarders.

She clasped his arm. "We need to warn the other women in the pictures. The ones who are still alive."

He pursed his lips, narrowed his eyes.

"Should we circulate their pictures? How will we find them? Especially the lady in the veil?"

He turned away from her, looking down the street. "The sketches are in Dresden's hands. It will be his job to find them. The man is stubborn, but he is usually thorough when given a credible lead."

"But—"

He started moving and she hurried to follow. "No buts. We will continue trying to find Jacob Worley. Leave the women to Dresden. Getting your brother released is our concern, those women are not."

His stride lengthened and she fell behind. "But—"

"Miss Winters? Marietta Winters?"

Marietta missed a step. Her body tried to freeze but her mind screamed at her to keep moving.

"Marietta Winters?" A hand grabbed her arm and she was spun to face the narrowed, gleeful eyes of Felicity Tercake. Her perfect bonnet shadowed her face from the sun, giving her an unimpeded view of Marietta. "It *is* you."

"Quite." She kept herself from gripping her shop girl skirt.

"Oh, this is *too* good," Felicity crowed. "You've turned to trade, dear cousin? Walking to the poorhouse, are you? Saying a final prayer for that brother of yours?"

"If you are quite finished."

"Not for at least a quarter hour more." She smirked. "What you've missed. You are the talk of the ton, my dear. You and your brothers. Nasty little business there."

"I see you are reveling in it."

"Oh, indeed. Never did like the lot of you. Hanging on Mother, begging for an invite to all the right functions. It is so freeing to be able to tell you how happy I am to see you cut loose."

"Your beneficence will surely be rewarded."

"Benton will be declaring for me any day now, so I'm sure it shall be," she said blithely, flicking the edge of her bonnet.

Unless things had changed drastically in the past few weeks, Marietta doubted it. "Lord Benton will hardly choose you. He could have a diamond, and you are anything but."

Felicity's eyes narrowed but she continued to smile. "As if you'd know a diamond from paste. How many offers have you had, Marietta? Oh, and how many invitations have graced your door of late?"

"None," Marietta said with a calm she didn't feel. "As you are well aware."

"I am," she purred. "Have you read the papers lately? They say you've turned to whoring." She looked her over. "I will be happy to confirm it."

"Such a nasty word for a *lady* to use."

Marietta jumped. She had temporarily forgotten Gabriel. He had been steps ahead of her when she'd been grabbed. Felicity startled as well, turning her bonneted head to see who had addressed her.

Felicity's mouth dropped an inch and Marietta watched the cogs turn as her lips pulled into a brilliant smile. Gabriel was the most . . . well, just the *most* man she'd ever met. She had little doubt the same was true for Felicity. "Goodness. My apologies, sir. You are most correct. My acquaintance here does tend to bring out the worst in me."

"Do you always blame your actions on others?"

Felicity's mouth dropped again, but this time from a different kind of shock. "I beg your pardon?"

"You just said that you behaved poorly because your acquaintance brings out the worst in you." He leaned toward her, and Marietta saw her cheeks redden, both from his proximity and words. "Hardly taking responsibility for your own actions, are you, miss? It sounds to me like perhaps you just behave badly in general, and then make excuses for it."

"I do not behave badly! I am a high ranking member of society, sir." She smoothed her hands along her skirt and looked up with a new smile. "I assure you my manners are perfectly acceptable."

"To whom?"

Her smile dropped and her eyes widened. "Miss Winters, cousin, if you'd be so kind as to introduce us?" She'd never seen Felicity so flustered.

Marietta shrugged. "I can't help you there, Miss Tercake. I don't know him."

"Weren't you walking with a man?" She looked Gabriel over. "Oh. Must have been a different man."

"Are you calling her a whore again? Are you sure you are a lady?"

"My father's Baron Kilden!"

"I'm not familiar with the name. Foreign?"

"Irish!"

Gabriel rocked back on his heels, saying nothing.

"Why am I bothering to talk to you! You are nothing." She seemed to have gotten past his face and looked at his clothes, his longshoreman apparel. Unfortunately, her cheeks were still bright and she'd made a fool of herself over him already. "And you." She pointed at Marietta. "Don't show your face at our door asking for help."

She marched away. Gabriel watched her go. Marietta watched Gabriel.

"I see why you would have picked a stranger to help you first." He looked back to her, his eyes unreadable. "Come. Let's go home."

Chapter 14

She flipped through the *Times* again. There were plenty of articles and opinions on the Winters brothers working together on their murder spree. Mostly ugly ones like Felicity had crowed about, but a few articles were creeping in, scattered throughout, proclaiming doubt in their culpability. Describing a few instances where they were at a party or another function and couldn't have been off murdering women. Nathaniel Upholt was the journalist responsible for writing most of the positive ones.

In the end, it would all come down to the sway of the tide. And there were only a few more days until the trial would begin. Not much time.

Marietta sneaked a look around the kitchen to make sure Gabriel hadn't popped in, silent as usual. She'd heard cats that were louder when they pawed across a floor. She pulled the journal from beneath a pile of the papers. She had fetched it from his room again. This time from behind the door. She'd almost missed it after a thorough search. Clever man.

L.D.'s husband returns tonight, and with him his per-sonal servants and guard. L.D. says we need to re-instill the need for total silence in our little avenger. This is a dangerous night. One wrong word and our house of cards may fall. But not without the ruin of our little avenger's family. Total ruin and persecution, what music to my ears.

If I weren't so smitten by our little avenger, I might try it just to see the pain in his gorgeous eyes. I so enjoy watching others fall. It reminds me of what my mother used to always tell me—that others are born to serve our whims. That we are born to make, use, and cut the strings of all. That the chessboard moves when no one notices.

Marietta twirled a lock of hair around her finger as she continued to read. It was all so deliciously awful. That these were the actual thoughts of someone.

The back door opened. She swung forward in her seat and spilled her cup of water over the right end of the table. She hastily shoved the book beneath a pile of papers and looked forward, mimicking the most innocent look she could dredge up.

"Marietta, you look as if you have been caught with your fingers in the cook's pie."

Relief sunk her elbows onto the table. "Oh, thank goodness. Jeremy, what are you doing here?"

"Dropped by to see how my favorite brother and my favorite client of his are doing." He smiled winningly and sat across from her.

She arched a brow. "I'm sure. He is your only brother, is he not?"

He threw his head to the side, his smile growing. "Small quibbles, small quibbles."

Marietta drew the newspaper back. She desperately wanted to keep reading the journal. The only times she was able to were when Gabriel was out of the house, and this time he'd only stepped out for a moment. He would always invariably find the journal—how, she didn't know—and hide it once more. She was surprised he hadn't burned it, but he seemed to take perverse pleasure in hiding it from her.

"How is the search going?" He leaned back in his chair, reminiscent of his brother but with a younger, cockier air.

She needed to figure out how to hide the journal now that Jeremy appeared to be in for a long visit. It lay perilously close to his position. "We found a man who seems suspicious."

"Really? Who?"

She examined the papers around him. Perhaps if she moved that one . . .

"A servant. From the Dentry estate."

His chair whacked against the floor, also reminiscent of his brother. "What?"

She looked up at the bang. "Why, are you familiar with the servants there? Oh, that's right. You are from that area, yes?"

Jeremy's mouth pulled up, but the grin was strained. "Yes."

She frowned. "I shouldn't have said anything. I thought Gabriel discussed the case with you."

He waved a hand. "I've been out and about the last

week. Why don't you catch me up? How did a Dentry servant get involved?"

A faint hint of uncertainty spread through her. She liked Jeremy. But he was acting oddly. But then so too was Gabriel. The whole case was making her think strange thoughts.

"He was stalking the last victim."

His leg started bumping up and down. "You know who the last victim was? They haven't said a thing in the papers."

"Gabriel found out through a fence. Something about the woman's—" Marietta could hardly call her a lady. "—necklace."

"Her necklace?" He swallowed. "Interesting. How like Gabriel to put the pieces together so quickly."

She frowned. "Are you well, Jeremy?"

"I'm feeling a bit under the weather, now that you mention it. Do you know the victim's name?"

She chewed her lip, her uncertainty turning into flat discomfort. "I'm not sure I should be discussing it with you, if Gabriel hasn't said anything."

He leaned forward on his elbows, his eyes round and earnest, desperation lining his face. He reminded her so much of Kenny, though a slightly wiser and more handsome version. "Please, Marietta. Gabriel tries to protect me, and he needs to stop. He doesn't—"

One of his elbows slipped on a bulge in the papers. He looked down, pushing them to the side and unearthing the journal. "What's this?"

"Oh, nothing." She nervously tried to take it from him.

He opened the cover before she could. She watched his face darken. "Who was the servant you were chasing and why?"

"Jeremy—"

"Marietta, please."

"Jacob Worley."

He stared at her. "And you think him responsible?"

She fiddled with the paper under her fingers. "I think someone is responsible, and it's neither of my brothers. This Jacob Worley had constructed an altar to the murdered victims."

"A what?"

"Some sort of shrine with pictures and notes. Like a madman who has fallen in love with the people he kills."

Disgust curled his face. "A shrine? To them? That is disgusting."

Again there was an undercurrent flowing through the room that she couldn't comprehend. "I know. What goes through the mind of someone when they kill another person and then set up a shrine?"

He blinked, as if that hadn't been what he was saying.

"Where did you get this?" He hefted the journal.

"From the woman's house. It's horrible. She was horrible." She held out her hand. He didn't move. "Jeremy?"

"You shouldn't read something like this."

She made an impatient motion with her hand. "Yes, yes, I've heard that before. Give it here."

He didn't move, so she reached over and pulled it from his hands.

The sound of the front door opening made her jump, and she shoved the journal right back under the stack of papers. Jeremy raised a brow.

Gabriel walked into the kitchen and stopped dead. "What are you doing here?"

"Good afternoon to you too, dear brother."

"I thought you were back at school."

"I took a leave."

"You what?" Gabriel's voice was forbidding.

"I will go back next term, if everything works out."

"Explain yourself. If what works out?"

"My project. I have something I've been meaning to take care of for a long time."

"What type of project?" she asked.

"No." It was the first time she'd ever seen Gabriel look even remotely frightened. His features changed, and there was something terrifying in his expression. "Go back to school. I will have the carriage take you and I will talk to the dean."

"No." Jeremy stood. "I'm staying in London. You can't control me, Gabriel."

"I can. You *will* go back to school."

"Next term."

"*This* term."

"No."

"Yes."

Marietta stood to leave.

Gabriel pointed at her. "Sit."

She sat. She immediately stood again, irritated with herself for following the command. "Why don't you listen to what Jeremy has to say?"

"Because I don't care what he has to say. He is going back to school *today*."

Jeremy's face was a picture of hurt and determination. "No, Gabriel. If you force the issue, I will cut off contact."

Marietta caught the devastation on Gabriel's face before it disappeared behind a mask of iron. "I'll cut off your allowance."

Jeremy opened his mouth. Whatever came out next from either of them was going to be unforgivable, she could feel it in the way their eyes flashed and their stances both turned into a mirror of aggressiveness. She cut Jeremy off and turned to Gabriel. "Why are you doing this? Just ask him what his project is."

"I don't *want to know* what his project is." She wasn't sure which was worse, the pain in Gabriel's eyes or the pain in Jeremy's.

"That's right," Jeremy said. "It's only your pain, Gabriel. Your way to ignore everything and maybe it will just *go away*." He swept his hand over the papers on the table, scattering them to the floor. A corner of the journal peeked from beneath the mess still on the scarred oak.

Marietta heard a trickle of water somewhere. They all stared at the journal. It just sat there staring back.

"Goddammit, Marietta!" Gabriel jerked the journal from the pile, spraying papers further. He stormed from the room and upstairs. There was a loud whack as he threw it against something.

Jeremy's eyes met hers. "Good-bye, Marietta."

"Jeremy, wait."

237

But he had already opened the door and slammed it behind him.

Marietta sank into her chair and looked at the papers before her.

Gabriel walked back in and clanged a pot on the high table. Then a spoon into the pot, then a container on the table. He started throwing things into the pot, and she stared numbly at his back.

He stirred the pot, his elbow making a small circuit. "We are going over to the East End tonight." His voice was completely calm, as if nothing untoward had occurred, as if the spoon wasn't scraping the sides and battering the metal.

"What?"

"Jacob Worley was spotted there. We are going to see if we can find him."

"What about Jeremy?"

His shoulders tensed. "What about him?"

"Aren't you going to do anything?"

"Yes, I'm going to find Jacob Worley."

"No! Aren't you going to do anything about Jeremy?"

"That is none of your concern."

"You made it my concern when you argued in front of me. When you told me to *sit*."

He continued stirring.

"You hurt Jeremy."

"Marietta . . . " His voice was forbidding.

She argued with Mark all the time, but Mark had always been slightly apart from Kenny and her. This was more as if she'd argued with Kenny. To see his face like Jeremy's had been.

"But—"

The spoon hit the bottom of the pot. "No!" His shoulders bowed forward. "You don't understand. Please leave it."

Her mouth parted. He had never said please to her before.

"Very well," she said softly.

She moved to his side, picked up an onion and began peeling the skin. His shoulders relaxed a fraction and she said nothing more.

The tavern was dim and filled with less savory types. The Clerkenwell area taverns, though raucous and bawdy, at least had none of this overt sense of menace. The patrons' shifty eyes and disappearing hands. Marietta touched the pistol in her pocket. Her lessons so long ago might finally be needed.

Gabriel threw a coin onto the table, and before she knew it two ales were in front of them. She worked up a smile. This ale looked about the same way the tavern did. Shady. There was something floating in the liquid that she didn't want to identify.

The man who had delivered the mugs stood before the table, a towel over his shoulder. Gabriel held out his hand, and when the man shook it, a glint of metal passed between them.

"We're looking for a man. About your height. Brown hair, blue eyes, with a scar running beneath his chin."

"I might know who you're talking about. What you want with him?"

"This is his sister. He hasn't been home in a fortnight. Family is worried sick."

Marietta read the look in the man's eye. He didn't believe a word, but then he didn't look as if he cared either.

"Bad business making family worry. Bloke fitting that description was in here yesterday. Talked to Denise." He pointed at a girl in a tight dress. "Moved off in a hurry."

Gabriel handed the man another coin. The man walked over and said something to Denise.

Gabriel leaned into her. "What do my eyes say, Marietta?"

She jerked to look at him. His eyes were smoky and bright green. "They say you are intrigued."

"Tut tut, Marietta. You are losing your touch." A bit of challenge entered his gaze.

She swallowed. "They say you are about to kiss me."

A slow smile worked over his lips. "Much better."

"But we don't need—"

His mouth swept hers. His tongue teased hers. His hands pulled her to him. Gabriel was never awkward or hasty. Always dominating. Always sure of himself.

He pulled away and she felt a quiver in her limbs. With one maneuver he could reduce her to jelly. No. Fire fueled her determination. She grabbed the front of his shirt and yanked him forward. Doing everything he had taught her. Pulling him into her and sending herself back.

She released him, breathing heavily. He stared at her, eyes wide, shock in the green depths.

"You still need me over here? Roger said you wanted to talk, but methinks you might be wanting something else," a voice said to her right.

Gabriel ignored the voice and continued to look at her, eyes back to regular size but unreadable.

Marietta gripped her mug and stared back.

Gabriel ripped his gaze away and motioned the woman to a seat. Denise sat. "Be needing a taste of another woman too? I can give you that." She cackled.

"It was said you talked to a man with a scar last night," Gabriel said, his voice clipped.

She took his measure. "Yeah, he was here. Took him home with me."

"You took him back to your room?"

She shrugged. "Seemed nice enough. Average tumble, but most days are like that, aren't they?" She gave him a once-over. "Other days promise a little more. Wouldn't mind being between the both of ya if you promise more of that display."

Marietta blinked.

"What can you tell me of him? Where did he go afterward? Did he say anything about where he would be?"

"Left right after. Most do. Said he would be back tonight. Not the first time that someone's made that promise and not kept it." She shrugged.

"Did he do anything odd?"

"Kept calling me Abigail. Told me to tell him he was a bad boy. Got to whip him. Right fun. Promised me more of the same." She shrugged again. "Don't really care what he calls me as long as I get me money. The whipping suited me just fine."

"You whipped him?" Marietta wasn't sure what she was more appalled by.

"Lor, some blokes like that. Where'd you come up from?" She looked her over, her eyes narrowing. "Ah, so you's one of them. Getting your skirt up for the adventure." She shrugged. "Might want to hide that accent."

Gabriel squeezed Marietta's suddenly tightened thigh. "Thank you." He slid a coin over.

"I'm here anytime you have need of me." She sent them a sly look and ambled off.

They left the tavern. Gabriel swore.

"He knew we'd be here."

"Maybe he just figured it was time to move on."

"No. Worley wouldn't miss the opportunity for more of the activities she described. Not from what the investigator's notes say. Somehow he knew we were coming."

"What will we do now?"

"He'll turn up if he doesn't leave London. And Dresden is after him too. The roads will be watched."

"Won't they hold off Kenny's trial, then?"

Gabriel grimaced. "No. We just have to provide enough evidence for him to get through it. I need to visit Cold Bath and give the latest batch of papers to Oscar. He will get them to your brother. Just hope that your brother will put his brain toward something other than the latest fashions."

Marietta peeked under the bed. She had only ten minutes or so to locate it. Gabriel always went through his tasks quickly and efficiently. And Lord knew, Oscar didn't waste any time on pleasantries.

It was always somewhere in his room where it didn't

touch his personal items. As if he couldn't bear to hide it amidst his belongings. She'd made the mistake of going through his things once. They all smelled of him. Warm and protective.

She crouched on the floor and peered underneath the serpentine chest, cheek pressed to the hardwood. Success! Her knees squeaked against the wood planks and she pushed her hand to the back, grabbing the edge of the leather and sliding it across the floor.

She was morbidly lost in the words as soon as she opened the tome.

We'll be moving to a new place for the summer. It will be painful not to see him, to hear his unwitting groans (how I ache just thinking of their music! so rare for him these days!) and to be away from his stoic glare, but we have a new candidate while we are away. Nothing like our little avenger, but enough to let us play. And a tantalizing step into a new caste. I don't know if it will be worth it, but C.F. assures that he will be.

Perhaps we can introduce him to our little avenger, should all go well. A.F. is anxious to have her titillations tested even before we've broken this one to the saddle. I see defiance already in the new one's stare. He thinks he stands upon the world, but will soon discover that we stand upon all.

Footsteps alerted her and she shoved the book under the chest, then quickly rose and moved away.

Gabriel entered, his eyes immediately falling on her. "Such a fair presence in a rather boring bedroom."

She smiled as brightly as she could manage.

"You were looking for the journal again, I see."

She said nothing. He moved to the chest and tossed his cap on top. He turned and leaned against it, uncuffing one sleeve as he watched her.

"Not even a word in protest? I'm shocked, Marietta."

She gave up her halfhearted pretense. "Why? You already know full well my purpose."

"But not the reason behind it."

She crossed her arms over her waist. "It's interesting."

"A madwoman's rambles?"

"She wasn't mad, not really. She was just not normal."

A dark smile graced his features. "So few of us are."

Frustration set in. "There is no reason for me not to read that journal. I'm a grown woman. You aren't protecting me from anything."

"Perhaps it is not you who I'm protecting." He said it in such a casual manner as he undid his other sleeve that she had to repeat the statement in her head to understand.

"Who would you be protecting? You don't know any of the people in the book."

He stepped toward her. "What would you say if I told you that I did? That I knew everyone in that book?" He circled around her. She hated when he did that. It made her feel out of control and small.

"I would say that you were lying."

"You wouldn't believe me?"

"You would be lying about *something*. Whether it be this or your lies of omission at the beginning."

"Ah." He trailed a hand along her neck. "And you don't forgive easily, do you, Marietta?"

"No." It was a failing she had never been able to overcome.

"You still haven't forgiven Mark. Or your parents. Or Kenneth. Or yourself."

She stiffened. "I have nothing to forgive myself for."

"No?"

"You are changing the subject. Do you know *anything* about the book?"

"Mmmm. Possibly. Possibly I know nearly every person referenced within."

She spun, but he somehow stayed right behind her, his lips brushing her ear.

"What would you do to me if I knew? If I knew exactly who killed all those women and chose not to let your brother go?"

So this is what it felt like to be launched from a cannon. "What?"

"Would you feel betrayed? Have you fallen for me, Marietta?" His hands slipped down her sides and pulled her against him.

"What?" she whispered. It was the only word she seemed capable of speaking.

His lips touched her neck. "Have you fallen for me, Marietta?"

Sudden clarity pierced her panic. "You utter bastard." She spun away from him. "You are testing me. Why do you do this? Have I not proven trustworthy?

Have I not followed you blindly? I even gave you my virginity!"

"Do you think that I seek blind followers?" His eyes were unreadable and dark. Watching. Testing.

"I don't know." She wanted to scream. She wanted to leave. What right did he have, the utter *cad*.

"That kiss in the tavern—what were you trying to do?"

"My kiss? You always kiss me like that! How dare—what—how—when . . . *argh*!" She gave in to the urge. "You will need to admit me to Bedlam when we are through. Do you do this to everyone you work with? I'll bet you did it to Oscar. He seems two steps away. What's wrong with Anthony and Frank and Clarisse and Mrs. Rosaire?"

"I never did a thing to them." The bastard had the nerve to look amused.

"I am the lucky one, then? Joy. So then, which is it? Testing me, or do you know who is in the journal?"

He looked away, toward the mounted clock. "I'm testing you, of course."

"Always testing. What will happen . . . after?"

He leaned back against the wave of the serpentine chest and worked at the buttons on his shirt, sliding one out through the hole, then another, without looking away from her. "After?"

She kept contact with his incredible eyes. "After Kenny is free. Or if—" She rolled her lips in. "Or if he isn't."

"Are you asking what will happen between the two of us in that case?"

"Yes."

He studied her. Then leaned forward and pushed a strand of hair behind her ear, his fingers curling around the lobe. "That too will be your choice. I make no promises. I can't. But I will not intentionally hurt you. To some, virginity is a sacred thing. For my own reasons I do not find it such. I value much more the choices one makes than the actual state of one's chastity."

"You have slept with so many?"

His eyes darkened. "Not so many as I see reflected in your gaze. While I find the pleasure usually to my taste, it takes much for me to find a partner that invokes it."

"Then Carla?" She had been wanting to ask that question for weeks.

He looked amused. "Your maid? No, not to my taste at all."

She thought of the pleasured noise the maid had made. The abundance of information he had gleaned.

"Ah, but you don't believe me." He tipped her chin up. "There is no way for me to prove it, and little reason for me to try at this stage. But I did challenge you to try and read me. And you were doing remarkably well."

She looked in his eyes. Read the fire and truth there.

"The end of this endeavor may be a slippery thing. But the challenge will remain."

His lips touched hers, just a fleeting touch.

"Do you continue to accept it?"

"Yes," she whispered. Confused and warm. She wanted to understand him. She wanted the comfort

247

and security she felt in his presence. She wanted him.

She just had to give up the control. Such a minor thing. Such a major thing.

He divested them both of their clothes quickly and pushed her against the wooden support of the four poster. Rocked her into it, teased her against it.

He took control just as he had before. Every time. Teasing and taunting her. Pulling her strings tight. Demanding her response. Responses her body was more than happy to give.

He laid her on the bed and connected them fully.

"What do you see in my eyes now, Marietta?" He pushed into her slowly. She could barely think straight. Could barely keep her eyes open and focused.

"What do you see, Marietta? Come, don't make me punish you." He withdrew so that just the tip of him was encased, making slow circles at her entrance, her hands bunching the sheets beneath to keep from hugging him and forcing him back inside.

"I want to know what those lovely brown eyes see." He made a quick stab, only halfway in, and her breath caught, a gurgle escaping her throat. "Tell me, Marietta, come on, lovely one," he coaxed.

What was he trying to get her to say? She'd tell him anything at this point!

He thrust all the way in, pushing her up the sheets, and her entire body moaned. Her hand wound around his neck, into the silky dark hair at his nape. He stopped moving, another form of torture. She tried to move beneath him, but he had her pinned below. He was leaning fully on his hands, the muscles in his arms bunched and tight, so the top half of her was free, but the pivotal point for her to move below was in his total control.

She squeezed him inside, desperately trying anything, intuitively doing the only thing left that she could. He went totally still. She squeezed him again, and a third time, the squeezes getting weaker but her desperation growing—hoping that they would make him lose control and move again.

He leaned down and chuckled in her ear, his hips rotating and making her forget to squeeze. "You are a naughty woman, Marietta Winters. I think your naughtiness should be rewarded. But first you have to answer my question."

He thrust deeply again. Darkness covered her vision for a moment, her mouth opened in a silent scream. He pulled back so that he was almost out. An ache throbbed through her so intensely that she nearly begged for him to end it. To continue it. To give her more.

A tongue swiped her nipple. His roughened cheek grazed her throat, her cheek, as his lips trailed across her and settled on her open mouth. She kissed him, pulling him against her, her hands still wrapped in the hair at his nape. His tongue invaded her mouth and claimed her. He slipped a little farther inside her from the movement and she tried to squeeze him again.

His mouth pulled away from hers and she found herself looking into brilliant green eyes, brighter than she'd ever seen them, almost too bright to look at, no more than a few inches above her own.

"I see desire." She licked her lips, the taste of him all over her. "And secrets still beyond my understanding."

"Yes. And?"

She didn't want to say what she saw there. It would be too embarrassing were she to be wrong. "Friendship?"

Now he just looked amused.

"Companionship?"

His lips quirked. He leaned down and his breath brushed her ear as he gently sucked on the lobe. "Interesting. Do you want your reward?"

Her heart picked up its beat once more. "Yes."

He moved inside her, a soft thrust that lit her nerves on fire. He moved again, slowly and deeply, hitting a place far up. Her cheeks were aflame, her throat on fire. There was a lovely feeling of completion moving toward her. It wouldn't take a minute more.

"Do you like that, sweetheart? Do you want a rolling wave or do you want to cap it off with an end like our table dance?"

She squeezed him again and something wild flashed through his eyes. She didn't get a chance to say a word before he pulled back and thrust fast and deeply inside her. And then again. And again. She moaned something or said something or shouted something as she went flying through the air, convulsing feverishly around him as he continued to fill and stroke her.

And she thought, maybe . . . maybe she'd gone and done the stupid thing and fallen in love.

Chapter 15

Marietta was awakened by a door slamming. The ceiling of Gabriel's room shot into view. Footsteps banged through the downstairs hallway, and she glanced at the empty pillow next to hers. Loud voices and something crashing against the floor had her pulling on her robe and running down the stairs.

She was surprised to see Jeremy and Alcroft in the kitchen, pacing back and forth in front of Gabriel. Even with their movement, Gabriel was the one who appeared to be on the prowl.

"This is serious, Gabriel," Alcroft said.

"I know that, John," he snapped.

She stood poised on the threshold, almost afraid to ask. "What has happened?"

Alcroft and Jeremy immediately looked her way. Gabriel did not, but she was sure he had known she was there. He always did.

Alcroft looked apologetic. "Another murder. A member of the ton." He glanced back at Gabriel, then focused on her once more. "London is in an uproar. All of the suspicion that has lessened toward your brothers is completely gone. They are calling for their heads. The trial is set to begin, and it does not look good, Miss Winters."

"Dammit, John!" His voice was harsh.

"She has to know, Gabriel."

"Who was it?" She walked farther into the room, the cold floor seeping into her feet, and then felt nothing, numbness setting in.

"Anastasia Rasen."

A pink fluttering bird flew across her mind. Marietta knew her. Not well, but she knew her. The whole situation just kept crawling closer.

"And they are blaming Mark?"

"They have no one else to blame. No other name on their lips." Alcroft's face was lined with sympathy.

"What about Jacob Worley?"

"We need to be hard-nosed with the papers. Whisper in the right ears. Reinvigorate the watch, put Dresden further on his trail. There is still a chance." Marietta wanted to hug Alcroft in that moment.

Jeremy's eyes were focused on the floor, but his gaze was vacant. Gabriel was staring at his brother's bent head.

"Why Anastasia Rasen?" she asked, for wont of anything else to say, her hands knotted in her robe.

Jeremy's mouth opened. Gabriel cut over the top of him.

"We don't know. Get dressed."

His voice wasn't unpleasant, but it was firm and brooked no argument. Closed and unapproachable, not how she'd thought the morning would be.

Before she could say anything he looked at her. His eyes closed briefly. When they reopened she read pain there. "Please. We need to hurry."

Alcroft and Jeremy's faces lit with surprise. She nodded and hurried back upstairs.

Alcroft whistled. "You are enamored."

Jeremy's eyes were narrowed as he nodded in agreement.

"I don't have time to deal with this," Gabriel said, pushing aside their questions. Tell me, what is happening? What type of damage needs containing?"

"The ton is beside itself, as can be expected," Alcroft said. "Would be even worse if they knew who all the victims were. Time is limited. They will figure it out shortly. You need to catch the man responsible."

Gabriel didn't look at his brother. "Jeremy, fetch the carriage."

Jeremy stalked from the room without a backward glance.

Alcroft watched him leave, and Gabriel worried that his friend knew exactly what was going on. "Catch the servant," Alcroft said, eyes serious.

"The servant is not responsible." Knives scraped across his skin at the admission. "We would be condemning an innocent man."

"An *innocent* man. Are you sure?" Alcroft asked, his eyes penetrating.

Gabriel stared at the scattered papers. "The net grows tighter. There is one place left to search. Two places, actually," he added.

"You are going to have to make a decision soon.

Will justice, protection, or revenge be your guide? Will you sacrifice the nobility you've always prized?"

"Justice has always been my guide." He could barely get the words out.

"Sometimes revenge *is* justice."

"I've taken my revenge. I did it without bloodshed."

"But another choice is upon you now. One thing you value will need to be sacrificed. If you could just let go of your damn nobility—"

Gabriel smacked the table. "It is all I have. All I've ever had."

Alcroft leaned closer. "You have justice. It doesn't have to end the way you think."

Gabriel stared at him. Alcroft was sympathetic, but he didn't understand. The mere thought of discussing it with his friend filled him with horror. Alcroft had led an easy life of privilege and respect. He would never be able to understand the conflict and despair.

Jeremy too had lived a life of privilege after those first years in hiding. Gabriel had given him everything. Had tried to keep him innocent of the situation. To protect Jeremy as no one had protected him.

"It doesn't have to end the way you are thinking," Alcroft repeated.

He had blamed his father for his blindness—the activities taking place right beneath his nose. His own son in trouble. His father had never argued the blame, his passive, upright control in full evidence as Gabriel railed. Their relationship, always formal and somewhat strained, had never recovered. But Jeremy didn't have that same strain. He visited their father often. He could have discovered any number of things during those visits.

"It is going to end just as I think. Unpleasantly."

The house on Wisteria Park was just as he'd expected. Frilly, pink, and gilded. Like a dying bird fluttering in its cage. He hated anything frilly and pink because it reminded him of Anastasia Rasen, and here he stood in the middle of her dollish kingdom.

The servants were blessedly absent, called to present themselves in front of their new master to see whether they would stay or go, but their absence wouldn't last long. And the danger of curious callers was ever present. There had been two knocks to the door already. They had to hurry.

"Why didn't Alcroft and Jeremy accompany us?" Marietta asked, poking through a drawer.

"I sent them on another task. We'll meet with them later."

He could barely look at Jeremy. He had never felt more of a coward. All it would take was a direct question to his brother. One question as to whether he was responsible and he'd know the answer. Whether or not Jeremy would tell him the truth, it would be apparent by the look on his face, the tone, the feel of his voice.

He'd never wanted to know an answer less. Jeremy's whereabouts were unaccounted for during the last two murders. He hadn't wanted to check the rest, the fear choking him. He hadn't tasted real fear in years, and yet here it was like an old friend come to call and deciding to stay for an extended visit.

His brother was what had kept him going. The person he was trying to save all those years ago. To lose him now was unacceptable.

"She always wore pink, but I didn't realize it was quite this level of obsession," Marietta said as she sorted through Anastasia's things.

He took a closer look. "What are you looking through?"

Marietta shrugged. "Her undergarments."

Women were strange.

"Why?"

"Some women hide things where they think men won't look. I'm hoping to find something here. What are we looking for, anyway?"

"Something to connect her to Jacob Worley. Anything unusual. Other than her overabundance of pink."

They spent another ten minutes searching when Marietta exclaimed. "I found a journal."

Cold seeped down his spine. "Let me have a look."

She clutched the book to her chest. "No. This time you can't use the excuse that she was a wretched woman."

He could definitely use that excuse, but his lips wouldn't form the words to connect her to him. He watched Marietta flip the first page. "Eighteen ten. She started her journal much sooner than Abigail, not that that has any relevance. 'It has come to my attention that it would be to my advantage to join a group of women led by Celeste F—'"

A crash downstairs swiveled both their heads.

"Stay here," he said, his heart drumming both from

the words she read and the unexpected noise. Would this nightmare never end?

Marietta watched him leave. It was probably a servant returning. How they were going to explain their presence, she didn't know. Gabriel had assured her he would take care of any servants, and if there was one thing Gabriel could do better than anyone else she knew, it was to charm someone to his way of thinking.

She looked down at the book in her hands. A group of women forming a group. A chill slid through her. She flipped the journal open to a random page toward the end.

Jane and I don't hold with this new addition. Mr. Moreton knows the boy, and should anything be said we will all be in dire straits. There are too many ties. Dangerous ties. I wonder if we've become too arrogant, too complacent. But it titillates Amanda—the thoughts of what we could do. To see him with our avenger.

Dear God. The journals were connected.

To see our avenger's extraordinary eyes darken to—

A hand covered her mouth and she was pulled back against a tall, hard body. "If you will kindly hand over the book?" a voice whispered against her ear.

Everything in front of her turned crystal and cold. The image of a man with a scar under his chin ran through her brain, colliding with the man gripping

257

her, though she couldn't see his face. Brisk fingers pried the journal from her fingers. "Thank you, Miss Winters. You've been a great help in recovering this."

She stood as still as she could, not knowing if there was a knife near her throat or a gun at her side. The hand around her mouth pulled her face to the side. "There is a lot you don't know about your *loyal* guardian. And what he will do. I'll be interested to see his choice in the end."

He shoved her and she fell face first on the bed. Complete terror raced through her and she pushed forward, throwing her body over the other side, falling onto her shoulder, scrambling to her knees to defend herself. There was no one there. The dark edge of a trouser leg disappeared through the connecting door. Faint footsteps treaded down the back stairs. She clutched the horrid pink coverlet, twisting it in her hands.

"Marietta? What are you doing?"

She whipped around to see Gabriel in the bedroom doorway, looking winded.

"There was a man. He grabbed me. Took the journal. Said—"

But Gabriel was already running past her, through the connecting door. Footsteps pounded down the back stairs. Surreptitiously, she looked around and backed herself into a corner to wait, staring at the rumpled covers, the divots and valleys in the clutched fabric.

He reappeared a few minutes later, disheveled and irritated. "He was already gone."

She examined the lines on her palms, the crisscrossing creases.

"Did you see what he looked like? He spoke to you?"

"He was behind me the whole time. He whispered." She traced a line. "He thanked me for finding the journal. They are connected, Gabriel. They were part of the same club."

Hands touched beneath her elbows, pulling her up. Fingers lifted her chin and eyes examined hers.

"That man was the murderer," she whispered, green eyes wavering in her view. "He had me."

Arms pulled her into his chest. "I have you now."

She hugged herself inside the carriage. She was glad they had taken the carriage for once. "Why do you think he let me go?"

Gabriel watched her. "If the journals are connected, then likely for the same reason that Kenny was left alive. That it is only his victims he intends to harm."

"He said—" She clutched the dress material under her fingers. "—that he would be interested to see who you choose in the end."

Though he hadn't been moving other than with the rocking of the carriage, his body stilled.

"What did he mean?" She watched him. Watched the flurry of emotions flit through his eyes.

He leaned forward. "Do you trust me, Marietta?"

Her fingers curled further into the material. Did she trust him? She had put all of her trust into him. If he betrayed her too, she didn't know what she'd have left. "Yes."

He ran a hand up her arm and loosened her fingers,

pulling them away and into his own. He repeated the gesture on the other side.

She let him pull her toward him, and he placed soft kisses on her neck, along her jawline, on her lips. He was trying to distract her, but at the moment she didn't care. She didn't want to think, just wanted to accept what he was offering.

He rapped on the trap five times in succession. They turned a corner, going in the opposite direction of the house.

He pulled her on top of him, so she was straddling him. The carriage rocked over the cobblestones, the swaying brushing them together. A thrust of her dress to the side and flick of his fingers across his own clothing and he was pushing inside of her, filling her, her body already ready. She kissed him fiercely and he clutched her hips, pulling her closer.

If he betrayed her . . . but no, how could he? Silly fears rearing like spitting snakes.

He hit that lovely spot deep inside. Over and over. And what was she doing thinking about trust and betrayal? She had hired him, she had come to him. He might not be hers forever, but he was at this moment.

He attacked her neck and she let her head dip back, clutching the hair at his nape as they rode to the rhythm of the stones. He kept pressing exactly where she needed him to, a lethargic, heavy, hot feeling overtaking her as she reached for that peak. She let him wash away the itchy skin and disgust of Anastasia Rasen's pink dollhouse, the sheer terror of the murderer's hands. Cleansing waves, but no answers.

She closed her eyes and let him push her over the

edge, stifling her breaths into his silky hair as she clutched him to her. He followed a second later, washing the lingering ill traces away.

She rested her forehead against the velveteen seat back. A mixture of drugged laxity and energy encompassed her. "There must have been something in Anastasia's journal."

He stiffened underneath her. "Do you really want to talk about that right at the moment?"

She smiled against the velvet, unable to see his expression, though she had no doubt it was put out. "I suppose not."

His whole body sighed. "There are a few places where we can inquire. Then I'm going to take you back to the house and make sure you can't walk for a week."

Marietta walked through the market, hair back in proper place, clothes back together. Gabriel was chatting with a crone selling trinkets in a ramshackle stall. He had stopped to chat with at least ten different vendors, none of whom would talk while she was present. *Too highborn*, one had said.

Gabriel had joked that she was bad for business. She couldn't help but begin to seriously agree. Any woman could take her place, following him around and going from tavern to tavern. Most women would do a long sight better at it than she. Her crisp accent did little to endear her to the lower classes and she was an anathema to the upper classes.

She was quite useless. And feeling quite maudlin, it appeared.

She sighed and touched a checkered scarf slipped

over the edge of a stall, her eyes skimming Gabriel as the crone handed him something. It seemed impossible that such a man could move between different levels of society so easily. Starting with only a smile—no, it was not hard to believe he could have started with his charm and succeeded with his intelligence and hard work.

Gifted by the heavens. Blessed beneath a star.

Though the shadows in his eyes, the expressions he sometimes tried to hide, said otherwise. Shadows she hadn't managed to breech. What would—

A hand gripped her arm and tugged her behind the stall and into a shallow alley behind the colorful rows.

Jacob Worley stood before her. Brown eyes containing a mix of earnestness and insanity.

She stepped back.

He stepped forward, and she readied herself to bolt. He held up his hands. "Don't leave." His voice was gravelly, unlike the night before. And his stature was somehow less. Smaller, less firm.

"Why would I stay? You've murdered five women."

His eyes grew watery. "I didn't. I'd never do such a thing, unless they asked it of me."

"Asked it of you?" The man was a bedlamite if she'd ever seen one.

"Following the rules. Always. So important. Miss Winstead and Mrs. Fomme and Lady—"

A flock of ravens cawed through the opening of the alley. Worley shook his head. "One more and then you are next. You must kill him before he kills you."

Hot terror flowed through her. "What?"

"Noble will kill you. Just like he killed the others."

Her jaw dropped. "You're mad."

He leaned forward and she pressed against the wall. "My ladies. Gone. His fault. Hates them. Wants revenge. Can't let him get the last. Melissande. Head of them all."

She couldn't gather breath. One part of her was screaming to run, the other was watching him in horrified fascination. He was like Abigail's twisted journal, only in reverse, the victim pining for the master.

"Kill him first. It's the only way. I tried. Too well protected from the outside. Must do it from within. You must. The only way. Must protect Melissande."

"Who is Melissande?"

But Jacob Worley was gone. Slipped back into the stalls to become a memory. A bad one.

Gabriel stood in the same spot a second later, eyes dark. "Marietta?"

Something spiked within her. New fear and lingering desire. "Yes?"

"Why are you back here? It's not safe." He motioned toward the market and she blindly followed him back into the crowded area.

How to respond? With a question, with the truth, with an accusation?

"I just had to catch my breath," she said.

Her mind had decided for her. Lied to him.

Worley's words circled her brain, battering and coy. Mrs. Fomme. Anastasia's journal had mentioned a Celeste F. Abigail's had mentioned a C. F. Celeste Fomme had been a dragon of society at one time, until something had driven her to the country. She hadn't attended ton events in years.

When Marietta had tried to mention the links between the journals, Gabriel had answered through seduction. He had pushed aside the matter, even with the overwhelming evidence of their import. She had let him push it aside, trusted him to return to it later.

The journal. She needed to read it. *Now.*

"I'm going to head back," she said, as nonchalantly as she could. "I'm only a burden to you here. I need to gather notes for Kenny's defense."

"I have already taken care of those papers. You approved them." His eyes turned unreadable.

She smiled. It took effort. "I thought I might go over them again and write out some memory aids. He stumbles when he gets nervous. He needs to remember what to say."

Hard green eyes watched her. His lips tightened, and for a moment she thought he would hold her there. "As you wish. Take the carriage. I will see you in an hour."

She bobbed her head and hurried away, her feet following her immediate need for flight instead of the more careful need to allay suspicion.

She saw Gabriel watching her as the carriage lurched forward. The carriage where they had . . . She shook her head, pulling her fingers from the soft cushions, the velvety blanket. She couldn't read his eyes from here, but his demeanor was dark. Accusatory. Murderous. Not like the lover he had been. A changeling. A seducer who always got his way.

It hadn't been Jacob Worley in Anastasia Rasen's house. It had been someone else. And Gabriel had been winded from running. Running from where?

An inkling of suspicion edged with terror seeped through her.

The carriage moved along the street. The horses seemed interested in a Sunday jaunt rather than getting her to the house in the speed she desired. She considered exiting and running ahead, but the horses were moving just fast enough to dissuade her.

She might need fresh running legs before the afternoon was over.

The carriage pulled in front of the house and she bolted from it before the horses came to a complete stop. The driver yelled something, but she just waved a hand and fumbled with the front door. It took three attempts of shoving her key into the lock before she finally managed to turn it. She flew up the stairs to his room and grasped blindly beneath the chest. There.

She scraped the journal across the floor and flipped it open.

January 2nd, 1813. L.D., C.F., J.M., A.F., T.R., and I have taken it upon ourselves to indulge in some fun. We have formed a club.

C.F. Celeste Fomme. A.F. Amanda Forester. J.M. Anastasia's journal had mentioned a Jane and Mr. Moreton. Jane Moreton. Anastasia? There was no A.R. She looked the initials over again and stopped. T.R. She had heard someone call Anastasia Rasen *Tasia* before. T.R.

All of the murdered women were part of this club and prominently mentioned in the journal Gabriel had been trying to keep her from. The journal he went dark over every time he caught her reading. He had reacted almost violently when she had read the part when they had found their favorite, the man of incomparable beauty with the gorgeous eyes—

The book slipped from her hands . . .

Gabriel. Archangel. Avenger.

. . . and slammed against the floor.

Chapter 16

Her heart stopped beating. She knew it did, for the house was entirely still. Nothing moving. Nothing making a sound. Not even her own heart.

How could—

What had—

This couldn't be happening—

Knock. Knock. Knock.

Marietta twirled on the hardwood and whacked her elbow into the chest. The staccato of raps echoed from the foyer.

What if it was Gabriel? Her pulse jumped, her heart kicking back into a full gallop. The pain in her elbow numbed as her breath grew short and her head grew light.

Knock. Knock. Knock.

No. Gabriel would simply walk in on cat feet. He could have murdered her where she sat, with her back to the door. She pushed off of the hardwood and gingerly walked through the doorway and into the hall. Her hand clutched the banister as the stairs rose to

267

view and she stepped on a creaky board that echoed her distress. Who would knock at the door?

Knock. Knock. Knock.

Mrs. Rosaire and Clarisse had keys. Jeremy seemed to possess one as well. And the servants from his Mayfair home—she had heard the one say he'd forgotten the key, so assuredly any of them would be able to enter.

Perhaps it was Jacob Worley come to murder her after causing her to separate from Gabriel. No, that didn't make sense. It hadn't been he in Anastasia's house—he didn't have the right build. And apart from that, he could have dispatched her in the alley. Besides, whether Jacob Worley was innocent or not, Gabriel . . . Gabriel had every reason to kill those women.

He had been telling the truth about knowing the participants in the journal. And then lied afterward, when he said he was testing her. She had thought him deliberately provocative, instead of playing some twisted game with her.

She hadn't seen his eyes. He had looked away when he said he didn't know the women in the club. That should have told her the truth right there.

Would you feel betrayed? Have you fallen for me, Marietta?

Dear God. She closed her eyes.

Knock. Knock. Knock.

He had every reason to kill those women. Maybe if he had told her that he knew them, explained—

"Gabriel, open the door," a cold distinguished voice intoned. "I know you are in there. You are slipping. I heard the floorboard."

Marietta paused at the top of the stairs, undecided. She could slip out the back, but what if this man, whoever he was, knew about the other door? What if there were others with him?

She made her decision, a safe one, and walked into her room. She secured her pistol and opened her window, sending a quick thank-you that it was facing the street.

She stuck her head through the open frame and looked down at the front stoop. A tall, severely dressed man was already looking her way, cataloging everything about her from the shoulders up. She said another thank-you that she hadn't changed from her servant's garb. She looked like just another maid in a house.

Albeit one sticking her head from a window.

"Mr. Noble isn't here presently. You can find him in the market. Good day."

She started to pull her head back inside.

"Hold." The man hadn't moved from his position, but his eyes had narrowed. "Who are you?"

"I'm Felicity, the maid." She took a stab at her distant cousin.

"You are not a maid."

"I assure you I am." She tilted her chin up.

"And I assure you that you are not. Come down from there, or I will assume that even though your speech and bearing are above a maid's, your manners are not."

Outrage washed through her, but she tamped it down, unwilling to let her pride be overcome by stupidity. "I do not wish to converse with you at present.

You may call for Mr. Noble at a future date or time, or you may search him out. Good day."

She pulled her head back through the frame and waited twenty beats of her racing heart. When she looked through the window again, he was gone. She grabbed her traveling case and pulled a shaky hand along her clothes. It would take her far too long to pack everything. She would have to abandon her things.

She glanced at her personal items. Notes, gifts, lockets, remembrances. No. She would have to take her memories with her and leave the physical representations behind. She grabbed only the items that were portable and held monetary value.

Tears pricked her eyes. No. Not yet. Later, when she was settled somewhere safe—a boardinghouse or neighbor who had never heard the name Gabriel Noble—then she would allow the tears to fall. Then she would figure out what she was going to do.

She gave herself five minutes to pack, and when the time was up, buckled her case and headed for the stairs, the journal secured in her shoulder bag. She would take as many of the documents in the kitchen as she could stuff into her bag.

Five more minutes. It was all she could risk. She had already been back at the house far too long. Gabriel could return any minute. He would walk through the front door. She would go through the kitchen.

She stepped into the kitchen and walked to the table, grabbing the first handful of papers and shoving them into her bag. Her hand was on the second handful when a voice stopped her.

"Lift your hand. Now."

She whirled to see the man from the front stoop standing in the shadows. Her hand went to her pocket, where she'd stowed her pistol.

"Don't move." He emerged from the shadows, pistol already in hand.

Marietta backed against the table as he walked toward her, tall and stately, examining her as if she were a bug to be squashed.

She wet her lips. "How did you get inside the house?" She knew she'd locked the door after her. And she hadn't heard a sound.

He remained motionless, the pistol held calmly in his hand. "I used a key. Who are you and what are you trying to steal?"

A small measure of relief rushed through her. He wasn't in the house because he was after her. He thought her a thief. Still a poor position to be in.

"I am simply a maid Mr. Noble hired. I'm cleaning up."

He raised a brow. "Gabriel never lets anyone touch his personal items or messes." He motioned at the table. "Let's try answering the question again."

Time was wasting. Gabriel could be home any minute. "You have to let me leave." She spread her hands. "I won't touch anything else. Everything I have packed is mine. I give you my word."

The journal might be stretching it, but it was hers, dammit.

"Why the hurry? What is your full name, *Felicity*?" His voice was commanding and conciliatory at the same time. As if part of him were in control and part in deference.

"My name is Felicity Rose. My brother is in trouble. I must get to him right away."

The last two statements were definitely true.

"Sit."

Marietta squared her shoulders. The man looked quite capable with a pistol in his hands, but she didn't think he would shoot her. There was something upright and noble about him.

Same impression she'd had about Gabriel.

She stepped forward before she could reconsider. "I must leave. Good day, sir."

"The documents you have just shoved into your bag are not yours. Remove them. Now. Then I will consider your request to leave."

If she could escape, it was worth it to leave them behind. She knew the facts of the case. Had already given Kenny what he needed to defend himself. The additional notes weren't worth her life. She nodded and pulled the papers out, quickly dumping them onto the table.

"There is still something in your bag. Remove it."

"It is only my journal. I had it before I appeared in this room."

The bag was ripped from her grasp and large hands deftly removed the book. He flipped the cover. An unidentifiable emotion flashed over his face. She pulled her own pistol from her pocket.

He looked up and his eyes briefly registered surprise before it was masked. "So you truly did have a weapon. Who would have thought a waif such as yourself so armed?"

"Quite." She motioned to the journal. "Put it in the bag and hand it back to me."

She needed the journal. It was the only link she had. And now that she knew the code, she knew all the answers were inside.

His pistol was back up and pointed in her direction in an instant. "We seem to be at an impasse, Miss Rose."

Damn, he moved quickly. "We do."

"How did you come to possess Abigail Winstead's journal?"

Surprise followed by deep terror was the only thing she possessed at the moment. "Her name isn't written inside. How did you know?"

"What I *don't* know is who you are and why you are here. Though I'm beginning to divine an answer to both."

The terror from his revelation and presence was offset slightly by his eyes, which mostly held curiosity.

"I need that journal, and I need to leave this house. Please."

"You are related to the Winters boy. Miss Marietta Winters, I presume? You have the look of your parents."

Her pistol wavered slightly before she steadied it. "You knew my parents?"

"No. But I saw them once."

"Who are you?" she whispered.

"Merely a butler. Or, I was a butler, I should say. Once a butler, always a butler."

That made an odd sort of sense. His mannerisms and carriage. The way he spoke. Dignified and censorious. Haughty, with a note of deference.

She licked her lips again. "Whose butler are, or were, you?"

"I was the butler to the Dentry estate. The personal butler of Lord Dentry." He gave a small bow, his pistol steady.

Dentry? She scooted around the table, keeping it in between them.

He cocked a brow. "Is something amiss?"

"You are the Dentry butler?" She laughed a little hysterically. "How do you know Gabriel Noble?"

Something passed over his face. "I see." His voice was measured. Darkness edged by resignation.

"What do you see?" She edged toward the door, bag firmly in one hand, pistol in the other. Her urge to leave the house suddenly outweighing her need for the journal.

The front door clicked open. Terror raced through her. Gabriel was home.

"I see that you know nothing about me," the man said.

She tried to keep her hysteria at a manageable level as she readied herself to open the door and bolt. "Why would I?"

"Gabriel? Marietta? You won't believe what I just found."

Marietta nearly sagged with relief at the sound of Jeremy's voice, then tensed again as she realized she couldn't trust him either.

Jeremy's handsome face came into view. He stopped dead, staring at the butler. "What are you doing here?"

"I'm here to discover what you two have become involved in."

"Nothing," Jeremy said quickly. "You should go back to the country."

The butler raised a brow. "I think not."

She reached forward and snatched the journal from him. Both men immediately turned to her.

"I'll let you two argue it out. Good afternoon." She inched toward the door again.

"Marietta, why do you have a gun?" Jeremy asked. "Why do you both have guns? What has happened here?"

"Nothing to worry over." She waved her free hand at him and clutched the journal, stepping back another foot.

"You are not leaving with that book, Miss Winters." The butler leveled his arm.

She forced her voice to be calm. "I am."

"Which book?"

The butler hesitated. "A journal that is not hers."

Jeremy stiffened. "Abigail Winstead's, then."

She wanted to scream from the frustration and absurdity, the secrets and lies. "I need it. I will send it to you after my brother is released. I promise." She clutched the book to her chest but held her pistol steady. "I won't tell," she whispered. "I'll do what I can to say nothing about him. I just want Kenny released."

Two piercing stares pinned her.

"I just want Kenny released—" Her voice broke.

"What do you mean, you'll do what you can to say nothing about him?"

She shook her head. The butler's eyes narrowed and he lowered his pistol. "You have the advantage now, Miss Winters. What do you mean?"

"I won't implicate him. As long as Kenny is released, we will disappear." Oh, God, Mark. She hadn't spared a thought to her older brother. Gabriel had him. He would be angry when he discovered her gone. And he could reach Mark before she could. Her brooch. She could trade it for a hack ride. She would make it. They could flee to the Continent. Or the colonies. Make a fresh start. Give up everything.

"Implicate whom?" the butler asked. It struck her that she didn't know his name.

Jeremy's face was pale. His lips tight. He must know.

She shook her head. "No." She inched toward the door and his gun rose slightly.

"I can't let you go until you tell me."

"No. I said I wouldn't implicate him, and I won't."

"Tell me."

Her head kept a continuous sideways motion, as if he would eventually understand.

"Yes, tell him, Marietta." She swung toward the kitchen door behind her and the pistol was ripped from her grasp. Gabriel stood there, leaning against the edge, arms crossed, pistol hanging loosely from his fingertips. "Tell him who you suspect."

Chapter 17

"**G**abriel!" Jeremy sounded strange, but she couldn't look his way. She could only stare at the man in front of her. He had come through the kitchen door after all. She couldn't even dredge up the emotion to call herself an idiot.

Gabriel didn't move, but his gaze shifted behind her, much as the butler had when she'd peered from the window. "Sir," he said to the butler. "I can't say I'm surprised to see you."

She slowly backed away from him. And away from the others—choosing the opposite corner. All exits blocked. No weapon. She felt around behind her for a knife—not that it would do much good against a bullet.

"As you shouldn't be," the butler said. "You should have notified me immediately."

Gabriel raised a brow. "It has been a long time since I've been under your control. I daresay I needn't have had to notify you at all."

Under his control? Marietta watched the byplay across the butler's face. Acknowledgment and pain.

"Jeremy sent you a note, I presume," Gabriel said.

"I didn't need a note after reading the papers."

Gabriel cocked his head in acknowledgment. "No, I don't suppose you would have."

"You knew I would show."

"There was little I could do about it."

"You could have *told* me."

Definitely pain this time. He practically exuded noble pain.

"There was no need," Gabriel said, negligently leaning against the doorway as if he didn't have a care in the world. "What was there to say? I ruled you out as the person responsible a week ago."

Ruled him out?

The man took a deep breath and drew himself up. "I see. I suppose I should thank you for your confidence, if not for your consideration."

Gabriel inclined his head. His eyes met hers and she froze in her search for a blade. "A veritable meeting of the damned. Shall we sit and discuss this like proper citizens, or begin shooting?"

The butler's pistol dropped. Jeremy shifted nervously before sitting. The butler took a seat as well. Gabriel still lounged in the door. "Well, Marietta, what will it be?"

"I hardly have a pistol with which to start shooting," she said with rancor.

"No, no you do not. I can't allow it, I'm afraid. Sit. There's no reason to be afraid. No killers in this house." His smile wasn't very friendly, all teeth and sneer, betrayal and hurt there that had no reason to be.

She walked stiffly to the table and sat as far from the others as her position allowed. Gabriel dropped into the remaining seat.

"Well, isn't this a happy scene."

"Gabriel—"

"A happy reunion, is it not?" Gabriel said, cutting the butler off.

She looked sharply to the others. Jeremy was still abnormally pale. Gabriel looked like a dark demon come to prey on their souls. The butler was impassive. His brows creased just the tiniest bit, just like Gabriel did when he . . .

The moment froze.

"Figured it out, did you?"

"Gabriel, leave her be."

She barely registered either remark.

"No," he said harshly. "I saw and heard what was happening before I entered. Answer the question, *Miss Winters.*"

"He is your father," she said numbly. "He is your tie to the Dentry estate. The reason you would have been around the estate so often. Why you would recognize Jacob Worley. You worked with him."

"A mere servant. Did I detect that part of the answer in your voice?" His tone was silky, dark, dangerous.

Jeremy shifted across the table. The butler—she didn't even know his name—remained impassive, though she detected a hint of disapproval as he too watched Gabriel.

"No, I didn't say that."

"Mmmm, sometimes there is no need to say so."

A lick of anger climbed her spine. "Whatever your

station in life, it doesn't allow you to play with the lives of others."

"I couldn't agree less." He leaned back, eyes hooded. "Your station in life directly impacts how much you can play with the lives of others and on what scale."

"That's horrible."

"Spare me your horror. The higher you are in society, the more with which you can get away. Own those people . . ." His eyes twinkled darkly. " . . . and you own everything."

The air grew thinner, harder to breathe. "No."

Gabriel, beautiful, and terrible in that beauty, leaned forward. "Oh, yes, *Marietta*."

"Gabriel," the butler barked. "That's enough."

"You are a guest in my house, Father. As mentioned before, I hardly need to take direction from you anymore." There was something black in his eyes. "Not that you ever showed much care for my direction, in any case."

The butler straightened, but even she could see, not knowing him at all, that Gabriel had shot him clean through. "Your mother and I—"

"Do not mention her in this." His voice was deadly. "If you had left us with—"

Jeremy's face had turned from white to red. "Gabriel, you cannot blame father for—"

"Really? And why not?"

"It's not fair."

Gabriel lifted a brow. "Fair? How interesting."

Marietta wondered if she had still been standing whether she might have been able to sneak out. Gabriel's eyes connected with hers, as if he'd read her mind.

"Don't even think it."

"Just let me go." Her voice was barely audible.

The skin around his eyes tightened. "No."

"Please."

Something flashed through his eyes and disappeared. "I think you have something to ask me." His tone was almost pleasant.

"No."

"Oh, yes. Ask me, Marietta. Ask me now."

Gabriel tightened his grip on the pistol. Her pistol, which she had been ready to use. From the corner of his eyes he saw the ends of a cobweb dangling from a thread, missed while cleaning. Unraveling now, like everything else.

I won't implicate him.

So he had come to this. Angrier at her than at his father, for no discernible reason. She had no reason to trust him. He had deliberately withheld the information from her. And yet, her response, without verifying anything with him first, without even *asking* if he had committed a crime, smacked of betrayal. He had known this girl barely a month. Had spent nearly every moment with her since, yes, but she was a speck on the carriage ride of his life. And yet . . . Yes, and yet.

Her lips pressed together more tightly. "No."

"Are you sure? Or do you just want to believe whatever your mind has conjured? Anything to get your brother released, correct? Why go after Worley, when you can present the watch—or even better, Dresden—with someone else? Someone Dresden hates? Someone society would love to see brought to his knees to make up for his galling success. A lowly son of a butler and governess. It would rectify the stain on society that I am. Another upstart removed."

"You are mad."

"A bit, I presume. Mad surely for believing anything of you." Bitterness. Fury.

Her lips pressed together and her eyes went watery. "Then we are mad together, aren't we? For I feel the same."

Jeremy and his father closed the door to the kitchen, their footsteps retreating through the house. Neither presence missed nor wanted at the moment.

"You were the one who came to me."

"And I thought I could trust you."

"No you didn't. You were brittle and edgy. You trusted no one. Don't rewrite our relationship."

"Our relationship? Is there such a thing? It seems you have been leading me around by the nose. Lying to me whenever it suits you."

"There is little point doing anything other than what suits me."

He watched the rage come over her face. The red and white mottled together, giving her color and depth and transforming the features he had long since abandoned thinking as plain into a face that was active and alive.

"You even lie to yourself."

"If it suits."

"You think that a dozen good deeds, a hundred, will make up for your sins?"

"It depends on the sin."

"Does it? Is that the justification you use?"

"That is the justification that everyone uses. Have you committed no sins to get your brother released, Marietta?"

"Yes, but I committed each knowingly. I didn't delude myself into thinking myself blameless. I didn't withhold information from you that was vital."

"You didn't have information that was vital."

"But you did."

"Nothing pertinent to you."

"It would have been pertinent to know you were raped! By five now very dead women!"

Silence split the air.

His fingers hurt from their grip. "And your question? Are you going to ask it now?"

Her heavy breathing filled the room. Strange, as he wondered if he would ever draw breath again.

"Those women. You knew them. You had every reason to want them dead."

"That isn't much of a question."

Her chest rose and fell, rose and fell. *She wasn't going to ask.* A strange sense of unreality gripped him. A feeling that he had been in this situation before, but standing on the other side. Unable to ask Jeremy. Unable to bear the answer. Unable to do anything except run away.

"They raped you."

He hated that word. The harsh sound of the long *a*. The way the *p* formed between puckered lips.

"Debatable, as I said before." He tried to keep his voice light, desperately fought against the emptiness in his head, in his gut.

"Not debatable. Not from Abigail Winstead's own hand."

"A madwoman's rambles?"

"Mad? Quite possibly. Rambles? I think not."

"You put too much stock in that book. Obsessed by it."

"Little wonder, when the object of it was with me all the time. Sleeping at my side."

"I seem to recall my bed being the one we shared."

Her color rose, angry and embarrassed. "I knew there was something about the book that called to me. Something in it I should read."

He buried his horror, his anger, beneath shallow disinterest. "I didn't realize you were into the perverse."

The pain and self-hatred not quite hidden as intended.

She reached out a hand to him and withdrew it just as quickly. Comfort automatically given, then consciously taken away.

He smiled bitterly. "Believe me, I don't need your comfort."

He watched her try to physically calm herself and it made him even angrier. She took a deep breath. "What they did was wrong."

"Spare me your pity. I hardly need it, any more than I need anything else from you." The tragedy of spite.

She looked down, pulled shaky hands together, then straightened her shoulders. "Very well."

"Your *question*, Miss Winters?" he bit out.

Her eyes connected with his. "Did you murder those women?"

He waited a few beats. "If not me, then who else?"

Her lips disappeared in a thin straight line. "That is not an answer."

"But if I give you an answer in the negative, that leaves you without a scapegrace. If I give you an answer in the positive, what will you do about it?"

"You were the one pushing for me to ask the question. Now *answer* it."

"Tell me, when would I have been able to murder the last two?"

She looked at the scattered papers. "You could have sneaked out to murder Anastasia Rasen while I was asleep."

"So stealthy, am I?"

"Yes, you are incredibly stealthy. Your upbringing explains that completely."

"The lowly servant that I am."

She gripped the table. "That's not what I meant."

"I see. You may want to rethink that in the future, Marietta. I think it is exactly what was meant."

"By my words, I meant that you have the stealth of someone who is used to getting around with no sound. Not bothering others."

"We can never bother our betters."

Frustration bent her brows. He felt little sympathy at the moment. The bile was there, choking him so that all he could do was spew it forth.

"Is that how you see me? As someone who thinks herself better?"

"Do you not? You think yourself better than Mark. Better than hapless Kenny. Better than your parents. Better than the others of your acquaintance who make mistakes. Tarred by your own tongue as judgmental and harsh."

The scathing words came so easily. The look on her face making him feel something other than his own pain. He ruthlessly shoved away everything that said he was hurting her. She was of the upper class. She had hurt him. She had pretended to care.

Why he had believed it was the question. Why had he bought into the thinking that she might have cared for him? *He didn't deserve it. He was tainted.*

"Nothing to say, Marietta?"

She lifted her chin. "You are right, of course. I am judgmental. And at times harsh. But I'm not a liar."

"Never?"

"I prefer frankness, even in my tactless, *harsh* manner."

"How refreshing," he deadpanned.

"How did you get me here? How did you convince Rockwood to send me your way?"

The unsettling sensation of something just beyond his reach fell over him.

"I didn't," he said succinctly. "You chose to come to me of your own free will. Unless that too you will lay at my feet. Have I overcome your will?" He leaned forward, lowering his eyes and cocking his head. "Made you do anything you didn't want to do?"

Her eyes hardened. "You use your sexuality well, Gabriel. I noticed it right away. It is hard to escape. Hard to avoid. You are good. Too good. Your teachers taught you well."

Anger, fear, something worse, coiled in his gut. It

looked like he wasn't the only one willing to get dirty in this game.

"Didn't you know?" she asked. "You look surprised. Sick, even." Her eyes were narrowed, something like grim satisfaction in the short smile. "You didn't honestly think that you weren't using all the tactics they taught you? Using them and hating yourself even *more* for it."

He was frozen to the spot.

"You didn't." Her voice held surprise. "Did you just expect that your self-loathing, your obvious hatred of the responses you get, was motivated by—what?" The grim satisfaction in her voice turned to pity and then hardened once more. "Well, Gabriel?"

"You have no idea of what you speak."

"Don't I?" She laughed, no humor in the sound. "Everything was as clear as the peal of a spring bell when I realized who you were. Who the man in the *journal* was. Abigail Winstead knew you well."

Gabriel snatched the book from the table. "She knew me well? She knew *nothing*." He threw the book so hard against the wall he heard the spine break. "She knew how to terrify little boys. She knew nothing about *me*."

Marietta swallowed and looked down. Gabriel heard an odd sound, then realized it was his own harsh breathing.

"Did you murder those women, Gabriel?"

"Right now I wish I had! But why would I *give* them that power over me? I *ruined* them. I made them *live* with it."

He had shocked her, it was written all over her face.

Right now he didn't care. He stood abruptly and tossed her pistol on the table, crushing a nut beneath. "Leave, if that is what you wish. Little rich girl gone poor and tattered. I'll get your brother out of prison and then *nothing*."

He didn't know how he got from the room.

Marietta wiped an angry tear as he slammed the door. The door hit so hard it clicked from its lock. She gripped the butt of the pistol tightly, dragging it across the exposed wood and spoiled papers. The heart of the crushed shell trailed beneath it.

The journal lay in the corner, crooked and awkward. Helpless. Malicious. Waiting like a predator feigning injury. The hapless prey sniffing near it only to be captured between crushing jaws.

Cruel. Terrible.

She pushed back from the table and stumbled to it, staring at it for a moment before picking it up between her thumb and forefinger. She dropped it into her bag.

The kitchen was silent. Eerie. She stood still. For once she had no plan. No course of action. Nothing to drive toward.

A noise, a muted voice, cut through the silence, and another joined it. The voices were far off, arguing, muffled by the nearly closed door.

Marietta found herself in front of the door. The one that led to the rest of the house, not the one that led away. She stared at the knotty wood. Her hand touched the oak—strange, as if the hand didn't belong to her. The hand pushed.

The voices led her through the hall and around the stairs to the small holding room to the west of the door. Four voices. Alcroft had joined the dysfunctional group, while she and Gabriel had been in the kitchen.

" . . . Worley is still out there," Alcroft was saying.

"It's not Worley," the butler said. She still didn't know his name.

"But Father—" Jeremy pleaded.

"He's right." Gabriel's voice was dark, eerily calm after his angry exit. "Worley worshipped those women."

"All the more reason to bring him to the magistrate," Alcroft said. "Something is off there."

"I agree with John," Jeremy was quick to add.

Silence.

"It's true, then." Jeremy's voice was tight, anguished. "You think I did it."

"Of course not." But Gabriel's voice was too dismissive.

Marietta felt something choke her. Like what she would have felt had a hot air balloon lifted from within her stomach.

"You're lying."

"Jeremy—"

"You are angry with Marietta for believing it was you, but how do you explain that you thought it was me, Gabriel? I am your flesh and blood. Your brother. And you think I am the killer, don't you?"

"I don't—"

"I didn't kill them, Gabriel." He sounded remarkably calm all of a sudden, just like his brother. "I would have happily dispatched them all to erase the past.

You didn't think I knew. Didn't think I *saw.* I *know* who saved me from them. I know more than you think. Father—"

"He had no right." Fury laced every word.

"—didn't have to say a word. I know more than he ever did. She approached me once, did you know?"

"Who?" Gabriel's voice was deadly.

"Lady Dentry."

Lady Dentry. L.D. Shivers ran through Marietta. *L.D.'s husband returns tonight, and with him his personal servants and guard. L.D. said we need to reinstill the need for total silence into our little avenger.*

His father had been the personal butler to Lord Dentry. She put her hand over her mouth as bile rose to hit the back of her tongue.

"I'll kill her."

"Of course. That will be perfect." Jeremy's sarcasm hardly reached her, as horrified and sick as she felt. The reality of the situation, of *Gabriel* being the man in the book, really hitting her.

"Out of all of them, she is the only one that remains."

"She never touched me. We left a week later. You succeeded." Jeremy sounded tired, bitter. "You remained the buffer, took all of the pain. Left me free."

"It should never have occurred in the first place." The butler's voice was filled with self-loathing.

"It did. None of this matters now." Gabriel cursed fluently. Creatively. A string of obscenities that lasted a good ten seconds. "And now, I have to. A nightmare come true."

"Have to what?"

"Alcroft, I need you to arrange an invite to the Dentry estate."

"What?"

"The bitch is the obvious next target."

"And you are going to save her?"

Gabriel remained silent. She felt the shock of the entire room. She wished she could see Gabriel's face.

"Gabriel, you can't possibly—" Jeremy started.

"I'm coming with you," Alcroft said.

"No. I need you to stay here. To delay the trial. Marietta's brother"—her vision filmed over at his words—"needs another day. Possibly two. Jeremy, I need you to help Alcroft."

"But—"

"I am accompanying you, Gabriel." Marietta felt the stillness in the air at the butler's pronouncement. "You don't need Alcroft to do a thing to get you onto the estate. You only need me."

"N—"

"And I will not accept your refusal. Once is quite enough in a parent's life to leave a child at mercy."

"I'm hardly a child. Besides, I've seen the bitch since, more than once."

"Nevertheless, you are not traveling without me."

Another long silence.

"As you wish." Gabriel's voice was subdued, neutral.

Marietta heard the scrape of chairs, the footsteps across the floor. She ran back to the kitchen.

Alcroft appeared in the door a few moments later, surprise on his face to see her. "Miss Winters."

Jeremy appeared behind him. "Marietta, we thought you'd left."

She could hear the front door close. Gabriel and his father leaving on their task. To see the woman who had spearheaded the club. To save the woman who had abused him.

"No." She met Jeremy's eyes. "Tell me how I can help."

Chapter 18

"I could hardly believe my ears, but here you are."

Gabriel said nothing as the blond, willowy woman walked through the door. Icy, amused eyes took him in from tip to stern.

"You look as delicious as the last time I saw you, Gabriel. What has it been, a year now?"

"About."

"Still as vocal as always." She laughed lightly as she stroked a hand along the brocade of a chair.

He watched her, leaning lazily against the wall, his indolent posture at odds with his heightened alertness. All emotions concerning Marietta pushed far below the surface—too easily used as weapons otherwise. "I see no reason to be loquacious with you."

"Oh, Gabriel." She walked to him. "Is that any way to speak to an old friend?"

"You are hardly a friend, Melissande."

"Mmmm . . . come, have a seat."

He waited for her to move toward the desk before

he pushed away from the wall. A few steps before she reached her desk she pivoted, smoothly turning into him, close enough to touch. He repressed the urge to clap at her strategy.

"Have you grown, Gabriel, since we last met?"

"Met? Is that your way of saying the last time you crawled into my town house, begging for me to pay you some attention?"

A laugh bubbled past her lips, her eyes glittering and focused. "You were always my favorite, Gabriel."

Smarmy bitch.

"The only one to give me a marvelous chase."

"I don't recall there being much of a chase."

"Chasing doesn't always mean in the physical sense." She tapped a long perfect finger against a button on his shirt. "Much too plebeian. No, the emotional element has always been more satisfying. The true test of character—who breaks last."

She moved to circle him. He walked forward and sat behind her desk, in her chair. He idly picked up a handful of documents, then put his feet on the edge.

He could see her lips pucker. She strode to the desk and sat in the chair on the other side. "I've taught you well, Gabriel."

"How to be a conniving bitch? Well, I can't let you take full credit. But have at it, please." He waved a hand over the papers.

"Though your manners have fallen."

"What are a few emotional acts of violence among friends, really?"

Her smile was tight. "Our little avenging angel."

He forced his muscles to relax. Her smile turned to satisfaction.

"You really did live up to the name. Ruined Celeste, Jane, and Abigail. Drove Tasia to drink. Ran Amanda out of the city. I'll bet it has always grated that you have been unable to ruin me."

She settled back in her guest chair, as if the hard back and seat were made of velvet instead of the purposely bony frame she favored—anything to keep her guests uncomfortable. "The coup de grace. The deviless. I was always flattered by the names you chose to call me. Drove Celeste crazy that you were angrier at me, even angrier at Abigail. Celeste always tried to think up new tortures to make you love her more." She smiled fondly. "Celeste was always a bit mad."

"She wasn't the only one, was she?" He smiled coldly and flipped through the papers fisted in his hands. Bills, correspondence. Ah, a half-finished note to someone named Tom. He would have to investigate to see who Tom was—and how old he was. Damn his missing investigator. Too long missing for it to be a coincidence.

Her smile continued its sunny path. "No, I don't believe she was. Jane is still a half step from Bedlam."

"Jane is firmly six feet in the dirt."

Her face froze, then recovered. "Gabriel, dear, have you been naughty?" Her eyes quickly scanned the desk.

He raised a brow. "Looking for something, Melissande?"

She smoothed a hand along the stomach of her dress, her figure impeccable, as it had always been. "Not at all."

"No weapon with which to defend yourself? Do you think your viper tongue will save you?"

At one time he would have fiercely celebrated the look of unease that crossed her face. Now he was tired. And angry.

"I'll bet you haven't heard from Celeste in a while? Or Amanda. Or dear, dear Abigail."

"What have you been up to, Gabriel? Truly living up to your name, are we? And here I thought you had always found it distasteful, despite your proclivities to help wretched souls too poor and desperate to deserve a second thought otherwise."

He crossed his ankles on the desk. "My, my, quite out of the gossip here, aren't you, Lady Dentry? Anastasia even made the headlines in London." He dragged his heels across the documents on her desk, skewing them as he halfheartedly searched. "Not even a recent paper? Has Lord Dentry finally caught on to you?"

"You wish it were so, Gabriel." She smoothed her hair, and he saw her surreptitiously glance around the room for something to aid her. She was far from stupid, and far, far from helpless despite her delicate looks and wide eyes. "My husband cares more for his political intrigues than his wife. He wouldn't notice if I chose to sleep my way through the ranks of the ton."

"You mean you haven't?" He feigned shock. "I'm disappointed."

She leaned forward. "Only the *young* men, Gabriel. Though I will always make an exception for you. I hate to admit it to you, but you *are* unparalleled." He watched how she leaned in, cocking her head just so, showing her best side.

Nausea stirred in him. He recognized that move. He had done it himself, just as he'd learned how to circle someone else and counter being circled. Something soul deep sickened at the realization. Other characteristics and gestures that he could identify marched through his head.

"You are next on the list, Lady Dentry."

Her fingers gripped the arm of her chair, though she was trying to project ease. "I assume that is why you are here, Gabriel. You always did have such a flair for the dramatic."

"I need the names of all the men who have received your 'favor' and perhaps been unhappy about it."

She froze. Her fingers uncurled. "Dear Gabriel." She laughed, relief flowing in her breezy voice. "You are here to save me. Oh how wonderful. The irony, the pain. Magnificent. Poor Abigail. Dead, you say? Pity. She would have reveled."

It took everything he had to sit in the chair. To wait her out. He could leave her to it. Leave her to her much deserved death.

"A list, Lady Dentry."

She leaned back, the relief strengthening her, and her innate confidence showing through. "Oh, but now that you are here and staying with me, we must renew our acquaintance. We have all the time in the world, Gabriel."

He tossed the papers on the desk. "You have ten minutes. Then I walk out the door. I couldn't care less if you live or if you die."

She raised a brow. "Then you wouldn't be here."

"I'm not here for *you*."

She smiled. "Do you know that out of all the young men we took under our wings, you were one of the few that didn't return."

"Somehow I doubt that."

"Some returned for more, slaves to our plans, two returned just so they could take their lives here. As some sort of statement. A deterrent to us? To me?" She waved a hand. "So messy, really. And Lord Dentry was not pleased."

"He knew?"

"Only that they stretched their necks, nothing more." She motioned to the desk. "And correspondence? I receive it by the handful from others."

He noticed an unopened stack in the corner and looked for an opener.

She waved. "My letter opener has been missing since last summer. I make Tom come in and open my mail." Her mouth curved. "The best thing, losing that opener. You should see what he can do with his tongue. Oh, don't look that way, Gabriel, Tom is twenty-two, plenty old enough to satisfy your absurd rules."

He split the top missive with his finger.

"Your brother is nearing that age, is he not? Jeremy was always so promising."

"You are nothing if not clever, Melissande," he said calmly. "Say another word about Jeremy, and I will complete the Middlesex murderer's final task for him."

He read the first line of the note from some fawning admirer, expecting her to retort. When she didn't, he looked up. Her face had gone white. A sliver of unease traveled down his spine. He finished reading the note, and by the time he was through, she had regained some of her color.

Her fingers shook as she ran a hand along the side of her hair, smoothing the imaginary escaped tendrils back into place. "What type of list did you say you needed?"

He twirled a quill and leaned back. "So compliant, all of a sudden? You'll make me think you cowed. Melissande Dentry, cowed."

"Mind your manners, Gabriel," she said calmly, with obviously more calm than she felt.

"Melissande, tut tut. You don't hold the power here."

"Even if you don't want your past uncovered?"

"I rebuffed your blackmail attempt at age twenty when you found me. It will hardly work now. I can simply play your game. I took what you so kindly 'offered.' A sixteen-year-old boy? Who would believe otherwise?" The bitterness and disgust made him twitch, and he moved his feet to the right. He smiled, a stock smile that he had learned from the master, one full of innuendo and guile. "Easy enough to make you the deviant in this story. Especially since all of your co-conspirators are dead."

"Our journals—"

He idly twirled the quill again, not feeling the ease he was trying to project. "There is only yours left. And I wonder what it shows? No doubt it is no credit to you. There is little that could be, if it is of your creation."

Her lips tightened. Fear and anger making her deceivingly lovely face twist into petulant lines.

He tossed the quill on the desk. "I grow tired of this. Whatever your ignorance of the fates of your 'friends,' you have obviously heard of the Middlesex murderer, judging by your reaction. I've never seen you so scared, Lady Dentry."

"I'm sure you are enjoying the moment, Gabriel."

He tipped his head back. "It would surely behoove you to think so."

The dark thought continued to swirl in his mind that he was doing exactly what Marietta had accused him of—using the tricks he hated. "Now give me the list."

She picked up the quill and dipped it. "I was so disappointed when we returned from London and you had disappeared. The club was never quite the same."

"Good."

"Your father was never the same either."

He said nothing.

"I always suspected he helped you and your brother leave. I punished him for it. I told you that I would."

"He accepted the consequences." Gabriel remembered their conversation. His father's anguish. His own mortification and anger, pushed onto a new target. There was still a part of him horrified that he hadn't stayed and saved his father the pain. One victim to take the place of more.

"He was the one person I couldn't directly touch." She smiled humorlessly at his surprise. "A bit of a bluff on my part. Your father was too close to my husband. Relied on far more than I," she said bitterly. "Still, I made things . . . uncomfortable for him. I'm quite good at that."

Gabriel slit the next note in her stack with his finger, not answering.

"You were always so fun. Deporting yourself like royalty. Full of knowledge garnered from your mother and with all the secrets of your father. Running around the estate with all of your friends, from low to high, and every female enraptured by you. A ravishing prince. I've seen no one like you since."

He continued to read. He knew that if there was one thing Melissande hated, it was being ignored. Her husband had never learned that truth, and therefore never learned why his luck changed whenever he slighted her.

"How is dear John? I haven't seen him in nearly a year. Still thick as thieves, you two? A miracle you were able to separate."

He could see that she was reaching the end of her tether, and decided to throw her a crumb. It was never wise to bait a dangerous animal. They had the tendency to find a way to bite you through the cage. "John is well. Ask him yourself."

"Away at school while you were stuck here under my thumb. Must have been hard." She continued writing. "Dentry's ward. As untouchable as your father."

John had been the lucky one. "With so many servants and village boys to choose from, I'm sure you didn't suffer."

"Mmmm. So who is the murderer?" She perked up a bit, either at the subject change or that he was responding to her.

"And I would know this, how?"

"Because you know everything, Gabriel."

Not everything. He had obviously not even known himself. "Why would I ask for a list?"

"Morbid curiosity? A way to help my poor victims?"

"I'm terrible at sympathy. I did what I could by stopping your club. While lacking in sympathy, I'm quite good at prevention and revenge."

"Lacking in sympathy? With all those pathetic souls you help? It's terribly amusing. Do you think you can compensate? Do you find peace? I hope not. All my hard work gone to waste." Her eyes glittered. "My favorite creation destroyed. It would break my heart."

"You give yourself too much credit. Abigail was far more terrifying."

He watched the spark go through her eyes. "You are a terrible liar, Gabriel. But I will forgive you."

"I feel indisposed to do the same."

"Pity." She pushed the paper across the desk. "There is your list. Woefully short. Most of the victims, as you deem them, quite enjoyed themselves."

"Especially the ones with rope burns across their necks." He scraped the list from the desk. "A *pleasure*, as always."

"You are leaving? You aren't staying here to protect me?"

Desperate for company as always, in the absence of her husband's regard.

He lifted a brow. "Prevention, Lady Dentry. Other than that, you are on your own. Perhaps you should inform your husband of the circumstances?"

Her lips squished together.

"No? I bid you adieu."

He found his father in the kitchen, chatting with the servants. He hadn't wanted to stay out of the confrontation, but Gabriel had refused him. It would have been a show of weakness to have been accompanied. Unacceptable.

His father didn't ask how he was, but he rested a hand briefly on his back as they walked, dropping it just as quickly. Still, the gesture filled Gabriel with warmth and shame. That he had blamed his father at all . . .

"What did you find, Gabriel?"

Names, familiar and unfamiliar, leapt up as he passed the list. There were a lot of things to do and people to contact, and not much time in which to do so.

"Two of these men were in London last I knew," his father said. "Lord Dentry will be back tomorrow. Let me talk to him."

His father still retained a relationship with the man.

Gabriel hesitated. Bringing in Dentry would complicate matters. "Very well."

Their trip back to London was mostly silent, but comfortable for the first time in a long while. They usually went through bouts of cordiality and strife.

His father separated from him as they reached the drive. "I will make inquiries into these two."

"I will see you back here later."

Gabriel strode into the Middlesex house. He wondered if Jeremy and John had finished their tasks. His steps echoed in the empty house, up the empty stairs. Empty of Marietta, who was somewhere else, somewhere his murdering self was not. Every one of his repressed emotions tripped over themselves, racing to the surface. Anger, pain, betrayal, longing, fear. He viciously tugged his cravat. He should have gone back to his Mayfair house and his valet. Why had he come here?

If she hadn't hated him before, she surely did now. Daggered comments. Cruel remarks. He'd taken his pain and rage and twisted it against her. And even though she had done the same, it still made him feel ill. Unforgivable.

Why had he come here?

He ripped the cravat from his neck and tossed it on the side table in his room, then worked on the buttons of his shirt. He opened the linen press to grab a change of clothing and froze as he looked into the mirror above the table.

"Marietta."

Chapter 19

Gabriel slowly closed the linen press and turned around. She was sitting in a chair in the corner—her legs pressed together and to the side, her hands folded in her lap—the calm presence of a lady but for the nervous twitch in her right foot.

"Gabriel."

He leaned against the press and fiddled with his cuffs, not looking away from her. "I thought you would be well away from here."

"I did leave—to help Jeremy and Alcroft with their task."

He watched her, unsure what was happening or where he stood. His freed emotions tore the foundations of the cage he had constructed for them. Perhaps for good.

"I returned," she said.

"I see." He carefully placed a link on the side table, like a hunter not wanting to frighten the hunted away with any sudden movements.

"Do you?"

He touched his other cuff, for once completely unsure of himself and how to answer. He shook his head without taking his gaze away.

"I know you didn't murder those women, Gabriel."

"That is good to know." He carefully removed the other link and set it down too, his eyes still on hers. "When did you figure this out?"

"I knew by the end of the conversation in the kitchen this morning." The word *conversation* was a bit off as a description. "And then I heard you speaking in the other room."

"Eavesdropping?"

Her right foot stilled. "Yes."

He nodded. "That doesn't explain why you are still here. I gathered that you wished yourself far from this house."

"And I gathered that you wished me far from here."

"Double the reasons for you not to appear. Why are you here, Marietta?"

He *wanted* her here. But he couldn't let things go. Couldn't let things stand. He expected, feared, that she'd walk from the room at his question.

"I came to apologize. For what I said to you at the end. About—About them. And for thinking you the murderer."

He undid the last button on his expensive shirt and shrugged it off, pulling one sleeve down at a time. "I was in a rather dubious position, as it was." He kept his voice even and calm, deliberately evading the first part of her apology and answering the last. "I shouldn't have expected you to trust me."

"You don't think highly of me, I know." Her head was high and she continued to meet his eyes.

"On the contrary, I think you quite extraordinary." He looked down and took hold of his undershirt.

"What?"

"I think you quite extraordinary." He used the action of pulling off his undershirt to hide his face. Bare to the waist, he didn't feel as naked now that there was more exposed than just his expression.

"I don't understand. I thought you said I was judgmental and harsh." The little bob in her throat betrayed her nerves and calmed his.

He tossed the shirt aside. "Those qualities combined with your others make you more extraordinary, not less."

"I don't understand."

"You told me I used my sexuality against others." He changed the topic and leaned against the press, his fingers touching the tops of his trousers.

"You do," she whispered, her body framed for flight. Or framed to stop *him* from flight.

"It is a very useful weapon. I learned to use everything at my disposal." He slid a finger along the button at the top.

"But you have plenty of weapons at your disposal now. You don't need to use it, if you don't want. If it bothers you, and I can see it does."

Something thrummed through him. Excitement. Increased nerves. "You are still watching me, reading my eyes. I don't know whether to be pleased or worried."

"It depends on what you have in mind."

"Yes, I suppose it would at that."

He undid the button and ran his fingers along the second.

"Gabriel, I—I still want to be part of the search. I know you told me to leave . . . " She looked at her hands. "I don't think you know how hard this is for me to say."

"I told you to leave if that is what *you* wished."

She looked up. "You said I was a little rich girl gone poor and tattered."

He saw the hurt in her eyes and wanted to soothe it, but honesty kept him still. "Aren't you?"

Her mouth set in a straight line and she rose gracefully. "It's hardly a flattering description."

"It won't take much for you to turn the poor and tattered aspect around. To be what you were bred for."

"Highly doubtful."

"That you have overcome your circumstances shows you are a survivor."

She searched his face. "And you prize that trait, don't you?"

"I do. That is why I help those who come looking for it. Those who are fierce in wanting it."

"And you saw . . . this fierceness . . . in me?"

He took in her bedraggled appearance. Bonnet askew, hem muddied, dress creased, just as she had looked that first night. Not pretty in the conventional sense, though there was something about her that he found beautiful. The set of her shoulders, her determined expression, the way her body reacted to his. The way his reacted to hers. How he felt when she was near, or when she spoke. Something indefinable. Something beyond appearance and determination. Something elemental.

He cocked his head back to rest against the press. "I still do."

She wet her lips. "Why?"

"Do you trust me?"

Her eyes narrowed. "Do you trust *me*?"

"What happened at the market?"

Her fingers gripped her skirt. "I ran into Jacob Worley."

He crossed his arms. He had thought as much. Had seen something in her eyes. Had been stupid to let her leave without him. As soon as he'd gotten the information he needed, he had run back. Gone around to the kitchen, *knowing* that something was off.

"And what did he have to tell you?"

"That you were the killer. That his precious Melissande was next, and then it would be my turn."

Dark thoughts wound through his head. "His precious Lady Dentry *is* next. But you should be nowhere on the list."

"Perhaps it was his way to scare me." She gripped her skirt. "It worked."

"Why did he think you were next? What did he say?" Fear coursed through him.

"That was all."

He walked forward and touched her chin, lifting it so he could see everything in her eyes. "*What did he say?*"

She swallowed, her eyes still locked with his. "He said I had to kill you first, or you'd kill me."

"And nothing else? He just mentioned me?" His knees locked.

"Yes."

He dropped his hand and stepped back, his fingers unwilling to relinquish touching her on their own. He opened the linen press door. "I will take you to the house where your brother is. It will take an hour to make sure we aren't followed. Gather your things now."

"What?"

He undid the other button on his trousers, letting them hang loose, and reached for a new shirt. A hand curled around his arm and forcefully tried to turn him. His shirt dropped to the floor.

"I am not going anywhere."

He turned the rest of the way toward her, her fingers burned his flesh. "There is the possibility you have been targeted."

"That makes no sense. I had nothing to do with—"

He grabbed the hand branding his arm. A strange tingle of panic ran through him. "It doesn't matter. We aren't dealing with someone who has a full set of faculties. If Worley is at all involved, he may have targeted you."

"But you said Worley didn't do it."

"That doesn't mean he isn't in the midst of it. What if he switches his ire to you? Instead of doing me harm, he decides to harm you instead?"

He could see the shaken look in her brown eyes, and it echoed in the pit of his stomach. "No."

"*Yes.* Now go pack."

She crossed her arms, the long smooth curve of her neck tilting toward him. "I'm not leaving."

"Now is not the time for heroics. You have helped your brother. We will find out who is responsible. Your family will be back together by the end of the week. You will be safe."

She poked him in the chest, hard, her fingertip resting against his bare skin. "I'm not leaving you."

"You are."

"You are in far greater danger than I." Her finger trailed an inch down his chest before dropping to her side.

"I'm in no more danger than I've ever been. Especially from myself, it seems."

She looked down. "Oh, Gabriel."

He bent over to pick up his shirt, unwilling to look at her any further.

"I'm so sorry for what I said."

"It was nothing that wasn't the truth," he said with forced lightness. "It should be I on bended knee before you."

She stopped him from putting his arm through the hole. "No. It wasn't the truth. Please."

There was something so heated and fierce in her eyes that he nearly lost control.

"You are nothing like them. Any gestures you might have picked up are just those—gestures. Not used in any sort of cruel manner. It is the will that is important. It's the intention behind the action. Pleasure, not guile. And when I look in your eyes, I see—I see *you*."

He threw the shirt down and pulled her to him, mouth fused to hers, and spun toward the wall, pressing her against it, her legs climbing his, her heel pressing into his calf, the disjointed slide of his trousers to

311

the floor. He stepped out of one puddled leg and insinuated it between hers, rubbing up, making her ride his thigh, causing those deliciously caught cries in her throat as her hands pressed into his hair, trapping his mouth to hers and pulling him into her. He pulled a hand down her side, down her back, cupping her buttocks and grinding her against him, pushing her back into the wall and forward onto him.

His fingers wound under the fabric and between her thighs, and she was wet and hot and pushing into his hand. He pulled his forefinger along her. God, she was hot and ready and all he wanted to do was to push into her so hard that she was permanently part of the woodwork. He pushed his finger back along her and curled the tip inside, the sound of it pushing him further over the edge.

"Please, please."

He wasn't sure who said it, but he brought his hand up to touch her cheek and aligned their bodies, hitching her higher against the wall, feeling her slide down onto him, fitting firmly over the top. He buried his face into her hair, her throat, and thrust upward, her cries breathy and stuttered against his ear.

He withdrew and pushed into her harder and farther. Incredible and frustrating. And just *there*. He wanted, *needed*, to be just a bit farther. He pulled her against him, away from the wall. She wrapped her fingers around his neck, her eyes drugged and unfocused, and he quickly spun them to the bed, pushing her down on top, bending over her, feet still on the floor, driving into her, and God, yes, this was what he needed. Her head thrust back, her dress crushed and splayed indecently between them. Her heels climbed the small of his back as he pulled out and thrust as deeply into her as it was possible to go.

She moaned and the bed shook, and for the second time the world stood strangely on end. She pulled him back against her with her feet, her arms out, searching to bring him toward her and then dropping to clutch the coverlet, her stained dress, her body pulsing around his in frantic waves. And he kept driving, heady and crazy until someone roared and he was coming into her with a force that he didn't think possible to possess.

Her legs fell to the side and he collapsed on top of her, breathing in deep clutching breaths, the echoes thrumming from her chest, her mouth.

He pulled her up with him as he crawled onto the bed, his knees crinkling the coverlet and her ravaged dress as he caught upon it, the dress pulling down to expose her neglected chest to his view.

She absently attempted to tug her dress back up, her gaze still unfocused. His position stopped the attempt and he leaned down to kiss her bared skin. Her breath hitched.

"Luscious Marietta, or Marvelous Marietta, perhaps that should be your new name?"

The tip of her breast peeked over the frill of her dress, and he ran his tongue over the top. She gripped the back of his head, her fingers pulling through the strands.

He rose on his elbow and lifted his knee to release her dress. She didn't move and he felt a warm current. He tucked her up to him and scooted them both up the bed. She curled into him. A blast of something—desire, devotion, freedom—spun through him.

"I think you should stay with your brother for a few days. It won't take longer than that. I can feel it."

"And if I refuse? Will you lock me up with Mark?"

He threaded his fingers through her hair. "No."

"And then?"

"We find the murderer and set your brother free."

Unspoken, echoing around them, was the question: *And after that?* But she said nothing, her fingers gripping the bone of his hip. And he followed. Uttering no promises that could be broken.

Tomorrow was a new and unknown day. Today had been rough enough without worrying about where he'd be, where she'd be—where *they'd* be—tomorrow. Things he needed to think about, and things he'd rather not mull at all.

Some things *did* need to be said, however. "Lady Dentry made a list. My father is trying to locate a few of the Londoners on it."

"How did the—the visit go?" Her voice was hesitant, cringing.

"She was her normal, lovely self."

"She didn't—do anything?"

He laughed darkly. "She can't do anything."

"Oh."

She was silent, but he could feel her curiosity, her desire to speak. "What do you want to know, Marietta?"

She ran a hand down his arm. "How did you get started?"

"Started with what?"

"With this."

He pulled two fingers along her leg, enjoying the catch in her breath, but she captured his fingers before he could continue.

"Not that. How did you start such an endeavor? To the point where people would spend ten thousand pounds for your services or offer you three future favors?"

He ran his fingers along her side and stared at the ceiling. That hadn't been the question he'd thought she would ask. He didn't know if it was an easier or harder question to answer, the topic flirting with the edge of the main issue.

"It didn't start with ten thousand pounds or the favors."

She said nothing, waiting for him to continue.

"I ran from the Dentry estate, as I'm sure you've deduced. Took Jeremy with me." He tried to keep his voice breezy. "We hid in London for a while. We had nothing to our names, but we had contacts, knowledge. I started with a smile and the comprehension of how to work with the different classes. Desperation breeds other types of knowledge as well. Something that was very useful at the Dentry estate and later."

The darkness hovered just at the edges, but it was lighter than it had been, less thick.

"I did a few favors, introduced people who could help each other, that type of thing. I didn't realize how useful the talent was or what I could do with it until later." His fingers skimmed her hip. "I had earned a little bit of money by then, a lot of contacts. I took a chance and charged fifty pounds to a man who could

315

well afford to pay. He did. It was the beginning. I just kept moving up. Kept growing."

He skimmed his fingers over her stomach.

"Soon I was able to easily charge whatever I needed. I had the network in place to get most anything done or discovered."

"Do you get a lot of paying clients?"

"Yes. Only the most wealthy."

She leaned on her elbow. "If you charged less, you would get more clients."

"I know."

"Why don't you?"

"I don't need the money. I have more than enough to have proven myself." He gave her a self-degrading smile. "Besides, I'd have too many people at my door."

She touched his side. "You are more interested in people who can't afford your services. Working class folks."

"Yes."

"Why did you take my case?"

He didn't say anything for a second. "From a purely predatory standpoint, I knew you'd be a strong asset with your blending looks, even if your cultured voice has proven a detriment at times. And you were determined and loyal. Interesting. Your brother's situation was also interesting. Rockwood must have known I'd think so."

"What did you do for Rockwood?"

"You'll have to ask him."

"He's rather like you about not wanting to be in debt to anyone, though he's on a tight monetary leash with his father. I assume whatever you did for him, his father paid?"

He didn't answer, instead moving his fingers along her rib cage. She arched into his fingers as they grazed her breast.

"Why had I never heard of you?"

"Too many people started requesting services. I couldn't keep up and didn't trust others enough to bring them into the fold. So I keep to a referral basis. The whole thing works better in secret, just under the eyes of the watchful."

"How did you know Rockwood had referred me?"

"Each card is different. Subtle differences, but that is the best way to avoid forgery and to verify the identity of the sender."

"You enjoy it too, the intrigue, the suspense."

He smiled faintly. "I do."

"What will you do when you want to retire?"

"I'll turn it over to Jeremy." He hesitated. "Or one of Jeremy's children, should he have any."

"What about your own children?"

"Jeremy seems more inclined to marry, doesn't he?" Gabriel rolled over so he was looking down at her.

"I suppose that is true."

He reached into her hair, tipping her head back on the pillow, pressing a kiss at her throat. "Is that all you wanted to know, Marietta?"

She wanted to know everything. It was hard to imagine the man ever being taken advantage of. She hadn't known the boy. That he wasn't interested in

317

marriage was no surprise, so why did she feel a pit in her heart?

Her fingers curled into the coverlet as he rained kisses down her neck. "I want to—I want to know what happened . . . before?"

He leaned back against the pillows, tugging her over so her cheek pressed to his chest, her eyes facing away from his. His chest rose, fell and rose again. "What do you want to know?"

"How did they—how did they get you involved?"

His finger moved in an agitated pattern along her hip. "The attention was flattering at first. I thought Lady Dentry had the softest cloud of blond hair. A diamond of the first water."

Marietta focused on her mousy brown hair. Vines of moss across his chest.

"I had some experience with women, though having the house butler as a father limited interaction. The maids were all willing, always batting their eyes, but father was strict and didn't condone relationships beneath the stairs." His tone changed. "There was nothing he could do abovestairs, of course."

She moved her cheek along his chest.

His fingers continued their tattoo of her hip. "Lady Dentry started her venture in the same way I later did, I suppose. With a smile. She started with willing villagers, visiting men. But revenge, power, and control are hardly to be found with the willing." The tattoo became frenzied and his fingers withdrew to the coverlet.

"Willing conquests became subservient men, and offered no challenge. But Lady Dentry realized her key one day with a young boy who wanted to marry a village girl so badly that he rebuffed her advance. She had to have him. She broke him, broke the girl, and moved on, salacious in her new quest. She wanted strong boys, ones who didn't have a choice in the situation in which she placed them, just like she didn't have a choice in her marriage. Under her complete power, the more subjugated and unhappy, the better."

She rubbed her cheek along his chest.

"She enlisted a few other women with similar interests, vain or vicious women, and formed a little club."

"And then you . . . "

His chest surged beneath her cheek a few times. "I wasn't the first." The clock ticked in the background, the only sound in the room for thirty ticks.

"But my fate was sealed the day I denied her, though she later said she would have kept me regardless. Jeremy visited for a week. Staying for a sennight while Mother went to town to visit friends. I saw the way Lady Dentry looked at him—only eight at the time—and then back to me. Predatory and all too sure. I knew at that moment that I'd never have anything to do with her after she looked at my brother that way." He laughed, an ugly laugh. "Naive. As soon as my father was out of the picture, traveling with Lord Dentry to his various estates, she made a . . . deal . . . with me."

"Deal?"

"Blackmail."

She didn't say anything else, waiting for him to continue instead of continuing to prod.

"Jeremy was safe. That is what mattered. Still is."

"But you weren't."

"Six reasonably attractive women, two of them in the range of diamonds, one a diamond of the first water. Any boy or man's dream, wouldn't it be?"

"No."

A chilling laugh shook his chest. "The sixteen-year-old body doesn't always agree. More's the pity."

She didn't know what to say to that. "What made you finally decide to leave after . . . after being there for so long?"

"Allowing it for so long?"

She stiffened and tried to look at him, but his arm held her in place. "That is not what I said."

"My mother died." His voice was so soft she could barely hear him. "Jeremy would have had to come live on the estate. I couldn't let that happen. And something was off with the . . . women. I never found out what, but there was a new intensity. Something different in their eyes. I let a few things slip to my father in a rage. My mother was dead, out of their reach, and my father could fend for himself. I couldn't risk Jeremy."

"Your father—"

"He figured it out quickly enough with the clues I'd given. He found me packing and gave me everything he had on him, which unfortunately wasn't much. Jeremy and I left that night."

"The women didn't try to find you?"

"Oh, they did. I can't imagine their faces. Their anger. But the servants' network takes care of its own sometimes. We hid in London, as I said. I started doing odd jobs, tutoring Jeremy. I fell into an opportunity that was a little questionable, but I parlayed it.

Eventually I earned enough money, enough favors, to take revenge, to put them down. Monetary or social revenge mostly—either by bleeding them dry around town or ruining them the same way. And the rest . . . " He waved his hand.

"You were very brave."

"Bravery had nothing to do with it. I survived." He drew lazy patterns on her back.

"They underestimated you."

"Most people in the upper classes do. You'll have to watch for that when you return."

"It is doubtful I will return."

"They will embrace you with open arms as soon as your brother is released. You'll be the talk of the ton. Able to have anything you desire, as long as you grab it quickly—society is nothing if not fickle."

"What if I don't want to grab some fickle fate? It has held me powerless for so long."

He tensed. "Take the opportunity when it presents itself. Always. And society *will* present itself. A marriage proposal or five, I wouldn't be surprised. Take the control when you can in a situation where you are otherwise at the whim of others."

She chewed her lip. "Am I at your whim now?"

His arm moved, and thus freed, she turned her cheek to look into his eyes. "Are you? " he asked instead of answering.

"Yes, I do believe I am." She pressed a hand against his chest as he moved to rise. "Your whim is not unpleasant, but I yearn to be my own woman. To control my own life and movements."

His eyes turned unreadable. She thought for a

second she had lost him. The second turned into two. Abruptly his eyes switched back to the watchful, slightly wary look he had long sported, but there was something else there too that she couldn't read. Trust?

"Then teach me what it is you want," he said. "Show me."

She blinked. "I—I have nothing to teach you."

"Do you not? Come. Teach me, Marietta. Don't let my body do what my eyes don't cede. Make me obey your will."

"But . . . " She bit her lip. "Won't that be—"

"No. Didn't you say it is the will that is important? If I put myself in your hands, I trust you to take care of me."

Shock, love, something crazy froze her stomach, working up her throat, choking her.

"You will go back to society, and things will change, but tonight . . . tonight is yours." He rubbed one hand along her cheek, capturing the movement as she leaned into him. He abruptly snatched his hand away as if burned. "Do you see? It is hard for me. Second nature to try and take control. Take it away." He moved beneath her. "Free me."

Love me.

She reached for him, her hand heavy and shaking. Everything culminating in this one moment.

Chapter 20

Gabriel watched her eyes as she reached for him. Wondered what she was going to do. Her long fingers moved over his body, flattening and pulling over the ridges of his stomach, the planes of his chest. Touching the hair at his ankles and moving up farther behind his knees, to his thighs. She paused for a moment, then her fingers curled around him, already alive with interest.

She moved her hand and fingers over the surface, eyes narrowed as she concentrated, her eyes darting to his stomach briefly before connecting back with his.

"Does this feel good?"

"Yes." Her fingers were smooth, a little too gentle, but that was to be expected. Better gentle than rough at the start.

Determined eyes held his.

"You don't have to do anything, you—"

Her tongue touched the head of him. He nearly shot off the bed at the sensation.

Sure, bravery was one of her dominating traits, but most women he had been with had eschewed this particular act, and it hadn't upset him. It was too open. His face too easy to read. Entirely out of his control. He had never even come close to orgasm.

Marietta grew more intrepid and began to investigate all parts of him. He looked at the top of her head fondly. Even if he hadn't known that she'd never done this before, it would have been obvious from her first tentative motions. It was the thought that counted though, that she would—

Holy—

Her lips slipped around the head of him, her tongue grazing the sensitive spot underneath. An accident, no doubt, her finding that spot. His stomach rose and fell in a higher arc than before. He tried to keep his breathing steady. She paused for a moment, and eyes peered up at him through a haze of hair shaded with gold in the lamplight. The sight of her like that, wanton and beautiful, was enough to tickle that coil of interest that usually stayed dormant under these types of ministrations. But it was Marietta herself who caused the coil to appear. It wasn't—

Holy—

The second time was *not* an accident. The touch of her tongue pressing against him, tentative yet strong, was entirely a question. His damn body responded with another spike of breath. She did it a third time, a stronger press, more confident, and when he breathed in audibly, she concentrated more fully on those spots she was touching.

His resolve, his control, started to dribble right out

of his ears, pushed out by all of the blood draining downward. She seemed to be cataloging each spot and its reaction, then systematically combining movements and finding new ones. Yet always basing subsequent actions on his reactions, on *him*.

That's what had been missing in every previous encounter. Every other woman quite content to let him fulfill all her desires, but none of them *truly* wanting to fulfill his. To learn what exactly made him jump and shift and groan.

Marietta *knew* him, knew enough to gauge his reactions, and gave every indication that she wanted to know more.

Something foreign hissed from his mouth as she took all of him into her mouth and her tongue pulled along the length of him, up, up, pressing into the top, lips caressing.

Her name was a silent litany in his head. And in about thirty seconds it was a verbal litany from his lips.

She picked up her pace, a combination of untried maneuvers and those with which she had already found success. And the sight of her . . . dear God . . .

He couldn't stop from pushing into the pillow, couldn't stop the groan from passing his lips, the harsh breaths as his body spiraled from his gut up toward his tip. His arm went over his face, to block his expression, to stifle his cry. Lips popped from around him, the movement nearly ending the battle. His arm was suddenly batted away.

"Stop that."

His eyes snapped open. "What?" He stared at her,

uncomprehending, breathing as if he'd just run the length of the Thames.

"I want to see you."

He could do nothing but stare.

Teeth nibbled her lower lip and she leaned one hand on the coverlet. "What you look like when you—" She moved her free hand in a circular motion, teeth worrying a soft track across the glossy surface of her lip.

He flashed a grin, his body simmering back to a controllable state. "When I what?"

She gave him a pointed look.

"You'll have to be specific, Marietta." Laughter bubbled within him.

Her eyes narrowed, and the next thing he knew, her lips closed around him and she took nearly the entire length of him into her mouth. His body bent backward without his consent, all laughter strangled. Her mouth pulled back up, a strong press of tongue to his underside, and he thought, quite possibly, the world was about to end.

He reached for her, but she slapped his hands away, entangling her fingers with his and pinning them to the sides of his head. "Now, now, you did say I was in control, did you not?"

The motion brought her over the top of him, and she jumped a bit when their lower bodies connected. They weren't in perfect alignment, like every cell in his body called for, but they were close to it. Too close. She looked down his body, her hair tickling his throat. He knew what she would see—his body at complete attention, glistening, straining upward. When her eyes drew back to his, he could see the knowledge, the desire, written on everything from her darting eyes to her moistened lips. Her right leg slid over his so she was straddling him. He barely heard her quick intake of breath as he slid along her heat, his own quick breath nearly drowning hers.

She repeated the motion so that he slowly slid along her, the motion slow and teasing. He gritted his teeth and pushed his hips as far into the bedding as he could, his body screaming to thrust up inside her, to make her wail and scream his name, to claim her once more.

She continued to hold his hands hostage and to rub against him. From the rose blooming in her cheeks, he wasn't sure just who she was teasing more. One movement aligned them perfectly and he nudged, just an inch, an innocent look on his face when her head snapped up. Her eyes sparked and she kissed him, sinking down another inch. He returned the kiss and pushed his hips up, just a tiny bit so as to not attract attention. She drew back.

"No, no, no, Gabriel. I'm going to earn that prime spot in your harem." She leaned down and flicked a tongue over the lobe of his ear as he had done to her many times. Dear God, had she paid attention to everything he'd done? Returning all of his seductive actions and words. "Three nights of sin and more."

She swirled her hips. *Ungh.* Something unintelligible burst from his lips.

Confidence fairly radiated from her. Confidence, passion, and other emotions he dare not name. A drink mixed with the most potent ingredients for seduction.

Her swirling hips lowered her farther still, and the

color fairly burst from her skin. Soft, breathy air escaped her parted lips. She freed his hands and planted hers above his shoulders.

"Touch me."

Her lips hadn't finished forming the words and he was reaching for her breasts, his thumbs rubbing circles that made her body shift madly and sink farther down. She pulled up an inch and the muscles inside her contracted around him.

"Mari— Bloody—"

And damned if she didn't tighten around him again.

He grit his teeth and narrowed his eyes. He dropped a hand to where they were connected and flicked a finger upward at the same time he rubbed her nipple. She gasped and sank fully on top of him.

He wasn't sure he had ever felt anything quite so wonderful as her contracting muscles and the feel of her, warm and wet around him. And never heard anything as wonderful as her ragged breaths against his ear.

"Not fair." It was more of a released breath from her than actually formed words.

He moved his hands to her knees to stop him from touching her further. "Better?" he whispered against her lips.

She kissed him, long and deep, then shifted back so she was sitting on him. After a few tentative movements she found a rhythm she liked, and one that made his stomach muscles clench and his fingers clutch her knees. She swayed and lifted, riding, eyes closed and chin tilted like some wild fairy. Rose spread down her skin, making it glow. Her cheeks, fiery blooms, her eyelids heavy with passion. No man in his right mind would call this woman plain. He had never seen anything so evocative and gorgeous.

She moved over him, her breasts swaying with each movement. Dangling in front of him like ripe cherries. A nipple brushed his chin and he captured it between his lips. She moaned, her forehead dropping to his, her hair curtaining around them, her pace becoming more erratic as she pushed down, sheathing him, then pulled up toward his mouth in trembling thrusts, as if unable to decide between which she wanted more. He sucked hard and she threw her head back, mouth open, beautiful beyond anything, giving him exactly what he wanted and taking exactly what he needed.

He drew his hands up her thighs, to the sides of her breasts, then down her waist, forcing her farther down, pushing farther inside her, as far as he could go, no longer playing the submissive, pulling them back to equal terms, exactly where they should be. He gripped her hips and pushed down on them every time she drew back up, thrust his hips upward to curve into exactly the right spot. She went wild in his arms, exactly as he wanted, but instead of only reveling in her responses, the ones he drew and caused and controlled, he reveled in his own as well. The sleek, tight feel of her, the unintelligible sounds she was making in his ear, the wanton bliss of her reactions, responding like she was born to it. Born to him. Not something out of a power game, but something forged by mutual desire and compatibility.

Her lips moved over his ear, over his cheek, connected with his mouth, fiercely kissing him. Pulling his lips between hers, swallowing his groan as she made a particularly long downward thrust and swiveled her hips.

"Gabriel, I—" He curved upward again and her eyes rolled briefly back, her chin tilting and breath catching. Her hands fell to his shoulders to keep her upright. She looked into his eyes, her brown eyes completely smoked with desire and emotion, but not hazy from incomprehension. "Gabriel, I—"

He captured her lips and framed her cheeks in his hands, his fingers curling into her hair. But he didn't make her eyes roll back, he didn't cause her head to fall to the side, none of the tricks that would make her look away or lose contact with his eyes. No tricks that would hide his own completion, the expression on his face, the power that would give her. Their bodies met, their eyes held. And when they both fell apart moments later, he never looked away, and neither did she.

Gabriel picked up Abigail's journal. He didn't even like touching it, but Marietta thought all the answers were inside, and he had somehow known it to be the truth since the journal's discovery. That was the reason he found himself unable to destroy it. And the reason he hadn't been able to look through it.

He had a copy of Lady Dentry's list. All he needed to do was go through the journal and check each name off, referenced with what he remembered of each. See if there were any discrepancies, any allusions to events that might have caused someone to become a murderer.

Turning the pages was a struggle, but he began to make headway. One servant identified. Another. A village boy. A summer guest. When he reached his own section, he began flipping the pages more quickly. He didn't need to read it to remember.

He paused, his fingers in the act of flipping a page. Marietta had read most of this. Had probably gone back when he wasn't looking and scoured the parts concerning him. She knew all of it, and yet she was still here. Still with him.

He flipped the page, his eyes barely skimming the pen strokes. Marietta saved her pity but extended her empathy. His feelings for her were already strong, but he had a feeling they were sliding down a terminal slope into the unknown.

Always searching for ways not to be broken, maybe he just needed the person who hid his seams.

And because he was skimming the entries that concerned him, he almost missed it. Only the hour chime of the clock woke him from his stupor.

His finger pressed into the page and the voice echoed in his mind. . . . *just last summer. Horrible, as usual.*

A firm knot settled in his stomach. The strange thing was the flicker of relief—from finally figuring it out, from never having to go through the journal again, from ending the nightmare. Only to begin a new one.

He pounded the table with his fist. And then did it again, for good measure.

Marietta ran into the room, scanning the space as if looking for a threat. "Gabriel?"

"I know who the murderer is," he said grimly.

She stared at him, mouth agape.

He started penning notes. "Did my father, brother, and John say where they were going?"

"They are completing the task of tracking down the names on the list."

"Good. When they get back we will need to discuss the plan."

"Who is the murderer?"

"I'll tell you when we are assembled."

She started to protest. He reached forward to kiss her, to thwart her, and abruptly stopped.

He touched her cheek instead, rubbing his thumb along her soft skin. "Soon. This will be over soon."

Marietta was nervous. She didn't know why. Maybe because the nightmare was nearing its peak. Maybe because Gabriel was not telling her something, but at least not hiding the fact from her. Maybe because he never hinted at anything in the future. Anything *after*.

Jeremy, Alcroft, and Gabriel's father returned around noon. They gathered around the kitchen table. Gabriel was twitchy, pacing.

"I was looking over the list and found a match. A stable hand. Lester Flume. He's mentioned in Abigail's journal, not by name, but Lady Dentry has all of the names written out by hand and he is on the list she gave me."

"How do you know she has all of the names written in her journal? She hardly seems the type to do something so foolhardy," Jeremy said.

Gabriel nodded, but his shoulders tensed further. "She threatened me with it. Before. Foolish, yes, but she considers it worth the cost. It's a way to keep track for her. I saw a page near the beginning of her journal when I was looking through her desk, and indeed there were names, dates, details. I let her take it back before I looked further, but I am going to return tomorrow, to confirm my suspicions."

"And you think she will let you have a look at the book, just by you asking?" Gabriel's father asked skeptically.

"No, I'll have to dream up a good story, most likely. Play on her titillations. She will let me see it in the end." He shrugged. "And if not, I will take it. Give it to Dresden to end this."

"You would allow your name to be ruined?" Alcroft asked, shock all over his face.

Gabriel nodded once. Decisively. "I am willing to take the chance."

Alcroft slowly nodded back. "Very well. I will support you, you know that."

"Yes." Gabriel's voice was soft. "I know you will."

"As will I," Marietta said.

All eyes turned to her.

"I will go with you to the estate tomorrow," she said. He nodded slowly.

"So will we all," Gabriel's father said. "Then we will find Lester Flume."

Jeremy and Alcroft nodded, and it was done. The date was set.

* * *

The other men had left not ten minutes past, Gabriel speaking to each one individually and alone before they left, while Marietta gathered papers. He hadn't stopped shifting and tapping at the kitchen table since, all the papers still spewed across the top in a disorganized fashion. He looked up. "I need to go to the Dentry estate."

"What, now? I thought you said we were going tomorrow?" she asked.

"We will. But I need to go now."

She was quiet for a second. "You think there will be an attempt made today? That we can't wait for tomorrow?"

"Yes."

She nodded. "I'm coming with you."

He shook his head. "Aside from the danger, if Lady Dentry sees you, she'll make it her mission to destroy you."

"Why?"

He looked away. "She just will."

"I will deal with it. I'm coming." She laughed lightly. "You can't get rid of me so easily now." She just hoped that was true.

Not twenty minutes later they were inside Gabriel's carriage and leaving London proper.

Marietta shivered. She remembered a poem she had read just last year. She was finally going to meet the wicked witch.

Chapter 21

U pon arrival, they were immediately shown into a spacious library. Gabriel barely needed to present a card. Glittering panes of glass encased one side of the room, while books rimmed the others. Display cases and stands with curios dotted the space.

An icy blonde stepped forward to greet them. Marietta had seen her before at ton functions but never spoken with her. Lady Dentry was far above her socially and had reveled in staying apart from the other women in the ton, standing in her own space, putting her beauty on display at each event. Removed—an icy diamond separated from the paste.

Her gaze swept Marietta and dismissed her. Then immediately connected back. To Gabriel's hand at her waist, to Gabriel. Wintry eyes narrowed on Marietta, and she suddenly understood Gabriel's warning.

"I've never seen you so protective, Gabriel. This little sparrow deserves more of my attention."

"You grow duller in your waning years, Lady Dentry, if you think that I will let you touch Miss Winters."

An unexpected tingle swept through her at his tone.

Lady Dentry smiled. It was a pleasant smile, all the more chilling for the complete insincerity behind it.

"Come. Have some tea and biscuits." She swept a hand toward the service on the table.

Marietta perched on a chair after Lady Dentry was seated and thought of the lesson of Persephone, never to eat at the dark table.

Lady Dentry smirked and sipped her tea. "Today is the day, is it, Gabriel? That I will be cruelly murdered? You, my white knight come to save me."

Gabriel was as tense as he had been from the first. Marietta wished she could squeeze him, hug him, do *anything* for him. She squeezed her hands in her lap instead.

"If the knight suddenly decided to save the dragon, I suppose your statement would be true."

Lady Dentry laughed, a light, breezy laugh. "Of course, dear Gabriel, of course." Her eyes watched him, pleased. "But you are here. You returned."

He tapped a finger on his chair's arm. "You would see it that way. At this point I find myself disinterested in playing."

Lady Dentry's eyes turned chilling. She switched her gaze to Marietta. "You must tell me about yourself, dear."

Gabriel spoke before she could answer. "We are only here to finish this, Lady Dentry. I doubt Ma—Miss Winters is interested in making your acquaintance."

His slip turned Lady Dentry's icy lips. Marietta

could see the satisfaction combined with the anger in her smile.

"That may be true, Gabriel, but here we are. And you did say you wanted to initiate how this drama would play. Go, shoo, while I chat with your Miss Winters."

Gabriel's face was unamused.

"La, Gabriel, your companion can handle herself, can't you, Miss Winters?"

Marietta nodded. She hadn't been dealing with Mark for all of these years not to know how to deal with difficult people and petulance. Even if Lady Dentry was above her set and had taken viciousness to another level, she couldn't show fear.

Gabriel seemed to understand this, and she had observed that he never interfered before allowing the person to take care of their own issues first. It was one of his many admirable qualities. He rose and walked to the fireplace. Lady Dentry rose as well, motioning for Marietta to do the same. She put her arm through hers. "Come view the gardens from the window, Miss Winters." She led her over to the window, and Marietta had to wonder if this was what walking to the gallows felt like.

She could see Gabriel watching them from the corner of his eye as he inspected the fire screen, crouching in front of it and looking over the top edge.

"The azaleas look lovely this time of year. And the roses magnificent. Do you enjoy horticulture, Miss Winters?" Her voice was soft, so it wouldn't carry to the other side of the spacious room. Not that it would stop Gabriel from eavesdropping, with his finely tuned hearing.

"No more than the average person, Lady Dentry."

"Please, call me Melissande. A close friend of Gabriel's cannot stand on ceremony."

"Mr. Noble calls you Lady Dentry."

"Is that what you call him when he is inside you, Miss Winters? Pushing cries and plumbing your depths? Seems a bit formal. Oh, Mr. Noble, your cock is so large."

Marietta tried to pull away, but Lady Dentry held firm.

"But then Lord Dentry has never called me anything but Lady Dentry. Annoying, don't you think? To be so formal?"

Marietta stopped struggling, suddenly understanding this game. "I think that you are jealous, Lady Dentry."

"I am, Miss Winters. Terribly jealous that you have my little avenger." The name rolling from those lips made her ill, made the bile rise again. "Not that he is little, no. He is terribly lovely in that department. In all departments. My jealousy is boundless. He was delightful at sixteen, and he is delicious now. You must set him free."

"Set him free?"

"He is besotted by you." Marietta couldn't help but display her doubt. Lady Dentry gave a tinkling laugh. "You don't see it. How wonderful. And better that way. You two will never last longer than it takes for your brother—the younger one, if the papers I finally procured were correct—to go free."

She knew it was the truth, but couldn't help asking. "Why would you think that, Lady Dentry?"

She laughed again. "Oh, it is obvious why. You are from two very separate classes and spheres—in all respects. I do so hope you break his heart. Perhaps he will return to me."

"You are delusional."

"Perhaps. But it is all I have now." Her fingers tightened on Marietta's arm.

Marietta found herself free of Lady Dentry and beside Gabriel just as quickly as she'd been freed from Kenny so many days ago that it felt a lifetime.

Lady Dentry stuck one delicate finger into her mouth and sucked it, her lips making a little pop as she pulled it out. "Naughty, Gabriel."

"I grow tired of this. Hopefully the murderer will spare me your antics and show up soon."

A faint whistle echoed. He motioned toward the screen, which he had moved closer to the desk. "Marietta, behind the screen. Lady Dentry, sit at your desk."

Marietta immediately ducked behind, then watched Lady Dentry saunter to her chair, only her straight back and tensed shoulders belying her concern.

Gabriel crouched next to Marietta and they waited a moment. A minute. Two minutes. The room sat in silence, Lady Dentry even feeling the need to remain quiet and focused. Another minute passed. Marietta was about to say something to Gabriel when the door opened.

The person stepped into the room, the face going from the shadows into the light, and Marietta couldn't believe her eyes.

* * *

John Alcroft stepped into the room. Gabriel heard Marietta inhale sharply, and John's attention turned to their corner before his eyes shifted back, narrowing on Melissande sitting primly in her chair.

"Lady Dentry."

"John."

Marietta started to rise and Gabriel tugged her back, wrapping an arm around her shoulders to keep her in place.

"It has been almost a year since you visited, John. I thought you hated it here?"

"I do. This is an unplanned visit. I planned to wait another week, but matters have forced my hand."

John walked toward them, toward Lady Dentry, stopping suddenly upon seeing the journal on the desk, all buttery leather and malicious intent. His lips crushed together. "Gabriel."

"Have you decided to call me a pet name, John? How thoughtful, though I question the choice of moniker," Lady Dentry.said.

Gabriel silently swore at the bitch, her mocking not helping the situation.

"Silence," John hissed, his gaze gleaming and vicious. "Gabriel? Where are you? Under the desk? Down on your knees before her? How upsetting."

Gabriel squeezed Marietta's shoulder and rose from behind the fire screen.

"Ah, there you are. A preferable choice of seating, with the option to pitch yourself into the fire to relieve the irritation of her presence, at the very least."

"John."

"Gabriel. And Marietta too, I assume?" He looked to

the screen, and Gabriel cursed as her head popped over the edge. John looked satisfied. "And here we are."

"John, we don't need to—"

"Wrong, Gabriel. I think we do. How did you find out? And when?"

"Earlier. I read Abigail's journal. The entries concerning someone else, tied to me. The rest happening after I left. And then I remembered you saying you had been to the estate last summer. She"—he motioned sharply toward Lady Dentry—"mentioned losing her letter opener around that time. I remember that letter opener. Hideous, large." He looked at John's left hand, at the gilt tip sticking out of his sleeve. "It all made a sick sort of sense." He lowered his voice. "They got you too. I never knew."

"I know you didn't, Gabriel." John's chest heaved before he took a deep breath, shoulders straightening.

Gabriel took a step away from Marietta, putting distance between them and willing her to stay put. "Why didn't you say something? You never even pretended to know about their club before a few weeks ago."

"What was I to say? You *left* me there. You weren't the buffer for *me*."

Pain sliced through him. "I didn't know. I never thought they'd touch you. She said they couldn't—"

"They did," he said savagely, a growl erupting as Lady Dentry snorted, though her knuckles were white around the chair arms. "A week before you disappeared. I thought it a grand lark at first. I had no idea what was happening. Who wouldn't want six women panting over them? But they were planning other entertainments. I heard them whispering about it. Saw the looks. Read the journals, later, much later, their planned entertainments for the both of us. As soon as you left, things changed. I didn't understand why, but suddenly it wasn't just a weekend's lark. I was in their clutches. Couldn't escape. And you *left* me there, Gabriel."

"I'm sorry, John," he whispered. "I didn't know."

"You didn't even write to let me know you were safe."

Gabriel swallowed, unsure how to handle John's swing. "I was hiding in London. The network protected me until I rose to the head. Until I had more than enough power to deal with the likes of them."

John stepped forward. A friendly step instead of a threatening one. "It was magnificent of you, of course. I was ever so proud when I discovered your actions."

John's eyes were sincere. Lady Dentry chose that moment to show her continued disregard for life. "Gabriel is always magnificent. You never quite measured up."

The tip of the letter opener became the blade as it slid smoothly into John's hand, and he took a step toward her. Gabriel could have happily planted it between her ribs himself, but he stepped between them.

"John."

John stopped, cocked his head, and the blade merely tipped from his sleeve once again. "I should have anticipated you'd be here. I panicked. Bad decision on my end." There was something in his eyes . . .

"You sent Rockwood to Marietta."

John banged his free hand against the back of Lady

Dentry's guest chair. "There you go! Took you long enough, Gabriel."

"You *wanted* me to know."

John sat on the edge of the chair. His view of Lady Dentry thus impeded, he seemed almost relaxed. "You have incredibly good resources and a knack for choosing the right options. The emotion blinded you for much of this investigation, but even with that handicap I hoped you would figure it out. That you would join me."

"Join you?"

"You have as much a right to revenge as I do. We will have to get rid of that sycophant Worley, of course, as well as any of the other deviants. I had quite hoped you would do away with Worley a week past."

"How?"

"How what? How could you have killed Worley? Oh, any number of ways." He puckered a brow. "I suppose that having Marietta there was a bit of a damper, but a clean push from the roof would have put Worley to rights."

"No, how could you do it? Kill . . . them? And in that manner?"

"Very, very easily. And with no small amount of vigor and satisfaction." His eyes gleamed as they looked over Gabriel's shoulder. "Who do you think has the control now, my lady?"

That Lady Dentry didn't answer was all the answer needed.

"You could have taken your revenge in a different manner, John. Or moved on."

"Moved on?" He laughed. "As you did? Burying

yourself beneath case after case, helping those in need? You *took* your revenge too, Gabriel. I helped you with a few of those favors against them, though you had no idea I knew."

"How did you know about me?" Gabriel had wondered that all night.

John snorted. "They chattered about you ad nauseum. The journals were full of you. It was hardly a challenge to reason out. I had such high hopes. Especially when you started upon your path of destruction. When you shut down the club, I was thrilled. I loved you then. That we could rid the world of them." His eyes grew anguished. "When you stopped at ruining them, socially and monetarily, I could have killed you myself."

Gabriel could see the hate in his eyes. And the adoration. He didn't know which scared him more. "Why didn't you?"

"I couldn't kill you, Gabriel. There was still a chance, after all. And I had time. Time to plan and scheme. Time to change your mind."

"Why did you think you would change my mind, John?"

"Been missing your investigator?"

The abrupt change startled him for a second, before it fell into place. "You paid him off."

"Cost me a pretty penny too. But it is better for you this way. Better not to have someone disloyal on your payroll. Besides, I needed you to remain unaware. I knew you wouldn't go along with the first one. But given some time for the idea to sink in, for you to think your own brother the killer . . . with me feeding

Jeremy just enough information about the case for him to act guilty around you—for all the wrong reasons, of course . . . yes, then things might look different."

Anger choked him momentarily. "Different?"

"More acceptable. Enticing. Righteous. Don't lie. You would not have turned Jeremy over to the magistrates."

"Life has a strange way of making sure things even out. If Jeremy had been guilty, he would eventually have been punished regardless of whether I turned him in or not."

"Your punishment. Your justice. But *you* would not have allowed him to be tried in the courts and hanged."

"I would try to do the same for you, John," he said softly.

"We could kill her now, Gabriel. Together." The eager, pleading look was so strange on his friend's face that he had to force himself not to take a step away.

"You believe I will do it. That I will help you finish it."

"I hope." His hands ran along the flat side of the blade. "It's a funny thing, to have hope. I easily have revenge. Justice. Friendship. But hope is a precious thing. I left it to fate. Whether you would stay ignorant, join me, or be my downfall." His eyes were completely focused on Gabriel, his gaze piercing. "Are you my brother or my enemy, Gabriel?"

"I am your brother in life, John." His stomach hurt. His throat hurt. His heart hurt. "But I am your enemy in this."

John's teeth clenched, his lips trying to form expression and failing, pushing together into a straight line. "I see. This is rather an awkward moment, in that case. Will you at least step aside?"

John glanced to Marietta, as if suddenly realizing that she was still in the room. "Your brother will be released. I meant for it to happen with Abigail's death. There is no real reason they can hold him. And we can give them Worley, if it comes to that. I've been helping him evade Gabriel here and there this week, just to keep things interesting. To keep on track."

"No," she whispered.

"Come, Marietta, you know it to be true."

"John, leave her alone." Steel this time. Not even encased in satin.

John smiled faintly. "She is good for you, Gabriel. I won't harm her." He looked across the desk. "However, I do ask that you not stand in my way."

"John, I can't—"

"No, Gabriel! Do not disappoint me!"

He positioned himself to intercept John, whose eyes had gone wild. He crouched to leap forward. John's eyes were grim, his mouth tight. His body lines pitched for battle as well.

The door opened, turning all eyes to the oak. Lord Dentry stepped into the room, Gabriel's father and Jeremy behind him. Listening at the door or in a secret room this whole time, no doubt.

Gabriel's fingers curled into fists as Arthur Dresden walked in last, an uninvited witness to the events.

John stepped back, the thin blade of steel dropping to his side. "Lord Dentry."

"Mr. Alcroft. I am very disappointed in you."

"I am as well, Mr. Alcroft," Lady Dentry said, smoothing her hands over her dress and rising, secure in her safety. Six dark glares focused on her. Dresden's face was unreadable. "One would think after all we did, taking you in—"

"Silence, woman." Dentry's voice was flat. "I will deal with you later."

She stepped back, bumping into a display case.

"I can explain—"

"Silence, I said," he roared.

Lady Dentry visibly shrank, her eyes wide, a thin band of excitement in their depths. Gabriel curled his lip.

"Lord Dentry," John said. "I beg you to understand—"

"As much as I am . . . displeased . . . with what I've heard, and with my wife, Alcroft, I cannot allow you to harm her."

Lady Dentry smiled, a smug little smile.

"I, however, can do with her as I please." Unemotional eyes looked to her. "And I find myself inclined for once to do just that."

Lady Dentry's smile dropped.

"You have brought trouble upon trouble on this household, Lady Dentry. But I thought them petty things. When Mr. Noble, the senior, left my employ, I knew you were somehow responsible for his sudden want of retirement. I allowed him to leave, however, handicapping myself in the process. I should have watched you more closely, I see."

"You should have watched me at all," she snapped bitterly.

Gabriel said nothing to interrupt the interplay. Marietta's hand slipped into his and he squeezed it.

"I suppose I should have done just that." The rest of the room's inhabitants were silent bystanders. "Pity you should disgrace the name Dentry so."

She laughed, a wild, fierce sound. "It did not take much. And I enjoyed it." Her eyes swept Gabriel and John. "Every second."

Lord Dentry's face remained stern, taciturn, unemotional, but his hand fisted around the back of a chintz chair. "You will pay for this, Lady Dentry."

"My *name* is Melissande."

"This is a Bow Street Runner, Lady Dentry." He motioned toward Dresden. "Followed Mr. Jeremy Noble up from London."

Jeremy cringed and sent an apologetic look Gabriel's way.

"He heard the whole thing, which leaves me in a bind." Lord Dentry tapped a finger on the chair. "What shall we do?"

"I care little what you do," his wife said. Gabriel had never seen her as bitter as she was now. Utterly defeated, an ugly sneer on her face.

"Oh, but I think you do. And moreover, I care. I won't have you disgrace my name any more than you already have." He silently tapped for a few seconds, a large show of emotion from an altogether stern and unemotional man. "It would be in your best interest were you to be arrested, I will tell you that right now, for I am going to make the rest of your days quite . . . unpleasant."

Lady Dentry's face turned white, and Gabriel squeezed Marietta's hand as grim approval coursed through him.

Lord Dentry's eyes moved around the faces in the room. "The question is what to do now."

"He is the Middlesex murderer. He needs to be brought to justice," Dresden said, eyes narrowed on John.

Everyone in the room stiffened at his pronouncement. Gabriel closed his eyes. All their secrets would become public. He had put safeguards into place, but this situation was entirely bigger than what he'd planned for. All of London would know in one fell swoop. Printed in every paper and on the lips of every citizen. And John . . .

"No. You can't." Marietta stepped forward. "Please. Let Gabriel handle it."

Dresden's eyes narrowed on her. "Noble? I trust him no more than I do the rest of you. He'll release Alcroft as soon as they leave."

"He brought Worley to your attention. Deliberately put his own secrets at risk in order to help your investigation."

"He wasn't helping my investigation, he was helping his own."

"No." She shook her head. "Don't you see—it hindered him. You are a smart man; you put the pieces together enough to follow Jeremy out here. Why did you do that?"

Dresden's lips pulled tight. "That is neither here nor there. Why should I trust him to turn over the murderer?" He pointed a thumb at Alcroft. "His lifelong friend."

"Don't you see? Gabriel is the reason you know all of these things. He allowed you to know them. Took

349

the chance that under all of your stuffy, upright theatrics, you are a decent man."

Dresden was taken aback. Gabriel could only sympathize with that state at the moment. Could only keep his jaw from sagging as Marietta made her passionate declarations.

"And Lord Dentry." She turned to him. "Gabriel has said nothing publicly about your wife, nor your own unwitting part in this. Trust him to continue that. Support whatever story plays."

Lord Dentry inclined his head an inch.

"And you think he'll do right by you, do you?" Dresden's eyes were narrowed upon her.

"He has done right the entire time," she said simply. "He hasn't hurt anyone, when he could have. I've placed my trust in him, we all have." She looked at Jeremy and his father, then back to Gabriel. "And none of us have been betrayed." Her brown eyes were beautiful and clear. A spring shower washing away his sins. He nearly staggered under the impact. She looked back to Dresden. "Please."

The entire room seemed to take a breath.

Dresden's eyes scrunched. "I don't like people mucking around with the law. Mucking around with justice."

"No, not mucking. Just giving justice a chance to succeed in a different way. To prevent the innocents from being hurt."

Dresden looked around the room. "What innocents?"

"My brother, for one."

"It will hardly hurt him when he is exonerated by

Mr. Alcroft being taken into custody." But the corners of Dresden's eyes loosened a fraction.

"The innocents taken advantage of by Lady Dentry and her—" Her mouth turned down. "—club."

When Dresden's eyes softened another fraction, Marietta stepped forward. "Please. I know you want the letter of the law followed, but those victims, those boys, will never get their justice this way."

"And what of the women?"

"I didn't say that justice wouldn't be done. Just . . . just let Gabriel handle it." She took another step forward, her fingers spreading. "Please."

The faith in him, when she didn't even know what he would do . . . he could just let John go. His closest friend, his brother in all but blood . . . he could let him walk through the door. Marietta trusted him not to allow Kenny to take the blame, when it would all be so much simpler for him in this one, singular aspect to do just that.

"Mr. Alcroft needs to be tried and punished," Dresden said.

John wasn't looking at the Runner, he was looking at Gabriel. Gabriel stared back, thinking through plan after plan. John tilted his head, then nodded, tired eyes never leaving Gabriel.

Pain ripped through him. Gabriel stepped forward, at Marietta's shoulder. "He will. I will take him," he said, barely above a whisper. He cleared his throat. "Someone fetch a rope and a male servant's outfit."

"Why do you need—"

Gabriel held up a hand. "It will be easier this way."

No one responded to that, though Marietta looked up in confusion. Lord Dentry disappeared to retrieve the items.

"John, the letter opener." He held out his hand. John opened his palm, the long blade resting on top, and looked at the weapon for a long moment before giving it to Gabriel. Gabriel slipped it into his inside pocket, the cold steel pressed against his ribs.

"If you betray me, I will destroy you," Dresden whispered, his voice low and even behind him.

"I know," Gabriel said.

Lord Dentry returned and Gabriel handed John the coat, simple shirt, trousers, and shoes. "Put these on."

"Something for prison, Gabriel?" John asked. "How thoughtful."

He put on the borrowed garments and removed his pocket watch, slipping it inside his new trousers.

"No. Your watch." Gabriel held his hand out. "And your signet."

John raised a brow, but removed the objects and handed them to Gabriel. "Robbing me?"

"No. Keeping them for you," Gabriel said simply.

John narrowed his eyes, searching Gabriel's, then nodded. "Very well."

"Come."

They exited the house in a knotted formation, Dresden and Gabriel's father in front, Gabriel and John in the middle with Jeremy and Marietta at their sides, Lady Dentry clasped uncomfortably against her husband, bringing up the rear. Dresden and Gabriel's father spread to the sides and Gabriel entered his carriage, then motioned John inside. He could see Marietta's wide eyes and bitten lip.

He moved his eyes from her and nodded to Dresden, whose face was dark, shoulders tight. Gabriel understood the need for people in the law to view the world in terms more black and white than his own shades of gray. Although a softening of Dresden's edges would be more than welcome.

"You came by horse? Stop by the White Stag for a drink on your way back," Gabriel said. Dresden's eyes narrowed and darted between them. Gabriel wondered if he would go to the tavern or if he would follow behind, just in case.

His father handed him a strong rope surreptitiously, so that any curious servants would be unable to see. They had somehow kept the entire debacle within the two rooms and behind the thick walls of the manor, the servants none the wiser. Gabriel motioned for John to hold out his hands. He did so with another raised brow, though his eyes were resigned, haunted. Gabriel tied the knot.

His eyes connected with Jeremy's, which were as haunted as Alcroft's, but strength lurked behind the uncertainty. Gabriel nodded to him, held his gaze, tried to communicate everything he could in that one glance. Sorrow, apology, love, trust. Jeremy's face broke for a minute, then he nodded back, shoulders firm, head up.

Marietta's hands curled around the door's frame. "Gabriel," she hissed, trying to get him to lean out. "What if he does something to you in the carriage?"

"He won't." The sand was slipping through the hour

glass, his tongue unable to reveal his plan. Marietta understood honor. She'd understand later. He needed her to.

"But—"

"He won't. I'll see you back at the house." He touched her chin. "Everything will be fine."

Everything wouldn't be fine. But they all had to believe it to be.

They stepped away, as one, from the carriage. He closed the door and rapped the trap. The wheels rolled down the drive. Away from the beautiful estate with its ugly memories and unhappy inhabitants.

John was silent, staring at the rope binding his wrists. Gabriel didn't know where to look. Out the window, toward the setting sun, bloody and fierce. At his friend, a murderer, a victim. At the pristine bundle sitting innocuously at his side, waiting.

"How did you let it go, Gabriel? How did you become you, and not me?"

The afternoon had obviously drained them all. John's voice was reflective and even.

Gabriel stared through the window at the passing scenery. "I don't know, John. I never wanted them to win." He looked at his friend. "Their goal was to break us. I wasn't going to let that happen."

"You think me weak?" John's chin jutted forward; he looked more like his old self in that moment.

"No. I think you wronged. I wish . . . " He looked away. "I wish you had come to me. Or that—"

"It wouldn't have mattered if you'd stayed, Gabriel." John's voice was matter of fact and even more reflective, accurately guessing what he was going to say. "Did you read Abigail's journal? The parts where we overlap?"

"Some."

"Then you will know that it didn't matter. It would have been worse had you still been there, though I said differently earlier. You couldn't have saved me. I stopped blaming you during the day long ago." He gave a self-deprecating smile. "I sometimes still blame you at night, but we can't all be perfect."

"None of us are," Gabriel said quietly. "None of us are."

They sat in silence, the carriage rolling across Blackfriars, swaying over the stones as dusk fell.

Gabriel rapped the trap. "Is the Runner still following?"

"No, sir. He left ten minutes back and rode ahead. Haven't seen him since."

Gabriel nodded and stretched his suddenly tight fingers.

"Where are we going?" John asked, his head tipped back, eyes closed. "Cold Bath? Newgate?"

Gabriel shook his head slowly, watching his friend. "Greville Street."

John's eyes snapped to his and held for a long moment. He nodded. "Yes." His voice softened. "Thank you, Gabriel."

"Dentry and Dresden will take care of the rest. I'll make sure of it."

John's shoulders straightened and he dusted off the knee of his right leg. "Where shall I be going?"

"On a visit to the Continent. You shall take a liking

to Italy during your tour and stay there a few months. You will correspond with Lord Dentry and me every few weeks—and we will keep the ton abreast of your adventures, should they require news. If anyone inquires after you in Italy, you will move to France, and so forth."

John nodded. "My assets?"

"In a year you will have a tragic accident—"

"A racing accident, I hope. Fitting for me to go out on a horse, don't you think?"

Gabriel nodded, looking at his hands, foreign, clenched in his lap. "Fitting indeed."

"My documents are in order. There should be no trouble in a year. I've left everything to you anyway." John was calm, eerily serene. "Take care of my stables, will you? The horses. The trainers. I have a fine foal. Newmarket winner for sure. I would like it if you would race her, or sell her to a worthy buyer, should you have a care for me."

"I have a care for you, John."

He looked away, his throat working. "I know. I'm sorry, Gabriel."

"I know, John. I'm sorry too."

The carriage slowed. Hooves clomping to a stop. The turning of the wheels pausing for a moment, suspended.

John turned to him. "Marietta is good for you, Gabriel. I quite like her. Don't be a fool and let her go."

"I can do nothing *but* let her go, John. Sometimes love can only be given by setting someone free."

John watched him, then held up his bound hands. "You speak truly."

Gabriel paused, unsure whether he could truly bring himself to cut the rope. One cut through his bindings and it would be done. He pulled a knife from the bundle. His hand reached out, like a body part separate from his control, and cut the rope. The coil fell onto John's lap, then slithered to the ground.

They looked at each other for a long moment. Gabriel handed him a piece of charcoal, the cloth bundle with its two bulky objects bumping his thigh. John rubbed his hands over the charcoal, wiping streaks along his cheeks, his forehead, down his nose. Over his ears and around his neck. Over the shirt. Anyplace identifiable.

"I will have to do something to my hands," he said in a conversational tone.

"Yes."

"The street, maybe. A quick swipe to open the skin, to roughen idle fingers." His smile was self-deprecating.

Gabriel didn't respond.

John finished his ministrations and straightened his shirt, an unconscious gesture. "How do I look?"

Gabriel nodded, his lips unable to form words, his heart unable to beat.

John looked at him for a moment. A lifetime. "Good-bye, Gabriel."

"Good-bye, John," he whispered, somehow dredging up his voice. "May you find peace."

John smiled. A smile of old, like when they were younger, before Eton had separated them; playing on the estate, no cares in the world. "Yes," he said simply.

He held out his hands, and Gabriel placed the

bundle on top, the two objects clacking together, one heavy and one thin.

John's hand shot out before he could blink and pulled Gabriel to him. A fierce hug, a promise. Then he pushed him away and gripped the carriage handle. "Good-bye."

And he was gone.

Gabriel sat in the carriage. Staring at the opposite seat. Unable to tap the trap to tell his driver to move.

The carriage started moving without his tap. John had obviously not had such trouble. Gabriel allowed the motion to sway him back and forth. They rounded the corner. A distant shot rang out.

Gabriel didn't need to look back. To see. He trusted his friend. He smiled grimly. And wasn't that the crux?

Chapter 22

Middlesex murderer dead! Shot by own hand at the scene of a previous crime! Murder weapon found in his pocket— letter opener used on all the victims . . . Servant from the Dentry estate gone mad, an Edward Smith . . . though physical identification impossible . . . Arthur Dresden discovers murderer and claims the reward . . . whole story from his mouth on page four . . . Lord Dentry testifies! Kenneth Winters found innocent at trial and released! All charges dropped on both Winters brothers! Monetary settlement given by Lord Dentry . . . Statements on page six . . . London rejoices! Safe once more . . .

"Are you angry with me for not telling you before we left for the estate that John was guilty?"

Marietta pushed the special edition papers aside and looked at Gabriel, who was holding a mug of tea to his chest, the steam swirling up and around his face, as beautiful now as it had been the first time she'd seen him. Perhaps even more attractive now, if such a thing were possible.

"No. If you had told me about Alcroft after you made the discovery, I would never have been able to keep it a secret from him. I would have acted differently."

He nodded, his eyes falling to his tea, as if searching for the answers inside. "Are you leaving tonight?"

She wet her lips, her heart beating, unsure. "I can. Mark and Kenny are back in our rented house. Kenny said neighbors have been pouring in with congratulatory gifts and goodwill. Invitations are overflowing. Everyone wanting the first bit of gossip."

"You are welcome to stay here until the fury dies down."

"Thank you. I should probably go back, though. In case Kenny needs me." The last was more of a question. Would he ask her to stay?

"Best for you not to be caught here either. Everyone is probably wondering where you've been. Off to a friend's in the country. Stick with that story, no matter what your ratty cousin says."

She smiled, a strained, forced smile. "Yes."

"I know someone who will vouch for your whereabouts this past month, should you need it. A nice couple in Windsor."

"Thank you."

"Don't thank me. Please."

Silence.

"I'll help you pack."

Packing took little time. Not nearly as much as it had taken a month past. It was as if time had sped ahead to hasten their separation. She dreaded the activity of packing as much now as she had then. The pain in her heart markedly different, but still present.

The next thing she knew, she was at the bottom of the stairs, case in hand.

"It would be best if you go on your own. I'll have the driver stop a street or two over. You can catch a hack." He pressed a few coins into her palm, his touch burned. "I'll send your other things around later. In an unmarked carriage."

"Thank—" She cut herself off before she could finish the sentiment. Silence pervaded the foyer. "Will you be—"

"I'll be fine," he said.

She nodded and gripped her case more tightly.

Gabriel leaned forward, touching her chin, her cheek, brushing a loose strand behind her ear. His lips touched hers. Soft, yet firm. Warm and lovely. He pulled away, their bottom lips holding until the last moment and then disconnecting with regret.

"Good luck, Marietta. I know you will be fine. Remember what I said."

Find some nice young man to marry, comfortable, not a gambler, someone who will treasure you.

Someone who wasn't Gabriel. Someone with whom she could marry and raise a family. Someone she didn't love.

But also someone *she* wouldn't burden. Who wouldn't have to awkwardly reject her offerings. Who might come to love her someday.

"Good luck, Gabriel."

She walked into the carriage.

* * *

"This old thing? Why it is barely above a rag," one woman said to another, displaying her beautiful gown, obviously new and at the height of fashion. The two women blended into the crowd.

Marietta looked into the ballroom. She'd had to visit the retiring room for a bit, and even then found herself accosted by people wanting to *know*. Wanting to discover all of the salacious news before their neighbors. The night's festivities were in full swing, the ton euphoric over its new intrigue and gossip. Its notorious new *favorite* members.

She paused for a moment at the threshold. The doors wide open to her. The different groups of people standing in pockets. Each group would be delighted for her to join them. Like a storybook on vellum pages. She'd been asked to dance every dance, for once needing to turn down offers to save her feet. It was like a strange dream. And though the vellum was lovely, it was unsatisfying beneath her fingertips.

Two women chattered in chairs off to the side. "The Winterses are distantly related to the Duke of Shastmore, Earl Givet, and Baron Tercake. Lovely connections."

The other woman nodded and Marietta looked away. Of course now their connections were remembered. When it was convenient. The invitations that had dried up like the desert were now flooding their silver tray. The ton eager to unearth every piece of the scandal. Their fall from grace and triumphant return.

She saw Mark, still skinny, but not emaciated like Kenny, holding court to the side. Kenny stood next to him looking more uncomfortable than he would have in this situation six weeks ago, Mark, on the other hand, was acting as if he'd never left the bosom of the ton. As if he'd always had a small fortune, courtesy of Lord Dentry. She made her way to them.

" . . . and that is the exact thing I told him. Crandon, my friend, you don't put the bet on the sixes!"

The crowd around him laughed. She had heard the joke six times now, though, and was waiting for someone to finally catch on that it wasn't a very good one.

"My sister! Miss Winters. Have you met my sister, Plufield?"

The earl said no and they were quickly introduced. "Charming." "Delightful." "Handsome." She would start to think highly of herself if the new adjectives to describe her continued.

"I was wondering if I might have a word with you both," she said to her brothers.

The other men quickly excused themselves. Mark looked put out. "What are you doing, Marietta? Flushing the game into other yards?"

"No. I don't desire—"

"I have two offers for you already. And four more just waiting. Think we might even be able to bring Plufield up to scratch. My sister, a countess. Just think of it. We'll use the others to advance his suit, of course. And if a bigger fish finds himself in our net, well, then we will scoop him up."

"Mark—" she began.

"I'm the most glorious brother, I know."

"No. Why are you doing this?"

Mark's expression was half irritation, half confusion.

Kenny looked uncomfortable, but for the first time he didn't run off at the first sign of a fight, he threw his shoulders back and braced his feet. He would need to work on his neck and head, hanging lower and pressed forward, but all in all she felt a rush of pride. Kenny was finally growing up.

She knew who to thank. Gabriel had done something to him. Shoved a spine through his tail or pulled a string through his core. Kenny had gone to visit and thank him a few days ago and had come back a new man.

"The opportunity is there. We must grab it." Mark must have read her face aright for once, because his tone changed to disbelief. "You can't tell me that you don't want to be married. There are plenty of good matches here. Solid ones. I think you should wait for Plufield, myself, but if you think the lure is only good for a few weeks, perhaps we should take one of the others. Nice, ready blunt there. Good connections."

"Blunt is one of the things of which I wished to speak to you."

"Really, Marietta, I hardly think a girl need worry about such things, as I've told you. I have extra pin money for you," he said generously. "You can buy a new bonnet or some ribbons."

"You can't keep spending, Mark."

"'Course I can. I have the funds, don't I? Lord Dentry was quite considerate."

"Ga—" She cleared her throat. "Mr. Noble hired an accountant for the reward funds. The compensation and settlement. You will reach a cap on the quarterly funds soon."

"I'll just take a loan against the rest, nothing to it."

Anger pushed past her shields. "Have you learned nothing? We will be penniless once more. Beholden and ruined."

"Which is why you should marry Plufield. Or Ratching. They can keep us in funds. Won't let their in-laws starve."

"You are unbelievable. I can't—"

Kenny held up a hand, chin high. "Let me try to talk to him, Marietta."

She stared at Kenny, and out of the corner of her eye could see Mark do the same. She nodded slowly, elation and pride running through her. "Very well, Kenny. Thank you." Even if he couldn't talk sense to Mark, the shock of him trying was sure to keep Mark silent for at least a few minutes. Besides, maybe Kenny would be the one to get through to him. "I believe I shall retire. I'll send the carriage back."

Kenny nodded. Mark still looked flabbergasted, his long face even longer with his jaw dropped so far. With a satisfied smile she turned and walked outside, bypassing the well wishers, the gossip hounds, the suitors. It wasn't that the suitors weren't acceptable. There was even one young man on Mark's list who would make a solid, respectable husband.

But none of them were Gabriel. None of them were *hers*. And she was damned tired of trying to scrape her way, to dodge and plot and worry about what came out of her mouth at any given moment. Gabriel might not always be the perfect knight charging on his steed. But he was hers. She felt it deep within her. And she was going to let him know it.

She gave the driver the direction, ignoring his look, or the fact that he might tell someone that he hadn't dropped her off at home. The carriage moved. The wheels rolled forward. Hooves clomped. Closer and closer.

She stepped from the carriage as soon as it stopped. "Go back to the ball. I will be fine." She pressed a coin into his hand, then turned. The carriage rolled off behind her. She would have to hire a hack if this didn't work.

But it was going to work. She'd *make* it work.

She straightened her shoulders and marched up the walk.

The brass ring in the lion's mouth glimmered in the faint light of the gas lamps. Fierce yellow eyes surveyed her from above the loop, questioning her nerve. Marietta Winters curled trembling fingers around the bottom of the metal and forced it against the door knocker.

A large man answered the door, the light this time allowing her to see it was truly a butler, austere, but with the look of a man who could hold himself in a fight. His eyes traveled over her cloak, her shoes, her face, her hair. Chimes rang in the hall, giving the time as eleven in the evening. Too late to be calling, by any stretch of protocol.

"Yes?"

"I need to speak to Mr. Noble." This time her voice *was* strong, calm.

"Miss Winters, I presume?"

She blinked. "Yes."

"I'm sorry, Miss Winters, but Mr. Noble is out for the

evening." He looked behind her. "I'll have the carriage see you home."

Disappointment, sharp and deep, hit her. "I see. Thank you."

A different carriage from any she had ridden in previously escorted her back to her rented town house. Gabriel must be out with one of his others somewhere in the city. Seeing someone new perhaps?

The thought didn't bear thinking.

She entered the house and greeted the butler. Their new butler. Jeanie, the only servant they had rehired, passed her in the hall, her eyes unfocused and dreamy. Marietta shook her head. Jeanie was a good worker but a mite daft sometimes.

The door to her room was shut, and she opened it and slipped inside, heading for her dressing table. Jeanie had been prompt in lighting her lamps. She peeled off her gloves and reached to her nape to unclasp the necklace there. Movement in the looking glass held her motionless as she examined the image.

That explained Jeanie's behavior and the lamps.

She dropped the necklace to the table and walked back to the door, closing it softly and sealing them inside. She leaned against the door, her hands splayed on the wood behind her.

Gabriel was sitting on her bed, papers spread about in a terrible mess on top of it, leaning back against a pile of her pillows, looking wonderful, even with the dark creases under his eyes.

"Marietta."

"Gabriel. This is my bedroom, you did know."

"I confess I've been here before."

A tingle shot through her, very different from the one she had experienced the last time he was in her room, the night their partnership had begun.

"How did you get in?"

"I bribed your servants."

"Well, that will hardly do. And here I thought you had hired us some respectable ones."

He unfolded from his position and rose slowly, hitching his hip and shoulder against one of the bed poster poles and crossing his arms. "I bribed them doubly, so they would say nothing to your brothers or anyone else, should I stay for five minutes or five hours." Emotion flashed through his eyes, and she caught the vulnerability he tried so desperately to hide. "I suppose the poor servants are only as respectable as the man hiring them. Perhaps you should have checked his references."

He looked delicious. Hair falling into his eyes, the ever watchful look within them. Vulnerability and strength.

"Perhaps I still should. A full, *thorough* search."

He smiled. A full stretch of sensual lips—palpable relief combined with a predatory upward curl.

"That would be best. Tea?" He pointed to a service on her side table. He had obviously made himself right at home.

"No." She walked toward him, picking the pins out of her hair as she went. "I've had plenty of tea."

"You were supposed to be at the Smithertons' for at least another hour."

She arched a brow back, a second inkling that perhaps things *would* work out crossing her mind. "You are keeping track of my appointments?"

"Of course."

"You say it as if it's obvious. Why would you keep track of such a thing?"

He arched a brow. "I value my research."

"And what has it told you about me lately?"

"You have a number of offers. Good ones. Your brother is even hoping for an earl."

"He is. I met the earl tonight."

Something passed across his eyes. *Jealousy.* Her heart beat faster.

"I have looked into the earl's affairs," he said, fingers tapping on one crossed arm. "He is not a bad choice, all things considered. Jeremy, whose real London project happens to have two legs and a twittering laugh, was prowling a dinner affair where he met the earl. He commented that he was nice enough. My reports say the same. Moderate consumer of spirits and gambling. Plenty of money to keep you in style. The ladies report that he is not hard on the eyes. One of your others—Ratching, is it?—is also a decent choice."

She stopped a foot in front of him. "Yes. Both decent choices."

"Whom will you choose?"

She stepped forward a few inches more. "Who do you think I should choose?"

"Ah, but that is not my decision to make."

She closed the last six inches and tilted her head up. "I'm asking your opinion, is all."

His fingers curled into white knuckles. *Yes.* "And I'm not giving my opinion to you."

She pushed flush against him, her eyelids dropping to half-mast, his arms automatically falling and allowing closer contact. "Then I suppose I should determine my favorite with a kiss?"

He crushed his lips to hers, and she eagerly returned the kiss, the assault.

"I've missed you," he said against her mouth.

She pulled away an inch. "I've missed you too. I worried about y—"

He kissed her again. "I know. Talk later."

He turned and pushed her down on the bed, and she smeared papers beneath her as she leaned back on her elbows.

"I'll never find anything in that pile again," he said, his voice rasping as if he'd run ten miles as he continued to kiss her. He pushed against her, hard and delicious, and she pushed back, wanting the heat.

"You can't find—" She arched back as he freed a breast and sucked the tip. "—anything in those piles anyway, admit it."

"Never."

He pulled up her skirts, the layers of material ballooning and bunching around and between them. He stroked a finger along her, unerringly finding the exact spots that made her writhe against him, sneaking a fingertip inside her, on the path her body had already made. Fire and desire combining as he made her body sing. His body aligned with hers and her throat caught.

Fingers threaded through her hair and brilliant green eyes met hers. She looked in his eyes and read the honesty reflected back. The desire, the caution, the love.

"I don't want any of the others."

"They could give you the life you deserve."

"No." She shook her head. "They will give me anything but."

"I'm the son of a butler and governess, Marietta. Hardly someone that—"

She put her finger to his lips. "I love you." She felt the shock jolt through him, and barely kept hold of herself as the movement thrust him inside her an inch. "Love is what none of the others could give me," she said breathlessly. "I know you do not desire marriage. I don't expect—"

He placed a finger against *her* lips. "I never said that. I worded myself very carefully. I wanted to give you a clean chance to do as *you* wanted."

"I want *you.*"

"Are you sure?"

"Completely."

He smiled. A smile full of charm and roguish intent. Her pulse raced even as the happy light in his eyes made her heart soar. And then he was all the way inside of her and without looking away from each other they were moving together and cresting over the edge.

He pushed the papers from the bed, scattered leaves gently settling on the hardwood below. He held her to him like a warm blanket and she clung back.

"You do realize," he said lightly, "that once I commit to something, you'll never be rid of me?"

"I'm counting on it."

"Excellent." He traced a pattern on her back. "Now about those three nights . . . "

Next month, don't miss these exciting new love stories only from Avon Books

Under Your Spell by Lois Greiman

An Avon Romantic Treasure

Ella St. James is worried that a friend has been having clandestine meetings with a stranger. When she turns up dead, Ella is determined to discover the truth. Sir Thomas Drake bars her every move, and for a woman who believes that love is not only blind but also stupid, Ella's attraction to him is inexplicable.

Letters to a Secret Lover by Toni Blake

An Avon Contemporary Romance

Lindsey Brooks was a top romance advice columnist—until her own love life crashed and burned. Retreating to her home town to lick her wounds, Lindsey discovers a tasty treat in Rob Colter. But will going up against Rob in business rule out any chance for pleasure?

His Dark and Dangerous Ways by Edith Layton

An Avon Romance

Nothing very exciting happens to Jane Chatham—until her weekly dance lesson makes her the perfect contact for a former spy like Simon Atwood, Lord Granger. Now Jane wants to uncover all Simon's secrets . . . no matter how dangerous they turn out to be.

At the Bride Hunt Ball by Olivia Parker

An Avon Romance

Madelyn Heywood doesn't want to marry. So naturally she's reluctant to attend a ball held by Gabriel Devine, the Duke of Wolverest, to find a bride for his younger brother. But when it turns out that Madelyn and Gabriel have more in common than just an aversion to marriage, this ball may get turned upside down.

AVON

978-0-06-133535-8

978-0-06-144589-7

978-0-06-137452-4

978-0-06-134024-6

978-0-06-134039-0

978-0-06-111886-9